MW00411747

THE RABBI'S
IN TROUBLE

A NOVEL

CHANA SHAPIRO AND META MILLER

COVER DESIGN BY ALEX BURMENKO

DEDICATION

This book is dedicated to all the readers who asked us to write a sequel to *Fruitfly Rabbi*. In response, we offer a few new characters and more story twists and turns. We're delighted that Rabbi Joshua Stein provoked your interest enough to encourage us to continue his story.

We wish to thank the following people who helped us along the way. Nancy Steinhardt did a masterful job proofreading our book--twice. Her suggestions were wise and her critiques were gentle. Esther Rothstein's editing skills caught numerous missteps. Zvi Shapiro, Scott Steinberg, and Sophie Steinberg handled countless computer issues. Reverend David Richards' dialog suggestion came just when we needed it. Elayna Reed's careful reading helped clarify the title and strains of our story.

A special debt of gratitude goes to Alex Burmenko, owner and head designer at Switchworks Digital Media. Alex's graphic expertise and technical savvy were crucial to the book's production.

Finally, we are grateful and blessed to have wonderful husbands, Rabbi Zvi Shapiro and Dr. Paul Miller, who were remarkably patient and ready with encouragement.

Even though we didn't always agree on the conduct and nature of our characters, we had a lot of fun creating them. To that end, we assure our readers that the people and events described here are fictitious.

GLOSSARY

ADON OLAM ....Concluding Hebrew prayer

ALIYAH...Permanent move to Israel;
Torah reading honor

BARUCH HASHEM ....'Thank God'

BASHERT...Divinely intended

BAT MITZVAH ....Ceremony in which girls reach
Jewish adulthood

BENTCH...Prayer (commonly recited after
meals-Yiddish)

BIMAH ....Raised platform in synagogue
where Torah is read

BRIT MILAH ....Ritual circumcision

BUKHARI-STYLE KIPPAH ....Oriental-style embroidered
skullcap

CHAGIM ....Jewish holidays

CHALLAH ....Braided bread for Sabbath and
Jewish holidays

CHUPPAH ....Marriage canopy

DAVEN ....Pray

D'VAR TORAH................................Torah lesson

GET/GITTEN (pl) ....Jewish legal divorce(s)

GONIF ....Thief

HAIMISHE .... Pleasantly comfortable, homey
(Yiddish)

HASHEM...Euphemism for God, literally,
'The Name'

HAVDALAH ....Service ending the Sabbath

KIDDUSH..Prayer recited before Sabbath
and holiday meals; refreshments
served following services

KIPPAH; YARMULKA ....Skullcap

MAZEL TOV ....Congratulations (literally, "good
luck")

MECHITZAH ....Partition separating sexes in
Othodox shuls

MEGILLAH.......................................Term used sarcastically to
describe a long involved story
(literally, one of five scrolls in
the biblical canon)

MEZUZAH ....Encased prayer placed on Jewish
doorposts

MINCHA/MAARIV ....Afternoon and evening prayers

MINYAN..Quorum of ten needed for a
Jewish service

MITZVAH..................................Commandment; good deed

MOHEL ....Individual who performs Jewish ritual circumcision

PRUST ....Low-class; common (Yiddish)

PURIM ....Festival featuring in which Jewish people are saved from annihilation

REBBITZIN..............................Rabbi's wife (Yiddish)

REFUAH SHELAIMAH ....Complete recovery from illness

RESPONSA ....Written decisions by Jewish legal scholars

ROSH HASHANAH ....Jewish New Year

SCHMUCK................................Dreadful person (Yiddish)

SHABBAT ....Sabbath; time period from sun down Friday evening to sundown Saturday night

SHACHARIT..............................Morning service

SHANDAH FOR THE GOYIM ....Embarrassment in front of non-Jews (Yiddish)

SHEVA BRACHOT.......................Week-long celebrations following Jewish wedding

SHIVA ....Seven-day Jewish period of mourning

SHMOOZER..............................Gadfly; one who chats easily (Yiddish)

SHTIEBLE .... Small village (Yiddish)

SHUL .... Synagogue (Yiddish)

SIMCHA .... Joyous celebration

SUKKAH .... Temporary dwelling in which one resides during the Festival of Sukkot

TACHLIS .... The bottom line; essence (Yiddish)

TALLIS; TALLIT .... Prayer shawl

TALMUD .... Body of Jewish law and commentary

TEFILLIN .... Phylacteries

TORAH .... Scroll containing the Five Books of Moses

TZEDAKAH (BOX) .... Charity (Box)

VANTZ .... Lowly insect (Yiddish slang for a despicable person)

YAHRZEIT .... The anniversary of a person's death (Yiddish)

YENTA .... Gossip (Yiddish)

YOM TOV .... Jewish holiday

PROLOGUE

Rabbi Joshua Stein had been hired as assistant rabbi at Congregation Lev Shalom, a prestigious Orthodox synagogue in Chicago, Illinois, soon after receiving his rabbinic ordination. His family in Boston was disappointed that he didn't marry his long-time girlfriend or complete his postgraduate studies in genetics and join his older brother in his research lab. A family friend, Rabbi Mordechai Goldschmidt, who appreciated Josh's brilliant mind, guided him into Judaic Studies and, ultimately, the rabbinate.

In his new position, Josh slowly became aware of troubling events that had led Lev Shalom into financial difficulty. In addition, the growing conflict between the *shul* president, Bob Small, and the senior rabbi, Ephraim Halperin, drew Josh further into the morass. The synagogue administrator's daughter, Rachel Berg, and Josh informally collaborated to address the problems. Their insightful musings evolved into flirtatious meetings, and they became romantically involved.

In spite of efforts by many people with big hearts and good intentions, including supportive Holocaust survivors, the kibitzing restaurateur Kalman, loyal *shul* administrator Serena (Rachel's mother), and the president's candid wife, Sheila, troubles at Lev Shalom intensified.

Ultimately, Rabbi Ephraim and Bunny Halperin prepared to leave Chicago and retire to their apartment in Israel. Josh was appointed interim rabbi, while Lev Shalom sought a replacement for the senior position.

CHAPTER 1

Rabbi Ephraim Halperin and his wife, Bunny, sat wearily in their pan-elled library. Many of the shelves were already empty, and the archival boxes holding priceless manuscripts were neatly stacked in the corner. Bibelots of ivory and jade from their many travels were spread on a large mahogany desk among small ritual objects of sterling silver and crystal. The Halperins were packing all their worldly possessions.

Bunny was exhausted from pretending that everything was all right. She had maintained her usual composure and dignity during the Jewish holidays, and now all she wanted was to say goodbye to Chicago. Their apartment in Jerusalem, in which they had spent a month every summer for the last fifteen years, would now be their permanent home.

Rabbi Halperin, on the other hand, was leaving town reluctantly. He had delivered his last sermon at Lev Shalom, the congregation he had led for almost fifty years. The High Holiday cycle was over. Josh Stein, the young assistant rabbi, only in the job a few months, was understand-ably uncertain about his own future; however, while the congregation searched for Halperin's replacement, Stein was officially in charge as interim rabbi.

Halperin, himself, was resigned to starting over, but the circumstances under which he and his wife were leaving continued to plague him. He had willingly replaced the missing Holocaust Memorial Garden funds, and he had been exonerated from any criminal intent. Although the Halperins had always expected their departure to be honorable and poignant, they were leaving under a cloud.

"Thank God it's over," Bunny sighed. "I've had enough."

"It's not over yet, Bunny."

"What are you talking about?"

Fred leaned forward. "I'm not finished with our dear *shul* president!"

"Really? Bob Small? I just want to get as far away from him and Lev Shalom as we can. I thought we agreed on this."

"Bob Small and his insufferable wife can't be allowed to run things! I won't leave until I take care of him."

Bunny stopped her husband. "Fred, we're not going to talk about Bob, and you're not going to end up in the hospital again because of that bully. It's late. Let's get to bed."

But Halperin couldn't calm down. He kept pacing around the room of empty shelves. Plans and pictures of different scenarios in which he could prevail over his nemesis raced through his mind. He had to convince Bunny that there were still things he had to take care of, and he was sure that he was the only one who could bring Bob to his knees and at the same time restore his own image.

Bunny shrugged her shoulders. "I'm going to sleep. I'm begging you to let this go, Fred. We're finished at Lev Shalom, and I couldn't be happier about it. Leora's coming tomorrow and I'll need all my energy just to keep up with her. At least one of our children is able to help us. You know how she is about acting responsibly. Besides, she's the only one who can get away."

"Unfortunately," Fred sighed, "that's the problem. She's already thirty with no husband or kids. She needs to get out of the landscaping business and do something where she can meet different Jewish men, and not those Paul Bunyan types!"

"Well, she'll be here tomorrow and you can talk to her. I've given up. She's been with Aaron for too long. I don't like him, you don't like him, and frankly, I don't want her to marry him, and she knows that. I want her to get married as much as you do, but not to Aaron. Thank God she didn't bring him here on *Yom Tov*."

"It's all in God's hands, anyway, but she needs a push. Maybe she should move to Israel with us and get back to her interest in archaeology. I *will* have that conversation with her," Halperin declared.

"I bet you won't. You always left those kind of things to me and I'm all talked out with her. You can stay down here brooding all night, as far as I'm concerned, but I'm going upstairs."

As it turned out, Halperin fell asleep in his desk chair, amid the boxes of books in his beloved Chicago library, and he didn't wake up until late the next morning. Bunny was waiting for him in the kitchen, while he finished *davening* the morning service.

"Feel better after sleeping at your desk?" She asked, visibly annoyed, as her husband followed the aroma of freshly-brewed coffee.

Just as Halperin poured his first cup, the phone rang. He and Bunny looked at each other and agreed not to answer it. The Halperins were both anticipating a more relaxed and unscheduled life now that they were free from communal obligations. A phone call from an unfamiliar number was exactly what they didn't want.

The caller on the phone began to leave a message. "This is James Traub calling for Rabbi Ephraim Halperin. I'm a columnist with *The Chicago Journal*, and I'm looking forward to meeting you in person before you leave the country."

This was just the kind of intrusion Bunny feared. She was determined to spend the next few weeks packing and making final arrangements for their move to Israel. She had no intention of allowing her husband, who had done well during the High Holidays in spite of his recent heart problems and *shul* conflicts, to speak to anyone about anything having to do with Lev Shalom.

Bunny picked up the phone before Traub finished his message. "Mr. Traub, this is Bunny Halperin, the Rabbi's wife. We're in the process of moving to Israel, and neither one of us has any interest in talking about our synagogue."

"Mrs. Halperin," Traub cut in, "I'm not calling about the synagogue at all. I'd like to talk to your husband about his latest book. In fact, about all of his books."

Bunny answered, "*Pray This Way* will be reviewed in the Jewish media without any additional input from my husband. He's not planning to give any interviews before we leave."

Fred, his interest piqued by Bunny's side of the conversation, motioned that he wanted to talk. Reluctantly, she handed him the phone. She knew the signs. Fred was a pushover for media attention. He wanted to be known as a 'writer of importance', and he loved the spotlight.

"This is Ephraim Halperin. Do you have a question about my book?"

"I've read your other books," Traub lied, "and I'm a big fan. I'm Jewish, but never thought about the issues you so clearly write about. Your wife just explained that you're about to leave Chicago, and I'd like to interview you before you move. I'll meet you at your convenience, either at your synagogue, or I can come to your home."

Halperin caught himself, aware that he should discuss the meeting site with Bunny before he made any appointments.

"Let me think about your offer, and I'll get back to you as soon as I can. There's a lot going on in our lives right now, and my book isn't my first priority."

Hearing this, Bunny put her arms around her husband. She was relieved that he seemed willing, maybe even ready, to move on, and she had to take advantage of this sentiment before he was dragged back into old issues. She was disturbed that he believed he could settle scores with Bob Small, and she doubted her husband's ability to keep his ego in check when it came to talking about his books.

Traub, on his end, had an agenda, and he knew that this interview could strongly advance his career. He wasn't going to let Halperin avoid it.

"Why don't I call you in a day or two? A profile of you discussing your book will generate new readers, especially since you're leaving the country. As I said before, your book gave me a lot to think about."

As the Rabbi hung up, Bunny served the rest of their breakfast, thinking, *Fred should know better. That journalist wants much more than book talk, and if they meet, one of them will move the conversation to shul business. Is Fred foolish enough to try to use this interview to defame Bob?* She had a premonition that a meeting could really hurt her husband.

Bunny looked out the window. It was pouring, and she wondered if she could get any of her shopping done. She hoped this bad weather wasn't an omen of things to come. She couldn't wait for her daughter Leora to arrive.

CHAPTER 2

Fred and Bunny Halperin waited at baggage claim for their youngest child. Both of their sons were already in high school when their dreams of having a daughter had come true. Leora was raised practically as an only child, and whereas her older brothers' lives consisted of non-stop academics and sports, Leora was allowed to spend most of her time in art classes and volunteering at a community garden in the city. Bunny's hopes of a daughter who loved ballet and symphonies were eclipsed by Leora's love of rocks and plants. Her bold, confident nature fueled her individualism.

Leora was most comfortable in sandals, backpacks, and jean skirts. At weekly services and in the synagogue youth group, Leora was easily recognized by her long skirts, flowing shirts, and brightly colored socks. Her long, chestnut hair was always in a ponytail. She wasn't the least bit interested in makeup or manicures, but jewelry was another story. Multiple hoop earrings and lots of silver bangles were her trademark.

She had close friends, and even though she was clearly the most notice-able among them, she didn't flaunt it. Her creativity and down-to-earth demeanor were her chief attributes.

Leora, whose business and fiance were in New York, had been in Chicago with her siblings and their families a few weeks earlier on Rosh Hashanah and Yom Kippur. The entire Halperin clan wanted to spend the final holidays of their parents' leadership at Lev Shalom together.

Now that Fred and Bunny were moving to Israel, their children would probably never again *daven* in the synagogue where they had grown up.

As the Halperins waited for Leora at the airport, Bunny was uncharacteristically antsy. She couldn't stop checking her phone for a text that her daughter's plane had landed. Fred occupied himself with a book on contemporary Jewish thought, one of his favorite pastimes.

Leora surprised her parents by suddenly appearing. "Here she comes! Fred, put that book down! What's she wearing?"

Dressed in a knee-length black tunic over black leggings, Leora rushed into her mother's outstretched arms. She then turned to embrace her father.

"Lee-Lee!" Bunny exclaimed, "Are those diamond earrings?"

"Mom, you don't miss a thing," Leora laughed. "I guess I'm not totally different from you, after all! They're not as big as the ones you're wearing, but I'm only thirty--I still have time."

Bunny would have enjoyed staying on that subject, but her husband was ready to leave. Leora retrieved her suitcase from the carousel, and her father grabbed her backpack. With one woman on each side of him, the trio headed to his BMW.

"How's the packing coming along?"

Bunny let out a huge groan, "Not fast enough for me. Your father has all kinds of delaying tactics, but now that you're here, things will move faster."

Bunny gave her husband a withering stare, "With or without his cooperation."

"What's that supposed to mean, Mom?"

"What I mean is that in a few weeks all our stuff will be on its way to our apartment in Jerusalem. I hope your father's possessions will be on our lift, but if he wastes time here looking through his manuscripts and doing anything he thinks is more important, I'll be disappointed but not devastated. I'm going as soon as I can, no matter what."

Leora was confused. "Daddy, what's Mom talking about?"

"This discussion can wait for a different time. I have some unfinished business here in Chicago that I need to take care of."

The ride home from O'Hare took forty minutes. The family had never remained silent for that long, but each of them knew enough not to open the discussion any further.

Bunny and Leora went inside while Fred parked the car and carried in the luggage. Leora had a lot of questions, and she was relieved to have her mother alone for a few minutes.

"What's going on between you and Daddy? I've never seen you like this. You're always so supportive and composed. Besides, do you really want to fight, considering Daddy's heart?"

"I'm not the one to blame. We were supposed to leave Chicago right after the *chagim,* and now your father gets himself involved with a third-rate reporter who's pretending to be interested in the books he wrote. There's something between your father and Bob Small that you don't have to worry about and that I am determined to forget. But Daddy can't let it go. Nothing good will come of this situation, but you know your father. He's never been a quitter and he's not a coward. I used to think those were desirable qualities, but now they're coupled with a vendetta. Lee-Lee, I'm beside myself."

"Mom, let me talk to Daddy."

"I'll be interested to hear what he tells you, but believe me, he's going to make a fool of himself, and I don't want to be here when that happens!"

Fred Halperin caught the tail-end of the conversation. "Why do you think I'll make a fool of myself, Bunny?"

Leora and Bunny were embarrassed, and Bunny had no desire to get into an argument in front of her daughter.

It was Leora who spoke. "Daddy, we didn't hear you come in. Mom's worried and scared about the interview with that journalist, and you're a master of walking away from dangerous situations. I don't know what's going on between you and Mr. Small, but he's unworthy of one ounce of your energy. Don't get into anything with him."

"You're probably right, and your mother has made it crystal clear to me that she agrees with you. Frankly, I'm worn out from dealing with that man."

Bunny, a bit mollified, had heard enough. "Everybody knows Bob Small's low-class, and they also know that you aren't. Leora and I are going to continue packing, and you have plenty to do yourself."

Halperin looked at the priceless pieces of his lifetime collection of ancient manuscripts, which he had carefully organized for packing, but his heart wasn't in it. While he knew it was unwise and could be dangerously unhealthy to be obsessed with getting back at Bob Small, he was unable to shake it off.

He noticed a copy of his book, *Pray This Way*, lying among the parchments, and sent a prayer heavenward that he'd manage to keep the interview with Traub focused on his meaningful life in the rabbinate and on his literary works.

CHAPTER 3

A young man and woman walked into the office of Congregation Lev Shalom. He was wearing slacks and a striped, collared shirt. The woman, whose hair was platinum blonde, wore a light gray knit top with a charcoal pencil skirt. Both of them carried messenger bags. They walked purposefully to Serena Berg's desk.

"May I help you?" Serena asked

"Are you Rabbi Halperin's secretary?"

Secretary? Slightly miffed, Serena corrected them, "I'm the synagogue administrator," she declared. "I manage the office."

"Is one of the rabbis in? I'm James Traub from *The Chicago Journal*," the young man announced.

"Rabbi Halperin's on his way to Israel," Serena declared, refraining from revealing that the Halperins were still in town and wouldn't be leaving for another month or so. Serena had no intention of dragging the assistant rabbi, Joshua Stein, who was temporarily in charge, into this. Traub didn't mention that he had already contacted Halperin.

"We know the Halperins are moving. I'm a staff reporter, and Jenny Pittman is our photographer. It's a big story when a famous person suddenly announces his departure from a major position. Is it possible to meet with Rabbi Stein?"

"We want to get some current pictures for the paper," Jenny added.

Traub stopped her. "What Jenny means is that a good, well substantiated interview with photos will ensure a balanced story."

Substantiated? Balanced? Serena had heard enough.

"There's no story here. Rabbi Halperin retired, period. He had every right to leave whenever he chose, and that's exactly what happened. Rabbi Joshua Stein, our interim rabbi, isn't in the office right now, and I'm sure he can't add anything to enlighten you."

Traub was encouraged by Serena's defensive response. Now he was even more certain that there was plenty of dirt to dig up. He had heard rumors, and they must be true.

"Perhaps you know Sheila and Bob Small?" James smiled, mischievously.

"Of course I do," Serena said, cautiously. "Why?"

"My mother plays mahjong with Sheila. You know how some women talk while they're playing, right?"

Serena rose from her desk and faced Traub. "Anything you heard from Sheila Small is worthless hearsay. It's just gossip! I told you there's no story here, and now I'm getting back to work."

She furiously attacked her keyboard. As she did so, Jenny snapped a few quick photos, and James began to survey the surroundings.

Just then, a tall, slim, dark-skinned woman entered, and Serena greeted her warmly.

"Rabbi Stein's on his way. Please have a seat, Ms. Morales."

Unnoticed, Jenny quickly took a few snaps of Morales.

Just then, Lev Shalom President Bob Small burst into the office, demanding to see Rabbi Stein.

"I'm on my way to work and I have exactly three minutes to give Rabbi Stein his marching orders for the Holocaust Memorial meeting tonight," he blustered.

When Small was in a hurry, nothing was allowed to stop him, not the fact that he didn't have an appointment, or that he hadn't called from his car. Serena was in no mood to handle yet another unannounced visitor.

"Rabbi Stein isn't here yet, and he has a meeting as soon as he arrives."

Bob took a quick look around. He saw three strangers and couldn't keep himself from establishing his dominance, especially considering that one of the visitors had a camera.

"I'm Bob Small," he announced, "President and official go-to-guy here. What's happening?"

"Oh yeah, Sheila's husband," Traub whispered to Jenny.

"We're here from *The Chicago Journal*," Traub explained. "We're doing a story about your synagogue."

"Best Orthodox *shul* in the country!" Bob boasted, as Jenny caught his posturing on camera. Having had his picture taken, Bob's ego expanded accordingly, and his mood improved. He glanced at the dark-skinned woman sitting near Serena. He assumed she was there for a job interview, and he had no interest in pursuing a relationship with a non-professional. *But hold it,* he thought, *could she be waiting to talk with Rabbi Stein? If she wants a job here, she should talk to me, not him. Is something going on behind my back?*

"Tell the Rabbi to call me ASAP!" Bob ordered, heading for the restroom. *Nothing gets past me*, he thought, smugly.

Serena was on overload. As she prepared to eject the the first duo of interlopers, Rabbi Joshua Stein rushed in, obviously rattled that he was late for his appointment with someone named Kayla Morales.

Uh-oh, Josh thought when he saw the troubled look on Serena's face, *Something's up*.

Serena tried to signal Josh of imminent danger, but she was too late. As Josh and Morales stood in front of Serena, Jenny took their picture. Traub already had the headline figured out: 'Radical Changes for Major Jewish Congregation?'

Josh caught Serena's eye, and she understood that he didn't recognize the two people from *The Journal*.

"Rabbi Stein," Serena clarified, "meet James Traub and his photographer. They're here from *The Chicago Journal* to get a story about Rabbi Halperin's departure, but I already explained that there is no story. They were just about to leave."

Traub and Rabbi Stein shook hands.

Josh turned to escort Morales into his office, but not before Jenny caught the shot.

"We'd like to make an appointment to interview Rabbi Stein," Traub said to Serena.

What can I do? she thought.

"He can give you fifteen minutes next Tuesday."

"We'll take it! It was a pleasure meeting you. Really enjoyed your busy office," Traub beamed.

Just as James and Jenny left the building, Bob rushed back into the office, hoping he hadn't missed anything.

"Serena," he asked, "What's that black lady doing here with Rabbi Stein? I've seen her here before, right?"

Serena knew not to tell Bob anything he didn't have to know. In any case, she was sure that Bob would ask the Rabbi about Kayla.

"Ms. Morales is a future member here. She came to services once or twice and she's probably going to apply for membership."

"I sure hope she's really Jewish, and I hope she expects to pay membership dues. Let's see what kind of detective Rabbi Stein is. Halperin would never have gotten into this."

CHAPTER 4

Kayla Morales and Rabbi Stein sat at a small round table in his office.

"Sorry I was so busy with congregants during the High Holidays. Thanks for making this meeting. So, what's on your mind?" Josh asked.

" I have a bone to pick with you."

Josh laughed, "A bone to pick? With me?"

Morales allowed herself a small smile. "It's your synagogue that hurt me."

Josh was intrigued. "Tell me what happened."

Before Morales began her story, she looked around the room. She spotted a group of family photographs behind the Rabbi's desk. In each one, a young man stood holding a certificate of some kind.

"Are those pictures of your family?" Kayla asked.

"They sure are. I'm the kid in the middle, proudly flaunting my awards."

"I never saw a rabbi's office without Jewish artwork on the walls. Are you too religious for that?"

Josh laughed, "If you knew anything about me, you'd know that religion wouldn't be the reason!"

"What do you mean?"

"I don't own any art. The photos on my desk tell my story. My family thought I was going to be a geneticist, but obviously, it didn't turn out that way."

"I understand. My family expected me to become a famous artist, spending my life creating masterpieces. Hasn't happened yet."

Josh continued, "I've only been here a few months. Office decorating wasn't on the agenda when there were congregants to meet and sermons to write. I came as the assistant rabbi and now I'm kind of in charge. The senior rabbi retired and is moving to Israel, so I'm here as interim until the Board decides what to do. But enough about me."

"I know the senior rabbi, and I know how he feels about Jews like me," Morales began. "In fact, I met Rabbi Halperin with my fiance. Rabbi Halperin really disappointed me and hurt Daniel. In fact, he refused to continue to meet with us."

Josh realized that whatever he said now could cause more problems. He hesitated, perhaps a bit too long. Finally, he spoke. He was definitely curious, but he was going to go slowly.

"OK, Ms. Morales, now tell me about you."

"My maternal grandmother, Rose Weiss, was a white, Jewish woman who married my black grandfather, Joseph Thomas. They met at Pratt Institute in Brooklyn and married against the will of both sets of parents. In those days, the only place for a mixed-race couple to live, especially two artists, was Bushwick, a tough neighborhood in New York. They had one child, my mother, Hannah, who is Jewish, according to Jewish law. I grew up with multi-racial friends and family, but with no formal Jewish education.

"My father, Antonio, has a black mother and Hispanic father. Now you see that I'm tri-racial! After high school, I decided to figure out who I really was. I spent a year traveling and ended up working on an archaeological dig in Caesarea. I always knew that according to Jewish law, with a Jewish mother and maternal grandmother, I'm one hundred percent Jewish, but not everyone wants to accept that.

"When I was in Israel, I hung out with a lot of Ethiopian Jews. My friends knew much more about Judaism than I did, so I began to take classes. I learned to read Hebrew and I took the Hebrew name, Kayla, a derivative of God's name. When I moved to Chicago, I joined Bet Hillel, where Rabbi Elijah Dalton is the spiritual leader."

"I have a lot of questions," Josh interjected, "and they're going to seem superficial, but humor me."

"OK...shoot!"

"Before you took the name Kayla, what was your English name?"

"Rosalie, after my late grandmother, Rose Weiss. Next?"

"Rose Weiss! That's quite an identifying name, isn't it? How did you get involved with Rabbi Dalton here in Chicago?"

"I came here to teach art at Bet Hillel Day School, which is affiliated with Rabbi Dalton's mainly black congregation. I felt accepted and needed there. Now, I'm trying Lev Shalom because a mainstream Orthodox synagogue is where I want to belong."

"Go on…"

"You'd think that by now the Orthodox movement would be used to Jewish people of color, and that's what I expected. I came here for several weeks in a row, and people were friendly enough, but your esteemed Rabbi Halperin was cold as ice."

"On Shabbat morning, everyone wants to talk to their rabbi," Josh explained. "It's a busy time for him. What did you expect?"

"I expected Rabbi Halperin to greet me warmly, try to get to know me, and welcome me when I applied for membership. To my knowledge, that application is either still on his desk six months later, or more likely gone. At least I expected a call from someone on the membership committee, a member of the board, or even the Rabbi's secretary. But nothing! I have to say that I was surprised to get that return call from the *shul* office, offering to make an appointment with you. Now, there's one more thing I have to add."

Was there no end to this woman's complicated life? Josh wondered, but he said, "I'm listening."

"My boyfriend, Daniel, is white."

"Is Daniel also Jewish?"

"Of course he's Jewish! He felt completely out of place at Bet Hillel with Rabbi Dalton, so I brought him here. But Rabbi Halperin had no interest in us. Daniel and I want to get married here, and I want this to be our *shul*."

"You're telling me that Daniel's been here at least once? You mentioned that he met Rabbi Halperin."

"Daniel and I met with the Rabbi twice. The first time was unbearably uncomfortable, but I forced a second meeting. Total disaster. Rabbi Halperin saw us as this weird, unconventional couple, and we understood that not only did the Rabbi disapprove of us, but he actually wanted us to disappear."

"Ms. Morales, that doesn't sound like Rabbi Halperin's style to me."

"Trust me! That's exactly how it was."

Josh realized that his responsibilities as the interim rabbi would involve people and situations for which he was completely unprepared. He wanted to reach out to this sincere woman, and he knew that it would involve many more stressful hours. He'd have to meet Daniel, and even harder, he'd probably have to speak with Rabbi Elijah Dalton about Kayla's lineage. Even more important, Josh had to find out why Halperin had rebuffed the couple.

Kayla sat back in her chair with her arms crossed, waiting for a response. She decided to give this young rabbi a chance to do the right thing.

"Let me get you another membership form," Josh offered. "The office administrator will take care of you. And while you're at Mrs. Berg's desk, why don't you make an appointment for me to meet with you and Daniel?"

Serena had been sitting at her desk, wondering what could be taking so long. She had assumed that Josh would quickly run through the meeting and get busy with the load of work waiting for him. She had noticed Kayla Morales at services a few times, but had never found out anything about her. What did she want? Originally, Serena thought that the requested meeting had something to do with a charity or an ecumenical lecture request. That would have taken ten minutes at the most.

One more thing to distract the Rabbi, Serena thought, maternally.

CHAPTER 5

Bunny noted the caller ID and frowned. She reluctantly let it go to voice-mail; she wasn't the type to delete messages meant for her husband, even though this one was from James Traub asking for a specific time and place to meet. Traub claimed to be a great admirer of her husband's books, but she was sure that the reporter from *The Chicago Journal* was deceptive, determined to uncover any confidential information surrounding their departure. Fred was successful at using media to promote his work and interests, but Bunny knew that reporters could be cunning. Was Fred going to be the subject of further humiliation?

Bunny sat for a few moments considering her options, finally deciding to discuss the message with Fred after he heard it himself. They had built Lev Shalom together, and it was time to leave together.

Fred came into the kitchen with a smile on his face. He had attended morning services at a different *shul* from Lev Shalom.

"Guess who I saw at services this morning?"

"Aren't you glad there are other Orthodox synagogues in our neighborhood?" Bunny smiled. "You'll probably enjoy visiting all of them before we leave Chicago. Anyway, who was there?"

"Kalman ran up to me after *davening,* just like we were old friends. He was never one of my fans, but now that I'm no longer the star at Lev

Shalom, he thinks I'm going to go to his *shul* until we leave town. I almost laughed, but caught myself. We may come back to Chicago from time to time, and I have other *davening* options than at Lev Shalom. Maybe I will go to Kalman's *shtieble*."

Bunny didn't like the sound of that. Even the people who still supported and admired them had become uncomfortable in the last few weeks, hearing unsubstantiated gossip. *Enough with them*, Bunny thought.

Fred still had an axe to grind, and he believed that his learning and experience would continue to guide him. He had never hated anyone, yet he was unable to let Bob Small's belligerence go unchecked. Although the two of them had reached an uncomfortable detente, Fred wouldn't leave Chicago until he reckoned with Bob.

"There's a message for you," Bunny mentioned, as her husband reached for the newspaper. "Please don't let that journalist drag you back into the hospital. Bob put you there, and even if he regrets it, he'll never admit the role he played."

Halperin listened to the message:

Greetings, Rabbi Halperin. This is James Traub from The Journal. *We spoke briefly a couple of days ago, and I'm not giving up. Can you find some time to discuss your books and relate a few personal anecdotes from your many years in the rabbinate? I admit that I know very little about Judaism and nothing about Lev Shalom, so whatever you can tell me will make a big difference. How about Thursday morning? I'll come to you.*

Halperin immediately dialed Traub's number and agreed to a Thursday meeting at home. His knee-jerk response stunned his wife, who stared at him in disbelief. Then, without saying a word, she picked up her cup of coffee and walked out of the room.

Halperin followed her. "Bunny, stop! Let's talk about this!"

"It's your ego, Fred. We've been married all these years, and it's only gotten worse! After everything we've both been through this year, you should be too smart to meet with a reporter. If you really believe that he wants to talk about your books, you're kidding yourself. That man is going to use you to further his nonexistent career. He'll get a contentious, blood-sucking story from you, and he'll milk it for all it's worth. And he won't stop with you, either. Oh no, he'll go to Bob and Sheila Small, then to inexperienced, unsuspecting Josh Stein, then to your sweet, loyal administrator, Serena, and finally to every single member who'll talk to him."

Halperin had seldom heard his wife speak so vehemently and never with such venom. Nevertheless, he was confident that he could successfully direct the interview. In fact, he looked forward to focusing on his books and illustrious career. There was no way the reporter knew anything about the Holocaust debacle, thank God. But if he did, Halperin was ready to set him straight.

Bunny decided not to dwell on her anxieties. Rather than argue with Fred, she clarified her position.

"OK, Fred, if you're determined to jump into Traub's trap, I'm not going to allow him to control the interview. Whether you like it or not, I'm going to sit by your side the whole time, and when I decide he's crossed a line, it'll be over."

Halperin smiled. "If you want to be there, it's fine with me. I've been interviewed hundreds of times, and I've always been in control. Nothing will be different this time. At this point, I'm just interested in selling my books, and Traub can help me do that."

Bunny was still upset, but she had made her point. There would be one interview, period. She'd allow her husband to offer a few amusing stories about their years at Lev Shalom. She had more important things to do, and she was going to do them.

"Fred, I'm trying to protect you, and I don't want to talk about it any more. We have to finish packing the books. Jewish Lending Library is coming Friday morning for donations, and I want to give them everything at one time."

Halperin was smart enough to pick up his coffee cup and follow his wife. They spent the next few hours working side by side, making hard choices of what to keep and what to leave behind.

CHAPTER 6

As soon as Kayla Morales returned to Bet Hillel Day School from her meeting at Lev Shalom, she raced to the art room, where the students were already at work. She quickly put on her smock and made her way around the room, assessing the portraits they were painting. One of the students, Samuel, had decided to do a larger-than-life painting of George Washington Carver. He surrounded Carver's face with a halo of peanuts and had peanut shells glued to the canvas. Kayla burst out laughing.

"Sammy, that's the most unusual depiction of a famous person I've ever seen!"

"But why are you laughing at it?" Sammy was hurt.

"I laughed in delight!" Kayla exclaimed. "Tell me about it."

"Well, the halo is something George Washington Carver deserved. His discoveries helped a lot of people, black and white. And the shells give it just the right texture."

"Do you really understand what Carver did? He made other discoveries, too. He was a great scientist, and you might want to include some of his other accomplishments in your portrait."

"But you still like it, right?"

"I love it. You're a good artist and you're very original, but do yourself a favor, and find out more about your subject."

Kayla always tried to integrate the students' artwork with the school curriculum. This project was conceived in conjunction with the history teacher to highlight minority personalities. The object was to inspire the students to investigate important people who were unknown to them. The artwork was fine, but Kayla was often disappointed at how little the students knew about their subjects. She would have to do something about that.

Sammy interrupted her musing. "Ms. Morales, my report about Carver is due in two weeks, but I don't get the science part."

Kayla was aware that the science teacher was not a warm and open-minded educator.

She was sure Sammy would be reluctant to ask his advice, and she wanted to keep Sammy from relying on the internet. She had a great idea.

Rabbi Stein told me he has a background in biology, she thought. *I'm going to ask him to talk to my students. An outsider usually makes a bigger impression than an unapproachable teacher.*

When Kayla had her brainstorm about bringing Rabbi Stein into her school, she had no idea that she was adding one more complication to his life. Josh should be spending any spare time he had repairing his relationship with Rachel Berg. His confidante/girlfriend, Serena's daughter, was angry and he'd have to work hard to be forgiven.

CHAPTER 7

Rachel had reason to be angry at Josh. Rosh Hashanah lunch at Rachel's parents' home should have been perfect. From the soup to the honey cake, a lively discussion about Israeli politics, and an atmosphere of conviviality made the afternoon pass pleasantly for everyone. At least that's what Serena Berg thought. Her daughter, Rachel, on the other hand, disagreed, to say the least.

Rabbi Joshua Stein, whose family had come from Boston for Rosh Hashana, and Serena and Herb Berg, Rachel's parents, were dining together for the first time. Josh, exhausted after delivering his first High Holiday sermons, was oblivious to the activity around the table and longed to return to the solitude of his own apartment. He realized that the lunch had been a mistake. His head was splitting, his eyes were heavy, and his throat was sore.

"Serena," Josh's mother, Susan, gushed, "Your rooms are so colorful! I wouldn't have the nerve to upholster a sofa in purple velvet, but it certainly makes a statement!"

Serena didn't know if she was being complemented or criticized, but she liked Josh's parents and hoped that they looked upon her with favor.

Susan continued, "I just realized that your hair exactly matches your dining room walls! Isn't copper just the best color in the whole world!"

Serena still wasn't sure, so she decided to tweak the conversation.

"Actually, Herb was the force behind these walls," Serena stated. "I'm lucky to have a husband who cares about home decor."

Herb caught that last statement, but wasn't sure what his wife wanted from him. He wondered, *Serena must have something up her sleeve. Either she never noticed that I don't give a shit about home decor, or she's making some point with Josh's mother. Probably trying to impress the Boston crowd.*

"And I just love all the mirrors," Susan continued, "and the sconces."

Serena realized that Susan was trying hard to heap on the compliments, but it was too much. Herb changed the subject, and it was about time.

"Josh's dad and I were comparing notes about our rabbis, and we agree that Josh's sermon was spectacular, even though he's new at the job."

Josh didn't have the energy to express humility or gratitude. The best he could do was smile wanly. He caught Rachel's eye, hoping she'd take over.

Rachel, who had looked forward to the meeting of their parents, was aware of Josh's discomfort, but she was in no mood to feel compassion for his lack of attentiveness. Months earlier, she had made her matrimonial intentions clear to Josh's Boston mentor, Rabbi Mordechai Goldschmidt, but had not received encouragement. Nevertheless, her experience as an attorney had schooled her. She knew that every case can be settled satisfactorily if both parties find common benefit. Josh needed her, and she wanted him. That seemed like a mutually beneficial arrangement to her. And she was pretty sure that they were in love, so how could she move things along?

Josh's parents and his brother, Ben, enjoyed spending the afternoon with Serena and Herb Berg. Each mother fantasized about a moment in the future when they would stand under a *chuppah*. They sensed the closeness between Josh and Rachel who were deep in conversation after services. On the way to lunch, the couple slowed down and continued to speak privately. However, at the table, Josh's exhaustion overtook him, and Rachel was left to dazzle his parents on her own.

Dazzling was Rachel's forte. She was a whiz at work and in her volunteer activities. She was usually the smartest and most stunning woman in the room, and once she set her mind on something, it was her habit to achieve it. Josh's parents were clearly impressed with her intelligence and quick wit. Susan Stein noticed that Rachel was more than able to cover for her lethargic son, and she knew it was a valuable trait. Dan and Ben Stein both appreciated Rachel's ability to talk about Chicago sports teams and current events. In summation, she was a big hit with the Stein family.

In retrospect, Josh regretted that he had not contributed to the bonhomie of the lunch. He wished he hadn't been so worn out, but the fact that he hadn't fallen asleep at the table was amazing in itself. He was grateful that Rachel was there to keep things going. Even though both sets of parents would certainly be sympathetic, it would take a lot to gain Rachel's forgiveness.

CHAPTER 8

Rachel Berg, who, while at work, should have been strategizing for a partnership in her firm, was distracted. The lunch at which her parents met Josh's family had been far from satisfying. While the Bergs and Steins thoroughly enjoyed each other's company, Josh was barely present.

The young rabbi, who was already beloved by the active and demanding Lev Shalom teen group, and who never tired of hospital or *shiva* visits, showed none of his vigor at the *Yom Tov* lunch table, the very place Rachel expected him to shine. In addition, Josh had claimed to be looking forward to the meeting of their families. True, he was coming down from the intensity of two days of important sermons, prayers, and greeting congregants. It was also a fact that Josh worried about his future after the imminent departure of Rabbi Halperin. In spite of these concerns, Rachel refused to give Josh a pass.

Josh has plenty of energy for everybody else, Rachel thought, *but I should be the focus of his attention.* She had to admit that she was selfish, but so what? She still believed that she was in love with Josh, and she still believed that she wanted to be his wife and a congregational *rebbitzin.* She also understood that at most gatherings her mother carried the conversation. In fact, she had to admit that it was common for many men to depend on their wives in social situations, but she wasn't about to model herself after them. Besides, Josh was capable of more.

Rachel and Josh's easy conversation on the way to lunch could have led to a lively afternoon. Instead, the person who should have cemented the group may just as well have gone home. Rachel was in no mood to feel compassion. Because she found it impossible to concentrate on her work, and because she believed that confrontation is the best approach to solutions, Rachel took action.

Josh spent all day fielding phone calls and attending meetings. His talk with Kayla Morales lasted much longer than expected, and as soon as she left, he and Serena scheduled the rest of his week. Serena wisely avoided talking about the recent lunch with Josh's family (whom she really liked) or his relationship with her daughter. The lunch was past; it was back to business.

"It's after six," Serena announced, stifling a yawn and stretching. "Are you as worn out as I am?"

"I really appreciate your help, Serena. I'm just about overwhelmed."

"Let's stop for now. You have a day full of appointments tomorrow and a few hospital visits."

"And everything else," Josh noted. "Am I expected to be part of the farewell events for the Halperins?"

"Bob Small was clear with me," Serena explained. "I'm not to burden you or Bunny Halperin with plans. Bob has already selected his com-mittee. He's one *shul* president who loves to take over. I'm not surprised that Bob's making sure that we say goodbye to the Halperins for good, no matter what it takes."

After a full day, Josh finally found a few minutes to grab a snack from the *shul* kitchen, where there was always a supply of crackers, hummus, and soda left over from the Shabbat *kiddush*. He realized he hadn't checked his email yet, so he brought his food back to his desk. He noticed that Rachel had messaged him. He was pleased to end his workday with news from her, but when he opened her email, he couldn't believe the tone or content. It was the exact opposite of what he hoped.

Josh,

Why did you bother to come to lunch if you weren't willing to hold up your end of the conversation? Were you actually too selfish to talk to everybody? I thought you wanted our families to meet as much as I did. Do you think you owe anyone, such as my parents, an apology?

Rachel

CHAPTER 9

After sending her email to Josh, Rachel decided it would be better to face him personally. She considered stopping by Lev Shalom after work, but that would look too desperate, and she'd risk bumping into her mother or other congregants. It was Josh, and Josh alone, she wanted to see.

On her way home, she passed the synagogue. It was already quite late, and she was surprised to spot Josh as he was getting into his car.

Why not? Rachel decided, uncertain if Josh had seen the email she sent. *If he's seen it, I know he'll want to talk about it. If not, now's as good a time as any to confront him.*

Rachel pulled into the parking lot next to Josh's car, and he nodded when he saw her. He got out of his car and went to her side. She rolled down the window, eager to hear what he had to say. They looked at each other for a few seconds, seeing who would blink first. Rachel immediately knew he had read her angry words.

" Apparently you read my email," Rachel said.

Josh was hurt. "You're so critical. You knew very well how exhausted I was at lunch and you also know the stress I'm under. I was so out-of-it that I needed to depend on you to keep things going when our parents were together."

"And I did just that!" Rachel shot back. "You aren't the only one who's stressed. It's important to me that our parents get along, and I fully expected you to help. You could have forced yourself. After services at *shul*, with the congregants you were full of life; on the way to lunch, you seemed fine to me. It's like you have two different personalities."

Josh could tell that no matter what he said, Rachel wasn't going to calm down. He certainly wasn't in the mood to defend himself. This was a side of Rachel he didn't like one bit, even if she was right. Was every disagreement between them going to result in him being on trial?

Rachel didn't know what to do. She had expected Josh to be contrite, but he surprised her. Even if she had over-reacted, it was the principle of the situation. She had planned to present them as a couple, and Josh either didn't get it, or even worse, didn't want it. If she drove away now, would that be smart? If she stayed, the argument would probably get more out of hand. She waited for Josh to make the next move, and he did.

"We're both upset, and we have a lot to talk about, but not now. I hope to see you in services on *Shabbos.*"

He doesn't want to see me until Shabbos? I wonder if something else is going on, Rachel thought. *If he can wait, so can I.* She sat in her car and watched Josh leave. She was in no mood to go home, and she didn't feel like making small talk with any of her friends. She called her mother and asked to meet at Kalman's.

Herb Berg was only too happy to eat a sandwich and watch sport recaps in his favorite chair in the den. Serena met Rachel for dinner just as it started to get busy. Heading to their table, Serena was surprised to spot Kayla Morales. What was the woman who had spent such a long time with Rabbi Stein that very afternoon doing there? Serena recalled that

Kayla and a man had visited Lev Shalom a couple of times, and they had met with Rabbi Halperin, but those meetings had been short. Once again, Serena was aware that a lot of interesting things had taken place in Rabbi Halperin's office over the years, but she had never been privy to any of them. Now that Kayla had met Rabbi Stein, it was possible that Serena could find out more because, so far, he had proven to be more forthcoming than his predecessor.

After her talk with Rabbi Stein, Kayla was optimistic about becoming part of a mainstream Orthodox community in Chicago. She knew that Kalman's Kosher Dairy Restaurant was a popular neighborhood meeting place. When she called her fiance, Daniel Lewisohn, to suggest dinner there, he reluctantly agreed. Daniel, after being rebuffed by Rabbi Halperin, felt marginalized, and he had no desire to rub shoulders with people who would likely not welcome them as a couple. But he wanted to please Kayla. Restaurant owner, Kalman, delighted to welcome this new good-looking interracial couple, seated them close to the entrance, where they would attract attention.

Serena was curious about the couple. Kayla had left the Lev Shalom office with a synagogue membership application. Was she interested in conversion? Was it possible that she was Jewish? And wasn't the handsome young man with her the same one who'd been with her at Lev Shalom? Serena decided to stop at their table, while Rachel stood impatiently next to her mother.

Kayla and Serena recognized each other, and Kayla wanted Daniel to have a good feeling about the Lev Shalom administrator who had been so kind to her.

"Miss Morales, it's wonderful to see you again, and so soon!" Serena exclaimed.

Kayla was relieved that the first person they met remembered her and was so gracious. "Let me introduce you to my fiance, Daniel Lewisohn. Daniel, this is Mrs. Berg, the Lev Shalom administrator. The two of you met, but it was a while ago when we came to talk to Rabbi Halperin."

Serena remembered them. Completing the introductions, she added, attempting familiarity, "And this is my daughter, Rachel, the attorney." *Why did I say that?* Serena asked herself.

Rachel rolled her eyes and, frowning, subtly nudged her mother. Daniel stood to face Serena. He wasn't going to beat around the bush.

"Kayla told me that her experience this afternoon was completely different from the ones we had with the old rabbi. Kayla wants to join Lev Shalom, but it's not the right place for us. I'm the kind of person who likes to put my cards on the table, and it's going to take more than the new, improved, friendly rabbi and a smiling office worker to change my mind. I can spot phonies a mile away."

Rachel's adrenalin kicked in, and she knew she and her mother should move away as quickly as possible. She could see that Kayla was embarrassed by her fiance's inappropriate comments, and she was relieved that at least one of the pair had some sense. Rachel could just imagine the conversation that would take place between the couple when she and her mother left. She was sure that Kayla would put Daniel in his place.

Rachel squarely faced him, "Well, Mr. Lewisohn, I know you'll be candid, if and when you show up for services at our synagogue. It's reassuring to know that there's someone in the congregation keeping us on our toes. Too bad you can't use a scoreboard on Shabbat...or do you?"

"Enjoy your meals," was the best Serena could manage, concerned that Rachel always had to have the last word.

It was now Serena's turn to nudge her daughter. Moving toward their own table, Serena couldn't believe Daniel's rudeness, especially compared to Kayla who seemed so polite and amiable. *I wonder what their story is*, she thought.

Daniel was ready to leave the restaurant, even though they hadn't been served yet. "What a bitch! The mother seemed OK, but her daughter was messing with the wrong guy. I'm not intimidated by stuck-up lawyers any more than I am by pompous Orthodox rabbis. Let's go."

Kayla, too, was upset. Her intention to ease her fiance into the Lev Shalom community was already backfiring. *What just happened? Daniel has to control his anger and sarcasm, but that pompous Rachel didn't have to egg him on, did she? I'll have to call the Lev Shalom office first thing tomorrow, apologize to Serena, and make an appointment with Rabbi Stein.*

As if on cue, Kalman appeared at their table and presented their meals with a huge smile. He sensed tension, but ignored it. He always knew how to deal with an uncomfortable situation, and he prided himself on the cheerful, *haimishe* atmosphere of his restaurant. He was a natural *shmoozer,* who knew every patron, or at least acted like he did. Everybody loved Kalman, and Kalman loved them back.

Kayla took Daniel's hands in hers. Daniel began to calm down after his opening salvo, satisfied that he had made his point. *I'm going to get Kayla away from that mother/daughter duo. She's such a pushover, but I'm not. She should be grateful that I'm here to protect her from these fakes. She better not fall under Stein's spell.*

"Right out of the oven! And just for you!" Kalman exclaimed, placing the baked ziti and breaded tilapia on the table with a flourish. "If you need more bread or anything else, just wave in my direction."

Across the room, Serena and Rachel ate their meals in silence. Serena wished that her outspoken daughter hadn't responded to Daniel's rudeness. While Rachel concentrated on her meal, periodically shooting arrows in Daniel's direction, Serena's mind wandered…

Does Rachel always have to act like a prosecutor? Other people's daughters are home putting their children to sleep, and here I am with my critical, beautiful daughter. No wonder she's not married. She can't ever let anything go. And what's the story between her and Rabbi Stein? She's mad at him for something, probably nothing important. God forbid, if I ask her about it, she'll bite my head off.

Kalman noticed that Serena and her daughter were uncharacteristically morose. They usually had so much to talk about that they were often the last to leave the restaurant. He grabbed two pieces of baklava and brought them to their table.

"I figured the two of you are so quiet tonight because you have a sugar deficiency, so I'm here to remedy that."

It worked.

Serena broke the ice, 'We're thinking about the couple sitting in front. I know them, but Rachel got a bad first impression. The woman seems very nice and refined, but the man isn't."

Kalman sat down at their table, all ears. "What happened?"

Rachel was only too happy to oblige. "I'm sure my mother isn't going to say anything else, but I will. That man insulted my mother and Rabbi Stein, not only in words but in his infantile attitude. What a supercilious jerk!"

"Have they been here before?" Serena asked.

"No, and I have to tell you that I hope they come back. Rachel, honey, I'm sure that if, and when, that man gets to know your mother and Rabbi Stein, he'll change his tune. Speaking of which, I haven't seen Rabbi Stein here for a while."

"I know where you're going with this," Rachel laughed. "You're not getting any dirt from me."

Serena sighed, "Nice try, Kalman. She doesn't tell me anything personal either, but the baklava will make the evening better."

"She's right," Rachel agreed, her mood improving. "Baklava is a universal medicine."

His mission partially accomplished, Kalman returned to the counter and got back to work. He had successfully cleared the air between mother and daughter, but he was no closer to finding out about Rachel and Josh Stein. Well, tomorrow was another day.

CHAPTER 10

While they ate, Kayla and Daniel were deep in their own thoughts. Kayla was good at reading Daniel's mind, and she was sure that he would do his best to separate her from Lev Shalom, Serena, and Rabbi Stein. It would take some doing, but Kayla refused to be dominated by anyone, even her fiancé. Daniel's initial experiences with Rabbi Halperin at Lev Shalom had been disastrous, but she was determined to fix it.

Kayla was used to running interference. Her siblings were often in trouble, and when she met Daniel, she was comfortable with that scruffy, shoot-from-the-hip, fast-thinking personality. They had met in grad school in Chicago, both in education, but at opposite ends of the spectrum. Daniel's understanding and love of sports could have led him to a career as a high school PE teacher and coach. That kind of life might have made him happier, but he decided to change directions and go into computers.

Kayla's life-long interest and hands-on experience in the arts led her to the studio, where, unfortunately, she was financially unsuccessful. She became an art teacher by default, and then discovered the joy of sharing her passion with young people.

As an art student from a working class family, Kayla knew she needed a backup plan, so she took education classes in the evening. They met when Daniel was a model in one of her life drawing classes. They dated for two years, and when she entered grad school full time, they started living together. Daniel was not happy that Kayla had started spending Sundays studying with Rabbi Elijah Dalton at Bet Hillel. In Daniel's opinion, she was already Jewish enough, and her growing interest in traditional Judaism irritated him.

On one occasion, Daniel had directly confronted Rabbi Dalton, claiming that he was interfering in their lives. The weekends had been Daniel and Kayla's only time together. Now, on Saturdays, Kayla was unwilling to do anything that contradicted Jewish law. Those were the very things that Daniel liked to do: attend sports events, go to movies, sample ethnic restaurants, and take long drives. Kayla had moved her focus away from him to Judaism, and Daniel wanted her back.

In spite of this, they stayed together. Daniel respected Kayla. She was smart, clear-headed and sexy. And Kayla admired his strength. After Daniel's father suffered a stroke, his mother was worn out from managing their shoe repair shop and worrying about her boisterous sons. When Daniel was fourteen, he and his two brothers found that they were destined to take care of themselves. Fortunately, Daniel's high school coach watched over him, becoming his mentor. The other brothers didn't fare as well, but Daniel wasn't stuck in the past. With Kayla in his life, he had nurse, confidante, and lover all in one. He would never let her go.

CHAPTER 11

The day after the unpleasant restaurant incident, Serena got a call in the office from Kayla, who was determined to head off the confrontation she was sure would erupt between her fiance and Rabbi Stein. Kayla hoped to prepare the Rabbi for the meeting that afternoon.

Josh believed he could handle Daniel. After all, he had learned how to deal with the contentious personality of the synagogue president. If he could work with Bob Small, he was pretty sure that Daniel wouldn't be a problem for him.

Kayla, on the other hand, had seen her fiance in action, and she knew that he welcomed any opportunity to demonstrate his machismo. She also worried that Serena would react to Daniel when they were face to face in the office. Kayla hoped that Serena would act professionally and not dredge up the confrontation at Kalman's. Damage control had become one of Kayla's hard-won specialties.

Daniel was waiting for Kayla after school. He was in a good mood be-cause he had secured a new client in his computer business. Kayla was relieved that he was smiling. Daniel told her about his new opportunity and boasted that it was a big coup.

Kayla seized the moment to plan the scenario with Daniel. "I'm bring-ing the synagogue application with me, and I've signed it already. I want you to join, too. I truly believe that Rabbi Stein is much more than a 'sweet-talking rabbi', and you'll like him if you give him a chance."

"I'm going to meet Stein with you, aren't I? What else do you want? You know that I make my own decisions, so we'll just see how it goes."

Kayla changed the subject. "After our meeting, let's check out the *shul* social hall to see if it's right for the wedding reception."

"It's going to cost plenty, no matter where it is. The budget stays as is. It'd be different if our families were kicking anything in. You don't agree, but both of us come from loser families."

That last statement hurt Kayla, whose parents and siblings struggled daily to maintain their self-respect and independence. She wished she could help them, but the best she could do was take care of herself. She had to admit, however, that Daniel's family was a mess. Daniel had a lot to deal with, and Kayla knew that she was the one who provided stability and order in his life.

Daniel and Kayla walked into the Lev Shalom office, holding hands. Serena quickly escorted them into the Rabbi's office. Josh greeted them and shook Daniel's hand, then the three of them sat at a small round table.

"I'm happy to meet you," Josh said to Daniel, who was clearly not pleased to be there. Josh realized that cordiality would not be flowing both ways, but he persevered.

"I'm sorry your initial experiences here weren't good ones. How can I fix that?"

Kayla tried to set the tone. "Rabbi Stein, we're here to get to know you better. I've decided to join Lev Shalom, but my fiance has reservations."

"I can speak for myself, Kayla."

"I'm listening," Josh said, encouragingly.

Daniel stood up to deliver his message. "Kayla, here, is obsessed with Orthodox Judaism, but I'm not. In fact, if it weren't for her, I'd have nothing to do with anything Jewish. I met your Rabbi Halperin twice, and each time I was given nothing but challenges, not to mention his icy demeanor when Kayla and I talked about marriage. Either he's racist or just plain full of himself. So, Rabbi Stein, now you know how I feel."

"I appreciate everything you say, and if I were in your shoes, I might feel the same way. I assure you that Rabbi Halperin is neither racist nor stand-offish, but apparently he hurt you. Last year was difficult for the Rabbi, and you may or may not know that he was hospitalized. However, that's irrelevant now."

Josh was certain that Rabbi Halperin had legitimate reasons for his actions, and he was also sure it was entirely due to Daniel.

Kayla rose, gently taking her fiance's hand. "I'm grateful that Daniel's here and that he's been honest. I feel that both Daniel and I can be comfortable and feel welcome at Lev Shalom. I want us to be married at this beautiful place. It means a lot to me; however, if Daniel can't find a place for himself here, I'll become a member and we'll get married somewhere else."

Daniel dropped Kayla's hand and got close to Josh's face. "I can tell you right now that Kayla's living in a dream world if she thinks everything will work out. It's her fantasy. I've already decided to give you, Rabbi Stein, one chance, and one chance only, to convince me that any of this is worth my time."

Josh had heard enough, and he stood up to face Daniel. "Mr. Lewisohn, this isn't some kind of a contest, so I'm not going to fight with you. I'd love to see you at services this Shabbat, and I hope that we can get to know each other. At least I'm interested in getting to know you better. I assume that an intelligent woman like your fiance would have a superior partner. I really mean it when I say that I look forward to learning why she chose you. I think it'll be helpful if you take off your boxing gloves and sit down again."

Daniel conceded, "OK, Rabbi, you won this round. You're tougher and might be more honest than the old guy."

Kayla wanted to end the meeting on a positive note. "Rabbi Stein, when can we get together again? I'll be at services this week, and maybe Daniel will come with me."

"Don't count on it, Babe," Daniel warned, "but go ahead and set up the next appointment with the Rabbi."

With that last comment, Daniel led Kayla to the door. Stein quickly reached for Daniel's hand and managed a quick final handshake. Kayla caught the Rabbi's eye and smiled at him as they left.

As they passed Serena's desk on their way out, Bob Small was standing there. He saw Kayla and Daniel, but disregarded the warning glance from Serena. Bob stopped the couple before they could escape.

"I've seen you before, right?" Bob asked Kayla.

"We met just the other day, right here, in front of Mrs. Berg's desk," Kayla reminded him.

"And you've been to services here, too, right?"

"You have a great memory, Mr…?"

"Bob Small. *Shul* president, at your service."

Bob turned to Daniel, still fishing. "And you must be somebody special to be with such a good-looking lady."

Daniel didn't appreciate being referred to as a tag-along, and he clearly understood that 'somebody special' really meant 'who the hell are you?' Kayla knew Daniel's habit of finding an excuse to get his feelings hurt. She was especially determined to keep Daniel from engaging in a pissing contest with yet another important Lev Shalom person. It would be the second time in one afternoon.

Bob attempted a handshake, but Daniel put his hand on Kayla's back to hasten their exit. Bob completely missed that gesture, determined to make a good impression on this interracial couple. He was nothing, if not modern.

Disregarding Serena's discomfort, Bob pushed ahead, smiling, "So tell me what brought the two of you to Lev Shalom?"

Daniel automatically placed Bob in the growing category of 'condescending synagogue phonies', adding him to Elijah Dalton, Ephraim Halperin, Josh Stein, and that red-headed secretary.

"I'm finished here!" Daniel announced, heading purposefully out the door, leaving Kayla to do damage control, as usual.

Once again, Kayla covered for her fiance. Daniel had never hit her. Of course, that would have been crossing a line which Kayla would never allow. But she was so used to the testosterone-heavy men in her family that she had become an expert in protecting them from themselves.

She really believed that these difficult males were victims of their own backgrounds, and she forgave them. Kayla had to move past the uncomfortable spot in which Daniel had placed them.

"Sorry," Kayla said, making sure to take both Serena and Bob into her apology. "Daniel came here as a favor to me, and it's been too much. Please forgive that outburst. He's really not like that," she lied.

Serena and Bob were sure that Daniel was indeed like that, but they liked this young woman and felt sympathy for her.

Bob had encountered many 'Daniels' in his life, but he wasn't in the mood to deal with this one. On the other hand, he wanted to be kind to Kayla, maybe even get her to join Lev Shalom without her fiance. He gave Kayla a reassuring wink and walked her out of the office, oblivious to the fact that Serena had witnessed everything.

Kayla turned and waved to Serena as she left.

Returning to the office, Bob was proud of himself, as usual. "Serena, you're lucky I was here. I know how to handle people like that guy, but why would that girl put up with him?"

Serena held her tongue. *If Bob hadn't been here, probably none of this would have happened. I would've just said a kind good-bye. Rachel and I had enough of Daniel at Kalman's. I'd sure like to know what took place with those two in Rabbi Stein's office.*

Josh came out of his office to find Bob standing at Serena's desk.

"I don't know who that guy thinks he is, but I handled him, didn't I, Serena?" Bob boasted.

Serena was at a loss. She really wanted to talk to Josh about the encounter, but she certainly wasn't going to do that in front of Bob. Serena took her new role as Josh's unofficial protector seriously. She was sure that he had managed Daniel Lewisohn well, but she also felt that her years working with Rabbi Halperin gave her experience she could share to Rabbi Stein's advantage. He wouldn't broach the subject with her, but Serena was strategically positioned to inform him of everything she witnessed.

"Good to see you, Bob," Josh said, deliberately redirecting the conversation.

"Nice try, Rabbi, but I just talked to that couple coming out of your office, and as *shul* president, it's my job to get the dirt on potential congregants. I'm sure that there's a whole pile there."

"The couple clearly doesn't conform to our typical membership, but I wouldn't assume anything about either of them," Josh cautioned.

Bob picked up on the Rabbi's comment. "The black girl was fine, although I'm guessing she's not really Jewish. But that's beside the point. The white guy's a *schmuck*, but I finessed it, didn't I Serena?"

Serena knew she had to say something, and looking at Rabbi Stein, she answered, "It's always instructive to watch Bob in action."

Satisfied that he had secured his position with a subordinate, Bob led the way into the Rabbi's office.

Serena sighed and leaned back in her chair. *Rabbi Stein better call Rabbi Halperin. If anybody knows what to do about that unusual couple, it'll be Rabbi Halperin.*

CHAPTER 12

It was Thursday morning in the Halperin's half-packed study. The Rabbi took off his *tallis* and *telfillin* and went into the kitchen where Bunny greeted him with a frown. She was deeply disappointed that her husband who, until a few months ago, had exhibited a strong sense of self-preservation, now was falling victim to his need for vengeance. She knew he planned to use the press to repair his image and, in the process, bring down Bob Small. Bunny was sure the plan would backfire.

"Fred, there's still time to call Traub and cancel. Do yourself a favor and spend the day with me."

"He's coming here to interview me about my books. I'm looking forward to it. Don't worry."

Halperin moved to the kitchen table to eat his bland breakfast. He missed the french toast his wife used to make him before his heart problems began. It didn't take him long to finish the oatmeal and dry whole wheat toast. He was impatient: He couldn't wait for the young reporter to get there.

At eleven a.m. sharp, the doorbell rang. Bunny answered it. She had intended to be present throughout the interview but changed her mind, knowing that it would diminish Fred's stature. Bunny had always trusted her husband in rabbinical matters and stood by his side through every kind of challenge. She hoped he would exhibit the self-control and wisdom of which he was capable.

"Come in, Mr. Traub. I'm about to leave the house, so you and my husband can make yourselves comfortable. Help yourself to some coffee and cookies."

Just then, Rabbi Halperin, impeccably dressed in a three-piece suit, starched white shirt, and silk tie, came into the foyer and extended his hand to Traub.

Taking in the boxes and wrapping materials around the rooms, Traub thanked the Rabbi. "I know my timing isn't good, but I really want to talk about your books and the strong legacy you leave behind. I didn't bring my photographer. My intention is to have an informal talk with you about anything that you'd like to cover. Is that OK?"

"More than OK, Mr. Traub. Come, sit down. Let's get started."

"Rabbi, please call me James."

Halperin led the reporter to a comfortable chair and took a seat beside him, offering Bunny's homemade cookies. "I recommend that you take at least two of these to start. They're the best cookies you'll ever eat!"

Traub liked the Rabbi's manner. He knew how to put a stranger at ease. This interview was definitely going to go well.

CHAPTER 13

Josh asked Serena to arrange a meeting with Rabbi Elijah Dalton at Bet Hillel. He was the rabbi of the first Orthodox synagogue in Chicago that Kayla joined, and he also directed the school where she taught art. Josh realized that if he wanted to help Kayla with Daniel's obstinate behavior, he needed information, and Josh hoped that Rabbi Dalton would give him insight about the couple.

Dalton was free late the next morning, and Josh headed to the southwest side of Chicago, the old Jewish neighborhood. Pulling into the parking lot of Bet Hillel, Josh saw two cars, a vintage Cadillac parked beside a recent model Toyota Corolla. *Which of these does Dalton drive?*, Josh wondered, as he headed into the synagogue.

The building itself, although in need of renovation, was majestic, with high ceilings, a mosaic floor depicting the Twelve Tribes, intricate moldings, and beautiful carved doors leading into the sanctuary. The original congregants were European immigrants, who modeled their house of worship after those of their homeland. There was a sense of holiness here, and Josh was reminded of similar classic synagogues back in Boston.

The office, on the other hand, was modern and utilitarian. Josh was greeted by a plump woman with intricately braided gray hair, colorful jewelry and a cheerful demeanor. Josh noted a plaque on her desk, *Sarah Bright*.

"Good morning, Ms. Bright."

"Shalom, shalom, Rabbi Stein," she greeted him. "You're exactly on time; very admirable! Hope you didn't have too much trouble navigating the morning traffic on Roosevelt Road."

I bet she's the one who owns the Cadillac, Josh decided.

She led him into Rabbi Dalton's office, which looked like a traditional rabbi's study, with the added panache of an art museum. Ethiopian tapestries and embroidery from Israel covered the walls. Hand-made pottery and tooled leather tomes shared the carved shelves with a full set of the Babylonian Talmud, ritual objects, and hundreds of other books in Hebrew and English. Some looked familiar, and some did not. The centerpiece of the room was a massive ebonized wooden desk.

Interesting, very interesting. I wish I could spend a long time here, Josh thought, taking it all in.

Suddenly, Rabbi Dalton burst into his office, touching the *mezuzah* on the doorpost, and immediately embracing Josh. Dalton was a broad-shouldered, beaming presence, in a dark gray double-breasted suit, striped bow-tie and an embroidered Bukhari *kippah*. His mustache and goatee were perfectly trimmed, and his tortoise-shell glasses sat atop his groomed salt-and-pepper hair.

"Shalom, shalom!" Dalton exclaimed. "So you're the new rabbi at Lev Shalom. I've been remiss in not reaching out to you before this. It's about time we see a new face there! I certainly admire the old guard, like your Rabbi Halperin, but I truly love welcoming young clergy into our rather stodgy ranks. I hope you've come about something meaty."

With this pronouncement, Dalton gave a hearty laugh, led Josh to a large leather armchair, and added, "So, Rabbi Stein, what brings you to our side of town?"

Dalton took the matching chair beside Josh and waited until his visitor got comfortable. Josh faced a mocha-skinned, handsome man, in his fifties or sixties. He seemed to be the kind of colleague who was not afraid to speak his mind, and Josh decided to skip small-talk and get right to the point.

"I've come for advice about Kayla Morales and her fiance, Daniel Lewisohn," Josh began. He could tell that Dalton was a seasoned listener, who nodded and gestured in all the right places. "She wants to join our *shul*, but Daniel's another story. They claim that before I came to Lev Shalom, they met with Rabbi Halperin, and he pushed them away. That's not Halperin's style. He's much more subtle and nuanced than that. Can you tell me anything I should know?"

"I'll tell you this much," Dalton answered, "Kayla's a vessel of gold, and Daniel's a bucketful of horse manure that she carries around. She has her reasons, but they're misguided and self-destructive. Kayla works in our school, and she's an excellent teacher, but her fiance brought trouble into our congregation. Daniel's not a nice guy. He picks fights over everything, and she puts up with it. My advice, Rabbi Stein, with all due respect, is learn from your old-time, seasoned Rabbi Halperin. Steer clear of those two."

"What if Daniel comes around and they both want to join our *shul*?"

"Without professional counseling, and I mean heavy duty, it's a bad idea. I made it clear to Daniel that he's not welcome here, and the guy actually threatened me."

"You mean it? Would he really do anything?"

Dalton took a minute to craft his answer. "Maybe yes, maybe no, but he's volatile. Here's my real fear: One of these days he's going to cross the line with Kayla, and that would be the last straw. Without her calming influence, anything can happen."

Josh couldn't help asking, "Did he ever hurt her?"

"She wouldn't allow that. She comes from a pretty rough family, and she knows how to handle herself. The truth is that without Kayla, Daniel couldn't keep going. She's stronger than he is."

"There's something appealing about women like that, isn't there?" Josh asked.

Dalton raised his eyebrows. He was amused but responded seriously, "Watch out, Rabbi Stein. You've just given yourself a perfect reason to stop seeing them."

Josh was surprised and embarrassed at his own admission, and he knew Dalton was right. During rabbinic training, he and the other students had been cautioned about getting too involved with congregants of the opposite sex. It had already happened with Rachel, and Josh didn't want it to happen again. He would have liked to continue talking with Dalton, but, having received important information, he had to get back to work.

"I appreciate your honesty and advice," Josh said. "I hope we'll continue to meet."

"I'm going to be on your side of town on Monday night," Dalton offered. "How about meeting me for some good kosher food?"

"Let's go to Kalman's," Josh suggested. "Do you know him?"

"Everybody knows Kalman. Unfortunately, I don't get there very often. I eat at home almost every night. My wife's food and company are far better than Kalman's, but I look forward to joining you there."

"Thank you for seeing me on such short notice," Josh said, gratefully.

"When I got a call that the new rabbi at the world-famous Lev Shalom wanted to talk to me, I knew it was big," Dalton joked. "Oh, one more thing…"

"Something else?" Josh had a flash of panic. What would Dalton reveal now?

"Now that we're friends, call me Elijah."

"With pleasure," Josh replied. "And from now on, I'm Josh. See you Monday, Elijah."

On his way out of Bet Hillel, Josh paused at the front desk. "Ms. Bright, you have a beautiful synagogue," he smiled, "and a beautiful car!" *Let's see if I'm right about that,* he thought.

"Oh, you like my old Caddy? It gets more attention than I do. Speaking of beauty, we also have beautiful members. Come back to meet some of them."

"I'll do that!" Josh answered, and he meant it.

"Shalom, shalom!" she called after him.

"Shalom, shalom!" Josh called back, and he meant that, too.

That's a great way to greet and say good-bye. I wonder if everyone at

Bet Hillel says that, Josh mused.

Getting into his car, Josh checked his cell phone, which he had silenced before the meeting. He took a look around the parking lot. Was he seeing things, or were there two flat tires on Dalton's car? *I didn't notice that before. When did that happen?* He texted the information about the tires to Sarah Bright and went on his way.

CHAPTER 14

Kayla was taking her usual lunch break between classes. In nice weather, she enjoyed walking from the school parking lot to the Bet Hillel lot. The usual two cars were in their regular spots, and she smiled as she passed Sarah Bright's huge Cadillac. Glancing at Rabbi Dalton's car, she was surprised to note two flat tires, and she had a disturbing suspicion. It was unlikely that there had been any vandals around that morning. The Cadillac was untouched. She was sure that none of the students in her school next door, who respected their rabbi, would have had the means or motivation to damage his car.

Kayla was worried. *Did Daniel do it? He's the only guy I know who's immature and angry enough to do something that childish. I knew that Rabbi Dalton's dismissal of Daniel would have a backlash. I really believed that they would get along and that Daniel could find a place for himself in Judaism. Rabbi Dalton's forthright style set Daniel off, just like all the other times with strong male figures. Daniel always has to feel like he's on top and the rules for everyone else don't apply to him.*

She pulled out her phone and called her fiance.

"What's up, Kalya?" Daniel grumbled. Apparently, she had disturbed him.

"Where are you now?"

"In my car. Why?"

"Aren't you working?"

"I always hated that job. I'm finished with it."

"Daniel, what's going on?"

"What are you, the work police?"

"Yeah, in a way I am. Now tell me what happened."

"You know how I feel when people dis me. I'm done with that. I'm sick of clients who think they're smarter than I am, and I'm through doing the computer dance and having to tolerate idiots."

"You're leaving your business? You just got a new client. Shouldn't we have talked about it? I had no idea you were so unhappy. I can't support us. Daniel, you have to have a job."

'Well, guess what? I'm not in the mood to have a job. In fact, right now, I might take a little trip and go visit my brothers."

"Daniel, what's happening? You're out of control. It scares me when you get like this."

"Don't give me that 'you're a bad boy' talk. I'll do whatever I want. I don't have to defend myself to you or anybody else."

"Were you at Bet Hillel this morning?"

"Why do you care?"

"Somebody slashed Rabbi Dalton's tires, and I think it was you."

"Maybe it was."

"This isn't a game, Daniel. If you cut his tires, you committed a crime."

"You gonna turn me in?"

"I'm begging you, Daniel, you're crossing a dangerous line. I'm making an appointment with Rabbi Dalton to speak with you about this. Even if I don't tell him, he'll probably figure it out all by himself. You keep threatening people, and you're the one who's going to get hurt."

"This conversation is over, Kayla."

"We have to talk about this later, but I've got to get back to class."

"We'll talk about it if and when I'm ready to talk about it. Right now, I'm headed out."

Kayla had experienced Daniel's periodic fits, but this time she was really worried. After school, she had to talk to Rabbi Dalton, and after that, to Rabbi Stein. Daniel might be veering toward disaster, but she wasn't going there with him. She was sure that he'd return, but she didn't want him back. She was almost thirty years old, and she had spent too many years mollifying him. If he disappeared, he'd be doing her a favor. But she was sure it wouldn't be that easy. She looked at her watch and ran back to her students.

CHAPTER 15

Josh stopped off at North Shore Hospital to visit a congregant and then headed back to Lev Shalom, where he encountered an antsy Serena.

"I didn't want to interrupt your meeting with Rabbi Dalton at Bet Hillel," she said, nervously, "but Bob Small's been calling here all morning and kept complaining that you didn't answer your cell phone. You'd better get back to him right away."

Josh wanted nothing more than a couple of hours in which to catch up on work and start composing his Shabbat sermon, but another lesson learned in rabbinic school applied: Do the hard tasks first, especially if they involve difficult *shul* presidents.

"It took you long enough to call!" Bob shouted. "Do you actually believe in coming to work and earning your salary?"

Josh decided not to answer.

Figuring that he'd made his point, Bob continued, "Get this!"

"I'm all ears," Josh allowed, expecting something dire about the Holocaust Memorial Garden where difficulties never seemed to end; however, Bob surprised him.

"A reporter from *The Chicago Journal* called me. I know about this kid,

James Traub, and he can be a real *schmuck*. His mother plays mahjong with my wife. Sheila's nervous when he's around because he asks too many questions. Anyway, she told me that 'Mr. Nosy's' talking to Halperin, and I can just imagine what our esteemed former leader will say. I also know that Traub's planning to cozy up to you. I warn you, Rabbi Stein, don't talk to him. I'm dead serious. If Halperin wants to open up the Holocaust business again, I'm only too ready to take him on. But you, sir, stay out of it for your own good. Send Traub to me."

Josh had already become used to Bob's bluster. "First of all," Josh affirmed, "Rabbi Halperin is much too smart to talk to a reporter about anything personal. He would never discuss the Holocaust money. I can't predict what Traub will get out of him, but I suspect that the Rabbi will turn the conversation into a plug for his books, and at the same time, mention all the great things he's accomplished in Chicago."

"I can't believe how clueless you are!" Bob shouted even louder than before. "I know Halperin, and you don't. He'll paint himself as a hero instead of the criminal he really is. I never should have given him a pass out of Chicago. He should be in jail right now!"

Josh disregarded that last accusation. "Would you like me to speak with Rabbi Halperin about the interview?" Josh asked, pretending he cared about any of this. *If Bob's right, which I know he isn't, would Rabbi Halperin want me to get into the fray or stay far away? Stay away, definitely.*

"I repeat, and you'd better be listening with both ears, do not talk to Traub. I'll handle Halperin by myself, period. Over and out!"

A sudden dead tone signaled Josh's release. *Well, that was fun,* Josh thought.

Josh grabbed his cell phone on his way to the small chapel for the afternoon service. There was a text from Bunny Halperin. *Oh no, what does the Rabbi's wife want? I hope nothing happened to her husband.*

He raced back to his office after the service. He texted Bunny, and she responded immediately.

I'd appreciate meeting you this week. I may need your help.

Did something happen to Rabbi Halperin?

Not yet.

OK. Where and when?

Fred will be out for a few hours tomorrow afternoon. Please come to our house around one p.m.

I'll be there.

Josh went to Serena's desk, but she was already gone for the day. He left her a voice message, and, just to be sure, he scribbled a note asking her to cancel his next afternoon's appointments. He knew the curt style would alarm her, but so be it. What could be going on with the Halperins?

CHAPTER 16

Bunny met Josh at the door and led him into the living room, which was stacked with boxes. She got right to the point.

"Rabbi Stein, there's a journalist named James Traub who met once with my husband. He works for *The Chicago Journal*. In the past, we've welcomed the press, who have always supported us. But this is different. Mr. Traub is one of those ruthless, young writers looking for a juicy story, and under the guise of talking to my husband about books, I'm afraid he'll lead him into troubled waters."

"What do you mean?" Josh couldn't believe it. First Bob, then Bunny, was concerned about the same thing, but for opposite reasons. *Is Traub actually that deceptive? Probably. I may as well tell her everything I know,* Josh decided.

"Traub has already tried to talk to me, and when I didn't go along, he made an appointment to see me next week. I should also tell you that Bob assumes your husband will tweak the Holocaust story to his advantage."

"Stop right there! Bob's involved?"

"Traub's contacting everyone he can," Josh explained.

"The reason I called you--and I'm still trying to decide if it was a good idea--is that I want you to convince this Traub guy to stop. He and my husband met once, and that's enough. My husband wants to get back at Bob, but you and I both know that it must not happen."

Josh continued, "This is really crazy. Bob's wife, Sheila, plays mahjong with Traub's mother, so Bob knows that Traub expects a career boost from an expose about your husband and Lev Shalom. He's probably heard a lot of dirt already."

Bunny was livid. Life was spinning out of control. She had fooled herself into believing that she and Fred could put everything behind them and move painlessly to Israel. *Wrong, wrong, wrong,* she realized.

Walking Josh to the door, Bunny thanked him for telling her what he knew, urged him to talk Traub out of provoking either side, and started to formulate a plan of her own. She'd figure out how to prevent further meetings between Traub and her husband. Fred would have to forget about pushing his books and career, and she would talk to Sheila Small. In fact, she decided to call Sheila while Fred was still out.

Even though there was no love lost between them, Bunny and Sheila had a common goal. Neither woman wanted her husband to talk to James Traub. They had something else in common, too. Both of them had strong-willed husbands who made their own decisions. The phone conversation didn't last very long because they both realized that it was out of their hands. Each did agree, however, to work on her spouse in her own way.

CHAPTER 17

Serena had cancelled Josh's afternoon meetings, but Kayla Morales, feeling desperate, showed up without an appointment and spotted him just as he returned to the office. Kayla was determined to stop him, but he didn't want to talk to her until he spoke to Halperin about her situation.

"Ms. Morales, Rabbi Stein's busy the rest of the day," Serena stated firmly, attempting to run interference.

"I just need five minutes of your time, Rabbi," Kayla pleaded. "Just five minutes."

Rabbi Halperin had always frowned on drop-ins, and Serena wondered what Josh would do. She was disappointed that he gave in.

"Serena, Ms. Morales and I will talk in my office now, and I want you to let us know when five minutes is up."

They went in, and Josh was careful to leave his door unlocked and slightly ajar. As unlikely as it seemed, there could be no suggestion of intimacy. He took Rabbi Dalton's warning to heart about being careful with female congregants.

Josh didn't sit down, and he didn't offer Kayla a chair. "I have no time to talk, Ms. Morales. What's up?"

"I want to tell you that I'm filling out a single application for membership. Daniel and I put our engagement on hold for a while, and I'm moving ahead by myself. I know I can *daven* here without being a member, so even if my application is rejected, and in spite of Rabbi Halperin's rudeness, I intend for Lev Shalom to be my synagogue."

"Where's Daniel in all this?"

"He's angry, but he's always angry about something. I do have one request, and that's why I'm here without an appointment. Please don't contact him or try to reach out to him. He tends to blame others when things don't go his way, so my decision to join Lev Shalom independently could be construed in his mind as having something to do with you."

"With me? How?"

"Daniel's against all rabbis, and you especially are a threat. He fantasizes that you're manipulating me. It's not the first time."

"Manipulating you? Who else does he blame?"

"Rabbi Elijah Dalton. Daniel caused a couple of incidents at Bet Hillel. Anyway, I want to join a more mainstream *shul.*"

Josh couldn't reveal anything about already visiting Dalton, so he asked, "What kind of incidents?"

Kayla wasn't comfortable elaborating, so she answered, "Bet Hillel was the wrong place for Daniel, so I didn't force it. I'm still a supporter of Rabbi Dalton and, as you know, I teach art in his school. Rabbi Dalton actually insisted that his *shul* isn't the right place for Daniel."

Josh realized that Rabbi Halperin had correctly understood the situation and was correct in discouraging the couple's relationship with Lev Shalom or himself. Halperin had probably seen it all before and knew when to stop it.

Josh sighed, "I know this is hard for you, but I think you should put your own membership on hold."

Kayla frowned, "I know what you're worried about, but Daniel won't be a problem here. We postponed our wedding plans, and he left his business for a while. He decided to visit his brothers, and now he's probably already far from Chicago."

Josh wasn't convinced of that. He looked at his watch and started to lead Kayla out, but she had more to say.

"There's another reason I'm here."

"And that is…?" Josh asked warily.

"My students have never met anyone like you. Rabbi Dalton drops by the school all the time, but you have a completely different background. I'd like you to visit our school."

"Why me?"

"Among other things, you can talk about your Torah values."

"Kayla, it's Rabbi Dalton's school. Shouldn't your invitation come to him?"

"I've been thinking. You told me you have a background in science, right?"

"That was before I started studying Judaism seriously. It's been a few years. What's with science? You teach art, right?

"Our students would benefit from connecting with someone like you. I want them to meet you and to talk to you about relating Torah and science. Please come to our school. I'll also set up a meeting with Rabbi Dalton. He and his synagogue are unique."

Josh would agree that Dalton and his synagogue were special, if only he could reveal his recent visit to Bet Hillel, but he was spared from giving an evasive answer, because the knock on his slightly-opened door saved him. It was Serena telling him that more than five minutes had passed.

"Serena, please schedule another meeting with Ms. Morales in about two weeks."

Serena kept her response in check, just barely.

Kayla was still standing at Serena's desk when Josh rushed out to stop her. He'd had a sudden, disturbing thought about the slashed tires outside of Bet Hillel and the possibility that Daniel could cause more harm. "You didn't, by any chance, mention my coming to your school to Daniel, did you?"

"I don't remember, why?"

"Just wondering," Josh answered.

Serena sent a concerned look Josh's way, and Kayla caught it.

"It's OK," Kayla declared, "it's all good. See you in *shul* on *Shabbat.*"

Serena really wanted to know more about Kayla Morales, but she knew her place. *Rabbi Stein is becoming more and more circumspect like Rabbi Halperin,* she thought.

Josh considered various options, then decided to call Rabbi Ephraim Halperin, who would be the best person to help him figure out what to do about Kayla and her maybe-fiance.

In a few sentences, Rabbi Halperin advised Josh to discourage any further meetings with Kayla and Daniel. When Josh told him that he was already somewhat involved with the couple, and had even discussed them with Elijah Dalton, Halperin was dismissive.

"Rabbi Stein," Halperin stated emphatically, "you already made two mistakes. First, you showed interest in Ms. Morales and thought you could help her. Second, speaking with Rabbi Dalton is going to be counterproductive and won't enhance your status or wisdom. That's all I have to say."

Josh was stunned by Halperin's response. Elijah Dalton had been as helpful as he could be to a new colleague, and Josh's should-be 'mentor', Ephraim Halperin, had only curt and dismissive advice for him. *Bob Small's opinion of Halperin isn't so off-base, after all,* Josh thought.

CHAPTER 18

Rabbi Halperin was in no mood to deal with old problems, even though Josh needed help. Stein was now in charge. Let him unravel difficult situations by himself. Halperin had his own agenda, and he sat waiting for James Traub to call about their second interview. His *Talmud* was open in front of him, but he couldn't concentrate. Bunny had begged her husband to cancel further meetings with the reporter, but he decided to go ahead.

Making Sheila Small an ally to keep their husbands from reopening the Holocaust Memorial debacle had failed. Sheila was right. Both Fred and Bob were determined to use Traub to hurt each other.

Sheila Small and Bunny Halperin were strong, realistic women who loved their husbands in spite of their flaws. Bob was a street fighter, and Fred was a master of finesse. They were both ruled by their egos. In the past, Sheila had been able to assuage her husband's fury, but not eradicate it. Bunny had been able to persuade her husband to retain his dignity even when angry. Could he do that now?

Sheila worried that Bob would again become consumed with destroying Halperin. It wasn't enough that the Halperins were moving to Israel. Bob still wanted him in prison. Bunny feared that Fred would suffer further heart damage from re-engagement with Bob.

Now Traub was in the picture, and it would serve him well to get those two adversaries in the ring again. What happened to the signed legal documents that should have ended the battles, allowing Halperin to retire without shame? It's as if none of that had happened.

As her husband waited for that phone call, Bunny voiced her thoughts. She placed her hand on the phone, willing it not to ring. "As soon as I finish packing my clothes, I'm moving to Israel--with or without you!"

Fred had underestimated his wife's wrath, but at the same time, he didn't believe her. "After all these years I assure you that I know how to handle an interview," he insisted.

Bunny would have none of his excuses, "I meant what I said. I even called Sheila Small. I found out that Traub is also talking to Bob about Lev Shalom. Do you think Bob will tell him that Rabbi Fred Halperin built a fabulous *shul,* and we hate to see him go? Oh no. That reporter's the best thing that could have landed in Bob's lap!"

"Bunny, he can't talk about the Holocaust Memorial money. You know we have a legal agreement. Anyway, any innuendo from Bob can be easily countered by me."

"And is that what you want?" Bunny demanded.

"All I'm saying is that I'm not afraid of Bob, and you shouldn't be either. You, of all people, know that I'm not easily intimidated."

"I'm through talking about this. I don't want to end up in the hospital, myself. I'm telling you, Fred, when Traub calls, don't have that interview."

Halperin watched his wife storm out of the room. *What's gotten into her? I'm sure she'll come to her senses after the interview.*

CHAPTER 19

Serena was looking forward to her regular Monday night dinner with her daughter. She was exhausted from the annual Lev Shalom sisterhood kick-off event. Between the week-long baking in the kitchen, the non-stop deliveries of linen and flowers, and her general management of the maintenance and office staff, Serena craved a relaxing meal at Kalman's Dairy Restaurant.

There was something else on her mind. Were Rachel and Rabbi Stein still a couple? She sensed that something had changed. Even though Serena had learned not to be her daughter's inquisitor, there were things that she wanted to understand.

At Kalman's, Serena led her daughter to a back table, hoping that no one would interrupt them. Rachel was uncharacteristically quiet, expecting that her mother would interrogate her about Josh Stein. She knew it was coming and she had prepared her response.

Kalman, himself, came to their table and greeted them jovially. "I see that you're sitting in back for a change. You must have important things to talk about."

"We do, and it's private," Rachel answered, looking Kalman in the eye.

"Sorry, Kalman," Serena added, "There's a lot going on at work, and I'm looking forward to spending time with my daughter, away from congregants."

Even though Kalman hated nothing as much as being in the dark about community gossip, he smiled and gestured for a server to take their order.

"I understand completely," Kalman assured the duo. "Let me know if I can get you anything special. My regular customers are like family to me."

"But as you know, Kalman, even family members have private lives," Rachel warned, catching her mother's eye.

Kalman slowly backed away from the Berg pow-wow, hoping that somehow he would eventually learn about their tete-a-tete.

Serena wasn't going to be put off by Rachel's attitude. "You know what I'm going to ask you, Rachel."

Before Serena could say anything, Rachel held up her hand to stop her. "I'll answer before you even ask. I've had it with Rabbi Joshua Stein. There's nothing going on, and there's nothing to talk about."

A server came to the table, "We have some new specials. How about a spinach-stuffed mushroom appetizer? Our soup this evening is squash-pumpkin, and our entree is pasta alla vodka.

Even though she was in a bad mood, Rachel was still hungry. Was Kalman now reaching out to the trendy vegetarian crowd? That would be a smart move. She decided to test his new menu.

"Mom, let's skip the mushrooms and share the pasta. I'm hungry enough for my own soup."

Serena wanted to lighten the atmosphere at their table. "I'll have what she's having," she told the server.

"And to drink? We just got a liquor license."

Rachel smiled to herself. *Will there be no end to these gastronomic surprises? What's coming next? Salmon en croute? Grilled artichoke hearts? Sole Provencal?*

Serena caught that smile and decided to spring for a bottle of Cabernet.

Rachel was impressed. She had never seen her mother drink anything other than iced tea in a restaurant. Maybe some of Kalman's new-found sophistication was catching.

Once the server moved on, Serena forged ahead. "Everything was so enjoyable when we had the Stein family for Rosh Hashanah lunch. We all got along so well. We like the Steins; they like us. Even your father had a good time, and you know how hard he is to please. What's gotten into you?"

"Do you really think Josh was part of what you call 'enjoyable'? Did he say more than two words to anybody there? Did he pay a bit of attention to me? It seems like you and I were at two different lunches!"

Rachel was losing patience with the conversation. She would have walked out, except for the nagging expectation that the food would actually be worthwhile. The wine was served just in time, and both Berg women quickly emptied their first glass.

"Rachel, grow up! It was your idea to have the Steins for a *yom tov* meal, and I saw you and Rabbi Stein speaking intimately as you walked together to our house. The idea was for the families to get to know each other, and we did. And, since we're on the subject, I worked damned hard to make the afternoon pleasant for everybody. I don't ask for any special thanks, but I do expect to be able to have a decent conversation with you. It wasn't Rabbi Stein's job to entertain us. He worked plenty hard at services. There's no reason for you to be disappointed or angry. I'm your mother. Talk to me!"

Rachel was surprised at her mother's uncharacteristic outburst, and she had enough self-awareness to know her tendency to be overly critical. Why did she always have to be in 'lawyer mode'? Sure, Serena wanted to understand, but unfortunately, there was something guiding Rachel that she couldn't fully disclose to her mother.

She had to protect herself this time, because she had once allowed herself to be vulnerable, and even worse, it was with a married man, Andy Meyers. As a reward, he broke her heart. She would never allow herself to be hurt like that again. If she and Josh were a committed couple and he hurt her, she'd want him to suffer just as much as she would. Better to end the relationship right now.

Two men walked into Kalman's, deep in conversation. They were led to one of the tables in front, and continued talking as the server took their orders. Kalman rushed over and welcomed them heartily.

"Rabbi Stein! Rabbi Dalton!" Kalman exclaimed, loudly enough to capture the attention of every diner. "What a pleasure and delight to see colleagues from different synagogues here in my restaurant."

Kalman looked around the room, just to make sure that his customers were aware of this unique duo who had chosen his establishment for a public appearance. Among those who were impressed was Serena Berg.

Josh felt the necessity to respond, "Rabbi Dalton and I figured that we could discuss subjects of mutual concern while enjoying a delicious meal. Now that everyone in the room knows we're here, I hope we can still have a private conversation."

"Of course, Rabbi," Kalman assured him. "We just received our liquor license, and I'm going to send over two glasses of scotch--the best in the house. Don't worry about a thing. You're in good hands."

"Did you see who just walked in?" Serena whispered to Rachel.

"Not only did I see Rabbi Stein, but I heard Kalman's proclamation loud and clear. Kalman has a knack for self-promotion, and he knows how to use an opportunity to his advantage. Who knows if he even likes those two, but they think he does."

Serena ignored her daughter's cynicism. "I'm going to their table just to meet Rabbi Dalton and say hello to Rabbi Stein. Of all the rabbis in Chicago, I would've never expected them to be friends. There's a story there."

Rachel grumbled, "Mom, are you for real? You might want to talk to them, but I guarantee that they don't want to be disturbed, especially by the Lev Shalom administrator."

Without uttering another word or reacting in any way to her daughter's negative attitude, Serena got up and walked to the rabbis' table.

Rabbi Stein stood to greet her, and with a broad grin introduced her to Rabbi Dalton, who leapt to his feet.

"Shalom, shalom! Honored to meet you, Mrs. Berg," Dalton said, exuberantly, as he bowed. "I've heard that Lev Shalom is a model of staff excellence, and I look forward to visiting your fine synagogue very soon."

Serena was charmed by Rabbi Stein's gallant companion. "I've heard that you built a beautiful community on the west side. I'd like to visit one of these days," she gushed.

During the brief interchange between Serena and Dalton, Josh saw Rachel glaring at them. He considered gesturing for her to meet Rabbi Dalton, whom she would have found interesting, but he immediately changed his mind.

"Thanks for coming over," Josh said to Serena, putting an end to her visit. "Please give my regards to Rachel," he added, as both he and Serena inadvertently looked toward the table in the back.

Slightly uncomfortable, Serena smiled and walked quickly back to her daughter. Rabbi Dalton was a master of observation and assumed there was something going on between Rabbi Stein, Serena, and her daughter.

As the server placed the scotch before them, the two rabbis resumed their conversation. Back at their table, Rachel let her mother know, without a single word, that all conversation for the evening had come to an end and they would not linger for dessert.

The Berg women finished their dinner, paid the bill, gathered their belongings, and headed out. As they passed the rabbis' table, Josh and Rachel nodded matter-of-factly to each other, Serena kept her emotions to herself, and Rabbi Dalton took it all in.

CHAPTER 20

Bob Small couldn't wait for the interview, and Sheila didn't know how to stop him. She had tried at breakfast. It was touchy because Sheila played mahjong every week with Traub's mother, and in the past, Sheila had discussed synagogue matters openly around the table. Of course, the group had a steadfast rule that whatever was discussed at the mahjong table stayed at the mahjong table. Unfortunately, Barbara Traub, the reporter's mother, didn't honor the vow. That's how her son got the lead to investigate Rabbi Halperin's departure from Lev Shalom.

Sheila was furious at Barbara Traub, but she continued playing mahjong with the group. She knew better than to say anything private in the future. She wasn't sure how much James already knew, and she was worried because, when they talked, Bob would never miss an opportunity to malign Fred Halperin. Sheila planned to do as much damage control as she could.

As she poured her husband's coffee, Sheila implored, "Please, Sweetie, take control of the interview with James Traub. Don't let him trick you into saying things you'll regret."

Bob laughed, "Regret? Fat chance of that! Now I can set the record straight about that *goniff*! Halperin might not be in jail where he belongs, but I'm gonna make damn sure that he leaves Chicago in disgrace. I never shoulda felt sorry for him."

"Bob, the man ended up in the hospital. And they have to give up their home. And plenty of people know what happened. Do you think the Halperins want to leave the life they've led all these years? Hasn't Halperin suffered enough?"

"That's your only flaw, Honeybun," Bob countered. "You're a softie to the core. It's a good thing that I'm the boss around here; otherwise, you'd give everybody a third and fourth chance. Not me! When I know what's right, I just do it."

Sheila kept trying, "I'm just worried that this thing could backfire and you'll look like a troublemaker, not the problem-solver you really are. Just tell Traub that you're proud that you handled Lev Shalom's difficulties, and now everybody's satisfied."

"What?" Bob exclaimed. "And make it look like Halperin and I are buddies? No, I'm gonna use Traub to set the record straight."

"Sweetie," Sheila whispered, as she put her arms around Bob, "aren't there other things you'd rather do than get sued?"

"Sued? Whaddya mean?"

"The gag order! You and the Rabbi can't talk about the details of his leaving."

Bob winked. He was amused. "Don't worry about the flimsy gag order. If I know Halperin, he'll be the first to break the deal. He'll tell all the lies he wants and then slither off to his fancy apartment in Israel."

Sheila didn't know what to say next, but she couldn't let Bob go ahead with his plan to destroy the Halperins. The rumors might continue for years, but she wanted to be through with the whole mess.

Uncharacteristically, Sheila changed her tone. She stood up and square-ly faced her husband. "Enough of this vendetta with Halperin! You did a great job of leading the *shul* board, and you still have Rabbi Stein and the search committee to work with. I hope...oh, never mind!"

Sheila walked out of the kitchen, leaving Bob at the table with his un-finished breakfast.

Bob experienced a new sensation. He and Sheila had been a team since their youth group years, and in spite of petty differences of opinion, he had always prevailed. *Why is this such a big deal to Sheila?* He won-dered. *She knows I handle everything right.*

The breakfast, which Sheila planned as a means of calming her hus-band, was a failure. Bob knew what he had to do, and he was sure that Sheila would come around to his point of view. Leaving his breakfast half eaten, he called James Traub to set up a meeting as soon as possible.

That afternoon, Bob paced furiously in his office, repeatedly checking his watch and cell phone, while he waited for the reporter to arrive. Traub was Bob's last hope in his desire to destroy Halperin's reputation. If he didn't publicly expose Halperin's malfeasance, no one else would do it.

Bob had more against the Rabbi than the Holocaust Memorial scandal. Many years ago, when Bob and Sheila became engaged, Rabbi Halperin counseled Sheila against marrying such a rough-and-tumble guy. Bob, who barely finished high school, had just bought his first truck, plan-ning to start a trucking company, and he was penniless. Even though Sheila came from a working class family, she was a pretty, intelligent, religiously observant young woman who had her pick of eligible young men. Rabbi Halperin couldn't understand Sheila's other side, the par-ty-going, fun-loving girl, which he was sure would disappear when she met the right man. In Halperin's opinion, she fell in love with exactly the wrong one. Bob was still pained by Halperin's feelings about him and now, finally, Bob was determined to turn the tables and play judge.

CHAPTER 21

Should I? Josh thought, as he pressed speed dial. *Why not?*

Rachel Berg was surprised when she saw the caller ID on her cell. She decided to let it go to voicemail, yet she couldn't wait to hear the message.

"Hi, Rachel, it's Josh. Sorry we didn't get a chance to talk at Kalman's, so how about lunch at Avi's one day next week? I have to tell you all about my new colleague, Elijah Dalton, the guy you saw me with Monday night. I'm sure a lot has happened to you since our unfortunate meeting in the parking lot. Give me a call when you get a chance. But, Rachel, if you don't call me, I'll keep trying. You know how 'trying' I can be."

While she really missed Josh, Rachel decided to let him stew. She'd held her ground in the parking lot, and she could hold out as long as necessary now. With Josh's message, she was free to respond, but not quite yet. Her legal experience had trained her to strategize and move judiciously. She would wait until she got home from work to return his call.

The rest of that day went slowly and it was impossible for Rachel to concentrate on her current case. It was the same for Josh. He knew Rachel well enough not to expect an immediate call back, but he believed that she was as eager to talk to him as he was to talk to her. At least he hoped so.

Serena noticed Josh's desultory mood, but she let it go. There was too much to do at *shul*. The Rabbi might be having his own problems, but as long as they didn't concern her or her daughter, he'd have to fend for himself. The high holidays had worn everyone out, and the entire staff was ready to get back on schedule.

Josh was relieved that Serena was occupied with work. Typically, she was the kind of employee who sensed and reacted intuitively to her boss. She had worked for Ephraim Halperin for so many years, that she had trained herself to read his mind and anticipate his every need. That wasn't Josh's style, but he appreciated her input and support, and tolerated her excessive attention. When Rabbi Halperin retired, Serena could have left; in fact, Josh had expected that, which would have been disastrous for him. Even though he was only the interim rabbi at this point, he was getting the experience that would let him know if he really wanted to lead a congregation. Serena had become essential to his ongoing rabbinic education.

Of course, this was unfortunately complicated by his relationship with Serena's daughter. If and when she returned his call, and they started dating again, would this affect his professional relationship with Serena? Josh had seen the knowing look on Elijah Dalton's face at the restaurant, and Josh had hoped that Dalton would advise him from time to time. Was his colleague going to start asking questions?

Josh closed his eyes; he was exhausted. *Wait a minute,* he thought, *maybe Rachel won't return my call. That would certainly simplify things. But I miss her, and weirdly enough, I think I need her. I'm going home for a while where a Corona's waiting for me. Maybe I can get Serena to cancel my four o'clock appointment and I'll come back later for mincha and maariv.*

There was a knock at his office door, suddenly pulling Josh back to reality. It was Serena, and she looked worried. "Bob Small is stationed at my desk and says he's not budging until he talks to you. Rabbi Stein, I can just about see the steam coming out of his ears. I think you better talk to him."

"OK," Josh sighed, heading out to the main office. He put a smile on his face and extended his hand to his glowering visitor.

"For your information," Bob declared, "the war's heating up, and you'll be in the middle of it. That reporter, Traub, is gonna get to everybody before he's finished, so be ready to stonewall him. I'm gonna handle everything."

Josh looked around and realized that the secretaries, a maintenance worker and Serena were pretending to be busy, but they were making sure they wouldn't miss a single word. He took Bob's arm and ushered him into his office.

"Bob, I'm very busy. I have a lot of congregants to attend to. I have calls to return and sick people to visit. I have to prepare a *d'var Torah* for services at a *shiva* house tomorrow. And, let me tell you, I'm not in a good mood, so this better be important."

Bob was surprised by the Rabbi's abruptness and confidence and thought to himself, *Well, mazel tov! This kid finally grew some balls!*

Bob was right.

CHAPTER 22

During James Traub's interviews, Bunny had kept Leora busy with chores away from the house. She wanted her daughter to remain unaware of the Haperins' problems. While they were still in Chicago, Bunny was determined to prevent savvy Leora from losing respect for her father.

After a morning of packing and discarding, Bunny and Leora decided to do their most difficult task so far. Because her husband failed to completely empty his office at Lev Shalom (which Bunny considered excessively Freudian), she decided to do it. She was strengthened by having her daughter by her side, and they marched boldly into the synagogue carrying folded cartons and packing tape.

Leora had grown up in Lev Shalom. Even though she was a couple of years older, Rachel Berg and she had been active at the same time in the youth group and had served as officers. Serena, herself, was fond of the Halperins' daughter, and felt close to her, even though the Bergs and Halperins didn't socialize.

The two girls differed in many ways. Rachel spent her free time reading fashion magazines and was an expert on famous media personalities. Leora, on the other hand, loved hiking and taught herself how to organize and maintain a garden. Rachel was stylish and knew everybody, while Leora preferred being outdoors with plants instead of people.

As a teen, Rachel's long strawberry blond hair and trendy clothes made her look older than her friend. Leora, whose favorite outfit was denim skirts, oversized T-shirts and sneakers, was only comfortable when her wavy chestnut hair was in a ponytail. Yet, in spite of their superficial differences, they had one thing in common: each of them was the smartest girl in her class and both wrote for the school newspaper. Popular Rachel, on the high school debate team, held a major office in their synagogue youth group, and Leora mastered planning outings and conventions.

There were occasional trips to the mall when the girls were younger, but they lost touch with each other when Leora went to Israel after high school. Whenever Leora visited her family, she considered contacting Rachel but somehow never got around to it because their lives were increasingly different. When they bumped into each other at High Holiday services, their conversation was superficial. Leora, who spent little time in Chicago, planned to remain for only a few days solely to help her parents with their move.

Serena ran to meet Bunny and Leora as they walked into the office. She hadn't seen Bunny since the High Holidays, and even though Leora had been at services, she didn't have a chance to talk to her.

"Leora!" Serena shouted. "How wonderful to see you so soon after the holidays! What's the occasion?"

"Lee-Lee came to help us pack, and that's why we're here. My husband is so busy at home, he asked us to do what we can in his office. We brought special boxes for the artwork."

"Let me help you," Serena offered.

"We can do it. You have work to do, I'm sure. By the way," Leora smiled, "Rachel looked beautiful at services. It was great to see her, but we didn't have a chance to talk. I'll be here for a week or so and I'd really like to get together with her. What's her number?"

Serena wasn't completely certain that her daughter was in the mood to renew that old friendship. Rachel had been so moody lately that Serena had no idea how her daughter would react to anything unexpected, and she didn't want Leora to get involved in the Josh Stein business, even if Rachel would confide in her.

"Rachel's schedule is so unpredictable that I never know when she can even find time for me. Let me have your number and I'll give it to her."

Leora gave her number to Serena, and she and her mother headed into Rabbi Halperin's office.

Josh heard activity in the office next to his and went to see what was going on.

Without knocking, he quietly entered Halperin's inner sanctum and was surprised to find Bunny and Leora, whom he remembered meeting during the High Holidays. It was clear that Bunny was uncomfortable when she saw him. There were papers in her hand which she held behind her back.

Sensing their discomfort, Josh eased the atmosphere. "What a surprise! I assume you're emissaries from the Rabbi helping with the packing. Can I do anything to help, or would I just get in your way?"

Josh turned to the smiling young woman whom he had met a few weeks earlier. "Leora, right?"

"You have a good memory, Rabbi Stein. I'm curious, do they teach that in rabbi school? If so, I appreciate it. Everyone wants to be remembered, especially by the right people," Leora said, purposefully.

Josh knew she was flirting with him, and he liked it. Bunny knew it too, and she didn't.

"Rabbi Stein, with all due respect, we have a very limited time to get the whole office packed, and I need Leora's full attention. You may know that she lives far away and seldom comes to Chicago."

Directing her attention to her daughter, Bunny added, "In fact, Lee-Lee, you probably won't ever find a reason to come back to Chicago after we move to Israel."

Leora had the feeling that she just might want to return to Chicago periodically. Her long-term relationship with Aaron Gordon was going nowhere; her twenties were behind her; the landscaping business practically ran itself now that she had a well-trained staff; and she grew up in Chicago. She was comfortable here. Besides, this Rabbi Joshua Stein caught her attention. Chicago seemed more and more appealing.

Josh knew he should leave, but he wasn't ready. "Where do you live?" he asked Leora.

"After I graduated from Stern College, I decided to figure out how I could afford to live on the Upper West Side of Manhattan; however, my clients are mainly in New Jersey. I'm co-owner of a landscaping company."

Josh appreciated the information. Leora went to an Orthodox college for women, and she had a business that generated enough income for her to live in a heavily Jewish section of Manhattan. He wanted to know even more.

"It sounds like hard work. Do you have time for friends? To socialize?" Josh asked.

"Things have recently changed in my social life, and I welcome the chance to travel more and meet new people," Leora stated emphatically, hoping that her intention was clear.

It was certainly clear to her mother, and Bunny jumped in. "Rabbi Stein, please excuse us. We have a job to do. I'm sure you understand how pressed we are for time."

Josh didn't want to leave it at that. Turning to Bunny, he said, "I'm happy that we had a few minutes to talk. I've been meaning to offer my services to Rabbi Halperin, but I'm swamped here without him. I'll call your house soon."

Relieved that they were alone, Bunny showed Leora some papers she was hiding from Josh. From the date and manual typewriting on one of them, Bunny realized that she and her husband had been in their early thirties when it was written. It was when they were raising their young family and trying to build their synagogue. It hadn't been easy.

"Look what I found!"

Bunny was holding several sheets of paper. Leora carefully read the top one and sighed. "Mom, did you know anything about this?"

"I didn't have a clue. I always thought that Daddy was happy here."

Bunny folded the paper and put it in her purse. It was a letter of resignation, alluding to some controversy in the *shul*, signed by Fred, but never sent. Should she bring it up to him? She wondered if he would even remember writing it, but more hurtful was that he had never shared his despair with her. Lev Shalom had been smaller then, populated by Holocaust survivors and families just starting their adult lives, most of them needing teaching and counseling that would stress any rabbinic couple. Money was tight and Halperin only had a part-time secretary to help him. He had his hands full, and he probably didn't want to trouble Bunny.

Were there other things over the years that Fred had kept to himself? He had not been honest with her about the struggles with Bob Small, and she had known nothing about her husband's using the Holocaust money. Were there other things, too? He had always handled stress so well, she thought, but her husband's recent hospitalization proved her wrong.

Bunny showed Leora the other piece of paper. Whereas the first was a bit yellowed and frayed, the second looked recent.

"I'm *really* worried about this one," Bunny said, handing the letter to her daughter. It was computer-generated, the words all in capitals, bold faced, and thirty-six point type. "Why in the world would anyone be angry enough at Daddy to write something like this."

"Mom, I bet powerful people get letters like this all the time. Let it go." Leora didn't want Bunny to dwell on the possible seriousness of the note.

YOU THINK YOU CAN GET AWAY WITH ANYTHING
BUT YOU BETTER WATCH OUT
IT'S ONLY A MATTER OF TIME
UNTIL YOU GET WHAT YOU DESERVE

"We have to ask Daddy about this one," Leora insisted. "I wonder if he took it seriously. It's possible that he's gotten upsetting messages over the years, but I can't imagine anything like this. Did he ever mention angry congregants or colleagues to you?"

Bunny shrugged. "Nothing that really worried him. He was respected by everybody...at least that's what I always believed. I can think of only two people who could have written this kind of letter, but it just doesn't make sense."

"Like who?"

"Well, one of them was the former executive director, Joseph Garber, who was fired for some trumped-up reason that I never understood. The only other person who is vitriolic enough would be Bob Small, who has never been one of your father's admirers, to say the least. But really, Leora, it's inconceivable that either one of them would do that."

Bunny was frightened. *So it isn't only the borrowed Holocaust funds that Fred never talked to me about. What else am I going to find out about my husband? Even worse, what will that reporter uncover?*

Leora had already finished packing several shelves of books and mementos, and she had started on the other side of the desk where her mother was working.

"Daddy didn't ask us to go through his personal papers, Mom. He just wanted us to clear out and pack everything. You'll save us both a lot of angst if you stick to the program."

"I wish I hadn't found that old resignation letter, but apparently he never sent it. What really worries me is that threatening one.

"If I were you, I would tear up the resignation letter and forget about it. But, to be honest, the threatening letter is kind of scary. It could be from anybody, especially with what's going on in the world now. It could be from somebody who doesn't even know Daddy."

"I have a feeling that it was clearly directed toward him, because it says,'You think you can get away with anything'. That sounds a lot like Bob Small to me."

Leora was more objective than her mother. She had heard many discussions at home over the years in which her mother had been quicker to jump to conclusions than her less emotional father. Bunny tended to be overprotective of her husband and was quick to identify challenges that were usually unfounded.

"Mom, let's show this one to Daddy. I bet he'll dismiss it as nonsense."

Bunny shook her head, "Then why did he keep it? If he thought it was nothing he would've thrown it away. He didn't throw away the first letter, either. I just have a bad feeling about it."

Leora wanted to change the subject, "Besides, I have something more interesting to talk about."

Bunny had an inkling, and she was in no mood to pursue it. "I saw how you and Rabbi Stein were looking at each other. For your information, I've heard rumors about him and Rachel Berg."

"Rachel? Serena's daughter? Is it serious."

"As I say, there's gossip that they have a very close relationship, and I think it's better that you live far away. You should know enough about the life of a rabbi to realize that it's not a picnic. I've done it for too long and I can't wait to leave."

Leora had never heard her mother talk like that. That didn't necessarily mean that she would follow her mother's advice. There were other ways to find out more about Josh Stein. She looked forward to spending the next few days packing her father's office. But, first things first. If Rachel and Rabbi Stein were dating, she would never get involved in that. Interestingly, breaking off her romantic relationship with Aaron happened just before she came back to Chicago. Was it *bashert*, meant to be? Had she shown up at just the right time or was she kidding herself?

Bunny was tired. "Let's go home," she sighed.

As the two women left Rabbi Halperin's office, Josh was standing at Serena's desk. He took a couple of steps in their direction.

"Will you be back tomorrow?" He asked, hopefully.

"I doubt it," Bunny answered, sharply.

"Maybe," Leora answered, coyly.

Serena caught Bunny's eye. After all these years, they finally had something in common. Neither one of them wanted Leora Halperin and Rabbi Josh Stein to spend any time together.

As soon as Bunny and Leora drove away and Rabbi Stein was safely back in his own office, Serena sent her daughter a text. *"Did you know that Leora Halperin is in town again? She and Bunny are cleaning out Rabbi Halperin's office, and she'll probably be here a lot. The two of you used to be friends, so this might be a good time to catch up."*

Serena's mind was racing. *I have dreams for Rachel and Rabbi Stein. They complement each other, and Rachel knows it. It's going to take a little more time until he understands. What nobody needs is a complica-*

tion. I've always liked Leora, but I hope and pray that she'll go back to her landscaping business in New York. The sooner the better.

CHAPTER 23

Rachel Berg was able to work and monitor her phone simultaneously. She saw that her mother left a message. She read it and immediately called her.

Serena picked up on the first ring. "Mom, why's Leora in town? Is Rabbi Halperin sick again?"

"No, nothing like that. Leora came to the *shul* today with Bunny to finish packing Rabbi Halperin's office. I watched Rabbi Stein's reaction to Leora's flirting, and there's chemistry brewing. I also noted Bunny's displeasure at that interchange, which of course, would make a relationship between them even more attractive to Leora, who you might remember hardly ever agreed with her mother. Don't you think you should do something about that?"

"And that's why you texted me in the middle of work?" Rachel said, impatiently. "I have a lot to do. I'm hanging up."

Serena couldn't do anything more, but at least she tried. Rachel, on the other hand, couldn't get back to the case she was working on. *Why did my mother have to tell me that? Things are already rocky between Josh and me, and now that Leora's in town, it gives him a chance to spend time with someone else. She's so laid back that she's probably perfect for him.*

Rachel dialed the Halperin's home number and left a message, "Hi, Leora. This is Rachel Berg. My mother just called and told me you're in town. If you're going to be here for a few days, I'd really like to get together. It'll be fun to talk about old times and anything new in our lives. You can call me tonight at this number."

Satisfied that she had handled the situation, Rachel forced herself to get back to work.

When Bunny and Leora came home, they saw a message flashing on the answering machine. Rabbi Halperin was out of the house that afternoon, and Bunny was looking forward to an hour or two of relaxation before he came home. As Bunny headed to the bedroom to change her clothes, Leora listened to the message.

"Hey, Mom," Leora reported when Bunny came back into the room. "Guess who that was? Rachel Berg's mother told her I'm in town, and she wants to get together with me. I'm going to meet her someplace tomorrow night after she finishes work."

Bunny knew something was going on. "You're only going to be here a few days. I know you were friends growing up, but you hardly spoke to each other over the High Holidays. Don't you think a phone call would do?"

"Mom, you know I've always loved Chicago. In fact, I've been thinking about staying here until you move."

"What about your business?"

"I'm ready to sell my half and start something new. Who knows what the future holds? You always hated the fact that I was with Aaron, so you should be thrilled."

It's true that the Halperins didn't understand Leora's attachment to her long-time business partner/fiance, but Bunny was determined to derail the possibility of Rabbi Stein taking Aaron's place. Today's scenario in the *shul* was upsetting enough.

"Before you get together with Rachel," Bunny warned, "remember that she and Rabbi Stein have been seen out together several times, and Rabbi Stein has also been a guest...with his Boston family...at the Bergs' over *YomTov*. So, Leora, don't get involved with Rabbi Stein. Just stick to your original plan of going back at the end of the week. I'm telling you this because I love you and I don't want you to get hurt."

Leora took a deep breath, determined to remain calm and not act like the teenager her mother was assuming she still was.

"Mom, I'm definitely meeting Rachel tomorrow night, and I'm sure I'll find out everything I need to know about her and Josh Stein. You didn't like Aaron. I've broken up with him. You always said I should give up my business in New York and meet a different kind of guy, and now I'm ready to do that, too. Let me also add that you brought me up to think for myself and make my own decisions. So that's why I'm going to talk to Rachel and, if I decide it's a good idea and nobody will get hurt, I might just try to get to know Rabbi Stein better."

Bunny was worried. First, her husband who couldn't wait to move to Israel, decided that he wanted to stay in Chicago longer to pursue those phony interviews. Now, her daughter, who always professed undying devotion to Aaron, announced that they broke up, and she was about to sell her share of the business. Worst of all was Leora's interest in Josh Stein. Bunny felt her world, the existence she had cultivated and to which she had devoted her life, falling apart. But she was still Bunny Halperin, and she was going to move to Israel with or without her husband of fifty years, far away from her misguided daughter. As for her sons, daughters-in-law, and grandchildren, she loved them, but she was just too exhausted to think about them now.

Resolutely, Bunny announced, "Leora, I'm going to get back to the things that are important to me. When your father comes home, it might be a good idea for the two of you to do something about dinner." Forcing herself to maintain control, she headed toward the den.

Leora stopped her. "I really don't want to upset you more than you already are. I do listen to you, but I don't agree. If you're uncomfortable with my decisions, it wouldn't be the first time, and I'm sure it won't be the last. I never want to disappoint you, and I'm certainly aware that anything I do here in Chicago will reflect on you and Daddy. You have my word, Mom, that I won't do anything stupid."

"You know what, Leora, I'm not interested in pursuing this conversation. I'm worn out. You're a grown-up; I expect you to act like one."

CHAPTER 24

Rachel and Leora decided to meet at a Starbucks away from their neighborhood. Both of them already knew something essential about the other and Josh Stein, but they each planned to elicit the information casually during the conversation. At the entrance, they hugged, and got in line to order their drinks.

"You look great!" Leora exclaimed, as they sat down with their lattes.

"You too!" Rachel responded. "I'm really happy to see you. We didn't get to say two words to each other during the High Holidays, and now that your parents are leaving, I wonder how long it'll be until I see you again."

"Actually," Leora said, "I'm playing with the idea of moving back one of these days. A lot of our friends from high school have returned and I know my way around the city. As expensive as it is here, it's much harder to afford a nice place in Manhattan, and I've always loved our *shul*."

"But don't you still have a boyfriend and business in New York? Is he moving here, too? And what about your work?"

"As it turns out, Aaron and I broke up about a month ago. It wasn't going anywhere, and we realized it. We were together too long, and we were both smart enough to know that it was over. As a matter of fact, Rachel, I wonder if you would be interested in meeting him. He's a great guy, he works hard and we're still friends. If he takes over the business himself, he'll probably expand it, maybe even into Chicago."

Rachel was surprised. "Aaron and I will never meet. Anyway, I'm kind of dating somebody now. Would you believe that I've been seeing your father's assistant rabbi?"

This was the moment Leora had been waiting for. "Really? You're dating a rabbi? You know, I always thought you'd end up with that guy, Andy Meyers, you went to law school with. Anyway, let's get back to Aaron in New York. I know he'll come to Chicago to visit if I stay here. As I told you, we're still great friends, and he'll probably try to convince me to open a branch of the business here."

Rachel decided to lay it all out. "Look, I'm focusing all my attention on Josh Stein. We had a kind of a misunderstanding recently, and I guess I over-reacted. I've dated a couple of guys from work since then. After spending time with them, I've decided to get back together with Josh."

Leora realized that the path to Josh Stein was barred, at least for now. She liked Rachel and didn't want to hurt her, but she was more determined than before to stay in Chicago longer than she had originally planned. *Let's just see how the Rachel-Josh relationship plays out. I wonder if Rachel might be fantasizing about a future that's completely unrealistic. I can't even imagine her, the high-powered lawyer, as a congregational spouse, but if I were in that role, I could do it. I know that my mother and I are nothing alike and wouldn't handle the rebbitizin role the same way, but I am attracted to that man. I know what his life will be like, and Rachel doesn't have a clue.*

CHAPTER 25

Even though Leora had decided to discuss as little as possible with her mother, Bunny's years as a congregational *rebbitzin* had trained her to read between the lines. Bunny knew Leora wanted to stay in Chicago because of Josh Stein, but she would have none of it.

Mother and daughter were going through family photographs, but Bunny's mind was elsewhere. She was determined to get her daughter as far from Josh Stein as possible.

"It's so stuffy in here. I've got to get outside for a while," Bunny exclaimed to Leora, as she walked to the door. "Come with me. We can both use a break."

Leora gladly stopped, and the two of them went outside to enjoy some fresh air.

Bunny started, "Lee-Lee, I don't know how to soften what I'm going to say…"

"Go ahead, Mom, I'm sure it has something to do with Rabbi Stein."

"Of course it's about Josh Stein! Honey, you have a flourishing business in New York and you've made good friends, and I still don't know what happened between you and Aaron. I'm not crazy about him, but at least he's a known quantity. You don't know a thing about Rabbi Stein, and you're ready to throw everything away to test the waters here? Does that make any sense? Oh, and let's not forget that Josh is practically engaged to your old friend. Have you lost your mind?"

Leora stopped walking. "I might be losing my mind, but I don't think so. I don't want to run my business in New York anymore, and I don't want to get back together with Aaron. I can't imagine him being the father of my children. For your information, our relationship was more business than romance. It became comfortable for both of us to be together and to rely on each other. You say I have a lot of friends in New York? For the last year or so, it's been more Aaron than girlfriends. So what, exactly, am I giving up?"

"What's going to happen to your business?"

"Aaron's agreed to run it by himself, and he'll do great. There are already people working for us who can take over my end. Aaron will buy me out, and then I'll figure out what I really want to do."

"Well, don't do it here!" Bunny insisted. "Just don't move to Chicago!"

Leora calmly turned and started walking back to the house; Bunny turned to walk with her, realizing that she had been as clear as she could be, and now it was up to her daughter to do the smart thing. She decided not to discuss this with her husband and to pray for the best.

She felt in her pocket and pulled out a five dollar bill. As they entered the house, she walked over to the *tzedakah* box and dropped the money in. The custom of giving charity in hopes of a good outcome was inbred in her DNA, and she needed all the help she could get.

Leora watched her mother with amusement. Her whole life, she had observed her parents utilizing that same charity receptacle in good times and bad. She wondered, *Does God really care if I stay in New York or move back to Chicago?* Leora had some loose change in her skirt pocket. She looked at it, dropped the coins into the box, and went back to packing the *kiddush* cups.

CHAPTER 26

Leora wasn't the kind of woman who waited for life to happen. Everything she had achieved, including earning high honors at college and using her love of the outdoors to create a successful business, had come to pass as a result of her grit and optimism. She had to know how Josh Stein felt about Rachel, so she called him. She planned to invite him to meet her for lunch before she left Chicago. The only number she had was Lev Shalom.

OK, why not? Josh can always say no, but I'm pretty sure he'll say yes.

At eleven-thirty, everyone in the Lev Shalom office was out for lunch, with Serena remaining to handle the phones. She was surprised when the caller, Leora Halperin, asked to speak to Rabbi Stein. After putting Leora through to the Rabbi, Serena began to worry about the conversation taking place on the other side of the wall.

If Leora gets involved with Rabbi Stein, it'll complicate Rachel's relationship with him even more, maybe destroy it. Rachel has to figure out how to get Josh back into her life, and she better do it fast. What does Leora have up her sleeve, anyway? She's supposed to be Rachel's friend, but it sure doesn't look like it. Rachel's going to say I'm jumping to conclusions, and maybe I am. Maybe the call's about Rabbi Halperin. Or maybe it's about the Holocaust Memorial Garden. It's probably nothing. Anyway, Leora's going back to New York. Why would she even want to get involved with the guy who's taking her father's place? She has no reason in the world to stay in Chicago after her parents leave.

Serena couldn't put her mind to rest. She had an idea which would excuse her intrusion. She knocked on Josh's door and entered as he was hanging up.

"I know it's none of my business, but when Leora just called to speak to you, I got concerned that something might have happened to her father."

Josh was no fool, and he laughed, "Trust me, Serena, if anything happens in the Halperin household, I'll be sure to let you know. It's wonderful that you care so deeply about the Rabbi. I'm sure you're relieved that their daughter's here to help them. Leora told me that she's a good friend of Rachel's, so you know what a sensible and caring person she is."

This was not music to Serena's ears. She had expected to be reassured, but it was the opposite. Josh clearly admired Leora! Returning to her desk, she started to reach for the phone but stopped herself.

At the same time, Josh was sorry that he had teased Serena. He went to her desk and smiled at her. "I'm sure you're still worried about Rabbi Halperin after working with him for so many years. You and I are both grateful that their daughter's here to help them. She also offered to send suggestions for the Garden from New York. I told her to stay in touch with you in case she needs more information. I hope that's OK?"

Serena was relieved. She wasn't sure if Josh had read her mind about Rachel or not, but she didn't care. What she did know was that the young man leaning against her desk was the kind of person Lev Shalom was lucky to have. He was smart and didn't want to worry her.

Of course, Serena had no idea that Leora and Josh were meeting the next day for lunch, and that it was Leora's idea.

CHAPTER 27

Josh was well aware that every move he made was observed and discussed by his congregants, especially when it involved a woman. Even
though Leora had initiated the invitation for lunch, Josh opted for The
Chosen, a kosher restaurant in Skokie, about twenty minutes away from
the Lev Shalom neighborhood. He didn't have to spell it out to Leora.
She immediately agreed to meet him at a non-local haunt.

Leora arrived right on time and was seated at a table by the front window. She saw Josh parking his car and rushing in. She appreciated that
he was the kind of guy who didn't like to be late. She too, made it her
business to be punctual, but it wasn't hard for her. She never wasted
time brooding about her makeup or ensemble. Her wardrobe was small
and practical. Her glowing complexion and athletic build were all she
needed.

Josh apologized as he joined her at the table.

"You're exactly five minutes late," Leora laughed. "I didn't think you'd
stand me up. I'm starved. Let's eat!"

Josh laughed, too, "You can't be as hungry as I am. I've never been here
before. What's good?"

"I happen to have their whole menu memorized. My family used to
come here for a little privacy because it's not in our ghetto, and I liked

to eat here with my friends because the food is great."

"Better than Kalman's?"

"The best thing about this place is that Kalman isn't here. Don't look at me like that! I love Kalman as much as I guess you do, but I like to eat in a place that doesn't have the town *yenta* as its proprietor."

"I get it. So, what should I order?"

"The tomato soup is perfect, especially if you have it with grilled cheese."

Josh didn't want to make a big show about ritual hand washing before eating bread, so he looked on the menu for a salad.

Leora read his mind and pointed to a basin and cup on the side of the room. "The washing station's over there."

Josh liked the way she handled his unasked question. He wondered if she would order a sandwich and join him.

As they waited to be served, Leora entertained Josh with anecdotes featuring her parents and the crazy situations in which they found themselves. Josh's favorite was the Halperin's first *Purim* in which the male congregants, half of whom were Holocaust survivors, got drunk during the *Megillah* reading. They convinced their new, young Rabbi Halperin to imbibe with them, while Bunny sat with the women and laughed along.

"You weren't even there. How do you know it's true?" Josh asked.

"When my mother tells me something about my father, it's always true.

It's not in my mother's nature to make up stories."

"And what about you?" Josh smiled, leaning toward her.

At that moment, the waitress presented the couple with their lunch. Both of them got up and went to ritually wash their hands. Leora surprised Josh by saying the blessing under her breath. She may have been impressing him with the washing, but she knew what to do, and he appreciated it.

Somehow, two hours passed very quickly. Josh pulled out his phone and accessed an app.

"If you're going to *bentch*, will you do it so that I can hear you?" Leora asked.

She sure does know the drill, Josh realized. He liked it and decided to tell her.

"I'm feeling completely relaxed, and I'm glad we came here. The next time you're in Chicago, I hope we can get together."

"It might be sooner than you think!"

Josh was happy to hear that, but on his way back to Lev Shalom, his rational mind kicked in. *What if word gets around that I'm spending time with Rabbi Halperin's daughter? Bob Small will go ballistic. In fact, the Rabbi and Bunny would be furious. What if Rachel gets wind of this? She's mad at me right now, but she's made her feelings about me perfectly clear. She won't understand my having lunch with another woman, especially one who's her friend. Rabbi Dalton knew what he was talking about when he warned me about my public role.*

Josh found himself inadvertently echoing Serena's and Bunny's thoughts. *It's good that Leora's going back to New York. Was she serious when she said she might be back sooner than I expect? For better or worse, I have plenty of other things to worry about.*

CHAPTER 28

Daniel Lewisohn was furious. Not only was his business faltering, but now Kayla was determined to bring him into a new synagogue. She loved the Orthodox Jewish lifestyle and apparently adored the Lev Shalom rabbi. Well, Daniel didn't love the synagogue or the rabbi, and even though he had agreed to give Rabbi Stein one more chance, there was no point.

It was time to leave, probably not forever, but Daniel had to get to a 'safe place'. Both his brothers were divorced, and their children lived with their mothers. Bobby and Will Lewisohn were renting a small house in Racine, Wisconsin, far away from their families and in a neighborhood they could afford. Daniel had only been there once, but he knew his brothers wouldn't turn him away. In fact, he'd make sure of that by calling them from the road and bringing plenty of beer.

There hadn't been a lot of love among the three brothers, and Daniel was surprised when he heard that Bobby and Will were able to live under one roof. Necessity had always been the driving force in his struggling family. Fortunately, their hard upbringing had prepared all of them to survive by their own hands and resilience. Daniel's brothers managed to find steady work in construction and, except for occasional lapses in their work when Daniel reluctantly had to help them, never missed a child support payment. At least, that's what they told him.

An hour out of Chicago, Daniel called Kayla and left a message. He hoped that he'd hear from her immediately, but when she didn't respond, it strengthened his determination to get away and stay with his brothers until she came to her senses.

Nobody answered when Daniel called each brother's cell, so he decided to go directly to their house, sit on the front porch, and maybe crack open a couple of those beers in his back seat. He must have fallen asleep because he was awakened by the sound of trucks pulling into the driveway. Obviously, neither of his brothers had listened to his message because the dumbstruck looks on their faces convinced him that he might not be as welcome as he expected.

"What the hell's going on, bro?" a surprised Will wondered, frowning.

"Kayla kick ya out?" Bobby laughed. "Not again!"

Daniel decided full disclosure was unnecessary. "I just needed a little break. Kayla's going through stupid changes, and she wants me by her side the whole time. You know me, I'm too independent to let that woman boss me around. So, I figured I'd come and spend some time with people who understand me."

Will was more shrewd than Bobby. He knew very well that it was Kayla who had had enough of his brother. "OK, Dan, get your stuff and let's go inside."

"I brought a lot of beer," Daniel offered. "I figured you guys would be worn out at the end of the day, so let's go downtown and get something to eat. My treat."

"Sounds good to me!" Bobby exclaimed, wiping his hands on his jeans. "I'm ready."

"Not yet," Will cautioned. "How long you gonna stay? And what are you gonna do while we're working? Just sit here drinking beer and eating nachos? We gotta talk about this."

Daniel couldn't believe it. He expected a certain amount of gratitude for all the times he had reached into his own pocket to help his brothers. But he needed them now.

"Maybe a day or two," Daniel answered. "I still have to fix some business in Chicago."

"OK, Dan, two days," Will stated. "Yeah, sure, you helped us when we needed you, but you're the educated one who always made the bucks, so it was easy for you. And you have Kayla, too. You have everything, so I think it's kinda weird that you're here asking us to take you in."

Bobby was starving. "C'mon Will, give the guy a break." Then, turning to Daniel, he smiled, "You're treating, right?"

"Not only that," Daniel added, looking at their dilapidated trucks, "but I'm driving, too."

Dinner at the Starburst Diner was short, greasy, and delicious. While Daniel went to the register to pay the bill, the brothers had a couple of minutes to themselves.

Will was concerned, "Something's wrong and I hope Dan's not in big trouble. I wonder how much he drank before we got home. I'm not in the mood to deal with Dan when he's drunk."

Bobby stopped him. "Dan doesn't drink the way he used to. Not since Kayla got hold of him." Looking at his watch, he added, "Wrestling starts in fifteen minutes. We gotta get home. Let's go."

Will and Bobby had been looking forward to an exciting night of snacks, beer, and their favorite wrestlers beating the crap out of each other on TV, so as soon as Daniel joined them, Will announced the evening's agenda. They had bets on their favorites.

The three brothers managed to work their way through all the beer and half a bottle of whiskey. Daniel hadn't been that drunk or tired in a long time, and when he felt like that, his mean streak took over. He began to accuse his brothers of misusing the money he sent them and of being selfish lowlifes, who never amounted to anything. Then, he started on their horrible parents, their disastrous home life, and their lack of ambition.

When Will grabbed Daniel to calm him down, Daniel broke away and ran to his car. He sped off into the darkness.

CHAPTER 29

Kayla Morales sighed deeply as she took a chair in Josh Stein's office. Even though she had come to schedule a time when he could visit her school and talk to some of her students, she had something else to tell him.

"You look worried. Is everything OK?" Josh asked.

"It's about Daniel. I finally heard from him last night. I told you that he was going to his good-for-nothing brothers, who are always asking for money, may I add. He called to tell me that he's going to be there for a long time, and I can give his stuff away. I don't know if I really want to yet, but I'll be honest, my life is a whole lot calmer now that he's out of town."

Josh was surprised. "Actually, if I can be candid with you, your involvement at Lev Shalom is going to be much smoother now. But don't you miss him? I mean, you've been together for a long time. You were engaged. You must have thought that Daniel would come around."

"I probably saw it coming. Rabbi Dalton warned me that I would always have to mother Daniel. Eventually, even after we were engaged and I agreed to marry him, I was on alert and uncomfortable a lot of the time. Nobody in my life ever needed me as much as Daniel does, and I always knew I was the strong one."

Josh nodded, "I'm sure you've discussed this with Rabbi Dalton who knows you much better than I do. Still, I think it's only fair to warn you that Daniel may come back more determined than ever to pull you away from the life you want. It's true that I don't know him, but you, yourself, told me he's a loose cannon."

"That's because he's so insecure. I'm probably the only person he's completely comfortable with. He's rough around the edges, but I know his softer side."

"So, you miss him."

"I don't think so, but I'm worried about him."

"I understand, and there's plenty to worry about. Forgive me for the question I'm going to ask, but does Daniel still have a key to your place?"

Kayla smiled, "I know where you're going with that question. Daniel would never hurt me."

"OK, you know him, and I don't. I'm sure that whatever happens is for the best, and you have your priorities straight."

Kayla was eager to change the subject. "Speaking of having my priorities straight, let's talk about you coming to Bet Hillel Day School."

Josh and Kayla spent the next fifteen minutes arranging his visit to speak to some of her students about Torah and science. They were both relieved that Kayla had aired her thoughts about Daniel, but Josh knew that it wasn't really over.

As Josh walked Kayla out, he saw Rabbi Halperin's door open. He spotted Bunny and Leora continuing their careful packing of the Rabbi's possessions.

Leora saw him and made a quick decision to risk angering her mother by seizing the moment. "Rabbi Stein!" she called out. "We didn't know you were here. Come in and compliment us on our industriousness. Look what we've done, and I bet we'll finish before the week's over."

Josh came in, maneuvering around Bunny who had quickly stepped between him and her daughter. Bunny knew what Leora was doing, and she realized that it would be easier to control Josh than her daughter.

"Rabbi Stein," Bunny cautioned, "sorry that we can't stop to chat, but we have to use our time effectively. Leora's only going to be here to help us another day or two. She has a business to run, and I think you know that work always takes top priority. You probably have quite a bit to do yourself, so we'll let you get back to it."

Even though her mother's feelings were clear, Leora jumped in, "My mother's right. I was going to ask you for a tour of the Holocaust Memorial Garden, so maybe we can do that before I leave town."

Josh was conflicted. He knew that Leora Halperin should be off-limits, and he also knew that he had some kind of relationship with Rachel Berg that needed attention. Yet, here was a Jewishly-committed, interesting, and good-looking woman who didn't seem to be as high-strung or demanding as his current would-be girlfriend.

There were questions that Josh wanted to ask. "The Holocaust Garden? Did you see it when you were here for Rosh Hashanah? I understand that you and Rachel Berg are friends. Did she tell you about the Garden?"

Bunny was clearly getting impatient, but Leora forged ahead. "Rachel and I grew up together. She mentioned it to me when we got together last night, and I realized that I don't know anything about it."

Bunny stopped packing and moved toward her daughter. "There's not much of the Garden to see, and who knows how long it'll take to complete. Let's finish with Daddy's desk. Now, Leora!"

Josh found himself in an untenable spot. He remembered one of Rabbi Halperin's many rules for the rabbinate: *If it isn't an absolute necessity to get involved in a conflict, and it's not your business to resolve it, walk away!* But, in this case, Josh didn't want to.

"I'll leave the two of you to your work. Leora, if it's not too late when you finish, I'll show you around the Garden and let you look at the plans," Josh suggested.

Bunny stepped in. "Why don't the two of you take that little tour right now while I stay here and get more work done? When I've had enough, I'll wait for Leora and then we'll both head home together. The Holocaust Garden was a special project, and I'm sure Leora's father would want her to see it before she returns to New York."

As they headed into the Garden, Serena watched with concern, aware that things were changing.

CHAPTER 30

Josh was used to getting to know people slowly, initially on a superficial level. Small talk was easy for him, but he was uncomfortable when there was no conversation. He and Leora walked silently along the path that outlined the Memorial Garden, with Josh only occasionally directing her attention to the site of a future sculpture or planting.

Leora didn't mind the quiet. She loved everything nature had to offer, which made her life as a landscape designer constantly fulfilling. Unexpectedly, she found the embryonic garden challenging and invigorating.

Leora sensed Josh's discomfort, and decided to take the opportunity that presented itself. "I'd love to get involved in this project. You mentioned showing me the plans. While I'm here, I might be able to give the committee some ideas. Do you think they'd be open to that?"

Josh was delighted. "I'm sure they'd love to hear from someone with your experience. As a matter of fact, you probably know some of the people involved. But you're going back to New York and I don't know how that could work."

"What you don't know, Rabbi Stein, is that I'm seriously considering selling my share of the business to my partner and opening my own place somewhere else."

"Really?'

"And I add, Rabbi, that my partner was also my fiance. We've recently dissolved our romantic relationship, and now I'm ready to dissolve our business relationship. Aaron and I are still friends, so I'm confident that if we restructure the business, it'll go pretty smoothly."

"And you're ready to leave New York? I always thought it was the best place for singles."

Josh realized that he overstepped the casual conversation they were having. *Why did I do that? Do I always have to play 'Rabbi'? It's none of my business where she wants to live, or if she wants to be single.*

Leora laughed. "Who said I want to live in a city that's great for singles? There are plenty of other great places to live. I was just talking to my mother about moving back to Chicago."

"Move back here, just when your parents are leaving?"

"Exactly! My timing would be perfect!"

Now they both laughed, and the air was cleared. They continued to walk the periphery of the garden, and conversation came more easily as Leora talked about growing up at Lev Shalom as the Rabbi's unusual daughter who loved the outdoors more than music and movies like the other girls. She continued sharing more funny moments featuring her family.

Josh was eager to get to know her better. "I haven't laughed this hard since I moved here, and I don't know if I should say this, but it's really hard to imagine either of your parents in the situations you just told me. Your story about your father's Chanukah gambling and your mother's doughnut obsession are almost unbelievable. But there's one person from the past who I'm really curious about."

"Let me guess...It's Bob Small, right?" Leora suggested.

"How in the world would you guess that?"

Leora had no problem responding, "I overheard an argument between my parents a couple of days ago. It had something to do with lies that Bob was spreading about my father, and my mother just wants to leave all of that behind. I'm sure you know all the details, but I don't know if I want to hear them."

Josh had to establish his rabbinic boundaries, even though he was uncomfortable doing it. "I'm not sure I understand any of it. Anyway, you of all people know that I won't discuss any behind-the-scenes happenings around here."

Leora nodded, "You bet! In fact, my parents never talked to us at home about problems at *shul*. You can imagine how surprised I was this week to hear my parents arguing about a congregant in front of me. But, just between us, Bob Small is always sure that he's right, and other people are wrong. So I'll tell you what I do know, and I know this from Sheila. Everybody, especially my father, was against her marrying Bob. Sheila was special in a lot of ways. She was kind of wild, but smart, good-hearted and adorable. When she met Bob, they fell in love, and it was real. From what I see, they turned out to be a great couple. I wouldn't be surprised if Bob still holds that against my father."

This was new information for Josh. It wasn't only the Holocaust money, after all. It was old wounds exacerbated by the missing funds. Bob was the kind of person who could never forgive and forget, and, interestingly, Halperin was the same. But, as a rabbi, he knew how to control himself, and Bob never even tried.

Even though Josh wanted to know more, he changed the subject. "So, how long do you plan to stay here?"

"I want to be with my parents for their last Shabbat in Chicago, and then I'll go back to New York on Sunday. After I take care of things there, I may test the waters for my business here."

Josh wanted to know Leora better, but if she came back, would that make his life easier or harder? A picture of Rachel Berg flashed through his mind. He wasn't ready to get involved with another woman, especially a friend of Rachel's.

Their conversation had reached a natural conclusion. As they headed out of the garden area, Leora summarized, "You've been great to talk to, and I really enjoyed our walk. You have a hard job ahead of you, and I wish you all the luck in the world."

Josh smiled, "Thanks, I'll need it, and I wish you the same."

CHAPTER 31

Rabbi Halperin sat in his favorite chair, once again facing James Traub. Halperin wanted to tell the reporter his story, and after so many years in the rabbinate, Halperin was an expert at maximizing interviews with journalists. Traub knew he had a story, and he, too, was eager to coax it out of his prey. In other words, each man sitting in the Halperin's living room was confident that he could use the other to achieve his purpose.

Traub began, "Tell me how you came to write your most famous book, *Pray This Way*. I actually read it, and I have to admit I feel like I really know you. Your experiences of counseling and mentoring were really powerful."

"I tried to pepper my lessons with pertinent anecdotes, and believe me, Mr. Traub, I have twice as many experiences that didn't make it into the book."

"Most poignant to me were the times you found solace in prayer. Can you tell me more about that?"

Halperin leaned forward in his chair. This was his chance. "There are times, and every rabbi has these, when the congregation pushes its leader to understand that he must be strong and stand for what is right. The spiritual leader summons his belief in the Almighty and thereby gains the courage to persevere."

"Tell me more. What do you mean by 'courage to persevere?'"

Halperin paced as he answered. "Only recently I had an opportunity to withstand false accusations, but I am always armed with the assurance that the Almighty is fully with me. I was maligned and even hospitalized because of a malevolent congregant."

Traub was delighted to have an opportunity to probe further. "An evil congregant? May I ask what happened? Is he in prison? What did he do? Or was it a woman?"

Halperin smiled at that. "Let's just say that every congregation has one or two rotten apples, and it's true that this kind of situation has the ability to spoil the whole bunch."

"How can a rabbi tolerate that kind of abuse? I always thought the rabbi was the boss of the synagogue."

"If only that were the case, Mr. Traub, the rabbi would be able to be the true spiritual leader he's meant to be. That's the way things were when I entered the rabbinate. And that's the way they were for many years at Lev Shalom."

"Do you mean that society has changed, and there's a general lack of respect for the rabbinate? Or is it something else? Has the population of Lev Shalom changed? I'm sure that you've maintained your own personal values."

Halperin sat down once again and sighed, "Fortunately, I'm strong and able to depend on my unflinching faith and years of work with all kinds of people to carry me through. Once in a great while, a really unpleasant individual achieves prominence among the laity, and unnecessary complications arise."

"Such as…?"

Halperin caught himself. "Let's just say that the squeaky wheel is the one that gets oiled, especially if that wheel is the biggest wheel."

"You mean an officer or another staff person?"

At that very moment, Bunny and Leora walked in. They had heard the tail end of the conversation and Bunny knew how to gently stop it. "Fred, let's take a break and have some dessert. Mr. Traub, I insist that you sample my chocolate cake. You won't regret it."

Leora left her mother to manage the rest of Traub's visit, which would definiely be shortened.

Traub was a seasoned journalist. He hadn't had this important job for long, but his years as a roving reporter had provided him with excellent instincts. He knew he wasn't going to get anything more out of Halperin now that his wife interceded. Traub made a dramatic gesture of looking at his watch.

"I hope we can continue our interview soon," he said to the Rabbi. "I'm really sorry I have to miss that cake, Mrs. Halperin, but I'm already late for an appointment across town. I hope I can have a raincheck."

Once James Traub was safely out the door, Bunny faced her husband. He expected a tirade, but that's not what happened.

"Fred, you've clearly lost your mind and you're about to lose your dignity," she said calmly. "I meant it when I said that I'm moving to Israel as soon as I can, and I want you to come with me. There's still a lot to do in the other room, so when you're finished with the cake, I'd appreciate it if you'd put it back in the refrigerator. Just remember to put the cake dome on it."

Halperin was aware that Bunny had stopped him before he went too far. He felt sure that Traub's respect for him was intact, and he considered that it might be wise to discontinue more interviews. He didn't like the part of himself that craved power and fame, and yet he had become a slave to it. What had become of Ephraim Halperin who built a little *shtieble* into a great, dynamic synagogue? He was proud of that person, and maybe he could recapture some of his former optimism and goodness when he and Bunny made *aliyah*.

Most of the Holocaust survivors who had been the core of his original congregation were gone now, and the few that remained no longer related to him the way they used to. But he knew that he was the one who had changed, not these elderly people who remained loyal to the *shul*. He had a sudden urge to go to the morning service at Lev Shalom and beg their forgiveness. He had promised Jacob Wohl that the Memorial Garden would be completed while Wohl was still alive, but that didn't happen. Halperin's ego had prevented it.

His mind wandered back to the very early days when Bob Small's father, Hyman Smolensky (which became 'Small' when the family opened a grocery store on Chicago's west side), brought a rescued Holocaust *Torah* to Lev Shalom. And yet, in spite of that selfless act, Halperin had tried to prevent Smolensky's son, Bob, from marrying one of the Halperins' favorite teenagers, Sheila Steinberg. Even though there was no reason for Bob to forgive Rabbi Halperin, Sheila had brought Bob back into the *shul*, and they had become generous contributors and leaders.

Now he and Bob were enemies, and no one, except Fred and Bob and the dwindling handful of survivors, remembered Hyman Smolensky. Bob had always marched with his late father's rescued *Torah* on the High Holidays, but this year Fred was so wrapped up in his own problems that he missed the opportunity to acknowledge Bob's deep connection to Lev Shalom's past.

Bunny reappeared. "Is anything the matter? I asked you to put the cake away when you finished, but you're just sitting here with that slice of cake still in front of you."

"I've been thinking. You're right that the interviews with Traub probably won't help me. If I continue meeting him, I'll end up saying things I'll regret."

"I'm worried about you, Fred."

"Don't worry, Bunny. Everything's going to change once we leave.

CHAPTER 32

Bob Small paced furiously up and down the wide marble hallway of his beautiful home. He paid no attention to the family vacation pictures and trophies on the glass shelving or the priceless collection of sports memorabilia surrounding him. Sheila was busy in the kitchen doing what she always did when she was nervous, making double chocolate brownies. Aware of her husband's unrest, she was doing her best to stay out of his way, even though she had made her feelings clear to him.

Bob's mind was focused on the visitor he expected any minute, and he rehearsed his agenda, oblivious to the aroma wafting from the Viking oven.

The doorbell rang at exactly two o'clock. Bob appreciated punctuality and opened the door with a big smile on his face. "Come in, come in, James. So let's get started."

Traub nodded and obediently took the seat Bob showed him. They sat facing each other, Bob settling majestically in his favorite easy chair, James on full alert in an armless chair, certain that Bob had important, maybe even provocative, information.

Feigning innocence, James asked, "Is it OK if I record our conversation?"

"That's exactly what I want you to do. Let me say right from the start that Rabbi Ephraim Halperin's departure is the best thing that could've happened for Lev Shalom. And let me tell you why."

Bob paused a second or two to make sure that he had Traub's complete attention. He relished the fact that this opportunity had fallen in his lap, and he knew how to use his business savvy to turn a deal to his advantage.

Bob began, "Rabbi Halperin treated our synagogue like a personal kingdom. He was self-centered enough to use our resources for his own gain. Yes, I admit, that he's one of the reasons our shul is famous and a model throughout the world. But all of us, the congregants and the board, worked our asses off to help him, and what'd we get? Ya see, James, that man is so sure of himself that he boldly disregarded proper procedures and believed he was above the will of the board of directors."

"For example?"

Bob stood up, ready to deliver the goods. "It came to my attention, as synagogue president and chief cook and bottle washer, that there was a missing sum of money...and it was large. You may already know that a number of our office staff and our former executive director were somehow mixed up in the mess, and that I had no choice but to fix everything."

James was taken aback by Small's last declaration. "Did you say members of the office staff?"

"Three staff members resigned because of their loyalty to the executive director, Joseph Garber, who I found out was in cahoots with our illustrious Rabbi."

"What about that red-headed woman I spoke to last week? Was she there at that time?"

"Forget about her! Serena Berg would lay down on the floor so that Halperin could wipe his feet on her before entering his sacred office. Naturally, she still refuses to believe the truth."

Bob realized that the conversation was straying and he wanted to get back on track. He was sorry that he had mentioned Garber and the others. He was through with them. It was Halperin's reputation he wanted to destroy.

Pushing forward, Bob refocused his soliloquy, "You've come here to find out more about Rabbi Halperin, right? Well, believe me, if I were free to tell you everything I know, you'd have a Pulitzer-winning, real-life expose."

"Why can't you tell me everything you know?"

"Everybody involved signed a non-disclosure statement. I was forced to do it in order to get rid of that *gonif* for good."

Traub was intrigued and decided to push Small harder. "*Gonif*? Are you calling Rabbi Ephraim Halperin a thief? That's a pretty strong word."

"I'm gonna tell you something, but you better not quote me," Bob warned. "I mean it--this is 'off the record'."

"Go on."

Bob reached in front of Traub and grabbed the recorder. After he was certain it was turned off, he began.

"My father, may he rest in peace, was one of the original founders of

Lev Shalom. There were a lot of other Holocaust survivors, too, and they hired a young, energetic rabbi fresh out of rabbinical school, named Ephraim Halperin. Eventually, after decades of building the synagogue, a goal of that group was to establish some kind of permanent Holocaust memorial. To this day, James, that memorial hasn't been built. And, do you know why? Let me tell you. The funding was there. Many Holocaust survivors were alive. And there are still a few hopeful men and women, and let me add their children and grandchildren, who pray that this will come to fruition. James, this is the mission I took on myself, and I swore to a survivor named Nathan Wohl, who gave a large sum of money to the project, that it would be completed before he died. Well, that never happened, and here's why. Rabbi Ephraim Halperin, in cahoots with his lackey, the synagogue executive director, Joseph Garber, used the money to hire a PR firm to represent Halperin so he could be famous and sell his crappy books."

Traub had been certain that there was more to the Halperin story than simply a fond farewell to a beloved clergyman, but this was unreal. Small's revelations were shocking, but could Traub verify them? *Maybe that red-headed administrator can be useful,* he considered. *I have to get to her right away.*

Bob clearly wasn't finished with his accusations, but because Traub was determined to establish himself as a serious journalist, he stopped Small's tirade to ask, "Do you have any objections to my verifying your statements?"

"Young man, every word I've spoken is God's honest truth!" Bob said impatiently. "Frankly, any reporter worth his salt would know who to trust and who will just give you the party line."

James knew better than to jump into murky waters, "There can't be any harm in asking around to support your information."

Bob hated being challenged, especially by some kid looking to get a scoop. He was finished.

"I've told you plenty for your story. If you waste your time poking around the *shul* to try to prove I'm wrong, you'll be sorry."

James wasn't easily intimidated. In fact, he was now even more determined to talk to Serena, Lev Shalom board members, and anybody else he could find to get to the truth. When he began the interview he had no idea what a big story it could be.

As Traub got up to leave, Bob fired his parting shot, "Remember what I said. If you start prodding anybody connected to the *shul*, you'll regret it."

Walking himself to the door, Traub couldn't help but smile. *I can't wait to get to the redhead and her new boss, Stein. This is going to be huge.*

After Traub left, Bob went into the kitchen, gloating. He put his arm around Sheila and winked, "I took care of that boy. He got the whole story, just the way I wanted."

Sheila had heard everything and was positive this saga wasn't over.

CHAPTER 33

After the holiday of *Sukkot*, Josh found time to talk to Kayla Morales' class. He was pleased that his talk generated a lot of questions from the students. In fact, he enjoyed it so much that he agreed to visit the Bet Hillel school again.

The class ended about a half hour before school was out, and Josh decided to go into the synagogue office to see Rabbi Dalton before he left. As he passed Sarah Bright's desk, she called out a hearty, "Shalom, shalom, Rabbi Stein!".

Dalton greeted Josh with the familiar Bet Hillel salutation, "Shalom, shalom, my friend! Ms. Morales told me you were coming today, so let me hear all about it."

Seated in Dalton's colorful office, Josh described his presentation and the students' spirited reaction.

Dalton was pleased. "I imagine your appearance in the classroom will give the kids something to talk about at home tonight. I'm not sure they've ever studied with a white rabbi, and certainly not one who knows a lot about science."

"It's about time they met somebody like me," Josh noted, kiddingly.

"And how about me? How many of your people, especially the young ones, have spent time with a rabbi like me?" Dalton posed.

"You're right!" Josh quickly replied, "We can fix that. In fact, let's do something even more radical. How about staying on our side of town and coming to Lev Shalom for an entire *Shabbat?* I have a feeling the sermon you give will be very different from the ones our congregants are used to hearing."

"I accept your offer before your board of directors hears about it and vetoes it. And Josh, I would invite you to speak at my *shul*, but your 'White Rabbi Sermon' would probably put everybody to sleep," Dalton joked.

"Actually," Josh responded, "that's my great strength. My hard-working congregants look forward to a guaranteed nap time."

Dalton was preparing his next jibe when Sarah buzzed his office to announce Kayla's arrival.

Kayla was all smiles as she rushed in. "Wonderful job, Rabbi Stein! The science teacher wants to know when you're coming back."

"That's great, but what did the kids say?" Josh asked.

"Actually, they want you to come back tomorrow!" Kayla reported.

"Shalom, shalom, Ms. Morales!" Dalton greeted her cheerfully. "How was your day, and what did the teacher and students really think about our young rabbinic visitor? We want the truth!"

"Nothing but praise. I just stopped to thank you, Rabbi Stein. I'm in a big hurry, but I plan to *daven* with your congregation this Shabbat."

As she left the office, Dalton raised his eyebrows, "So I see that our Ms. Morales has found her spiritual home at last. I don't know if her decision is permanent, and I'll tell you why."

"Go on."

"She's already a Shabbat observer who walks to our *shul*. If she becomes a regular member of your synagogue, she'll move into your neighborhood. Do you think her fiance will agree to that?"

Josh shrugged his shoulders, "If you're worried about Daniel, he's probably out of the picture. They broke the engagement, and Daniel's with his brothers now."

Dalton whistled, "Maybe *Hashem* decided to pay attention to our girl and handle that relationship for her. On the other hand, do we really know where Daniel is?"

Josh nodded, "Kayla just heard from him, and he's not in Chicago. That's what she told me, and I hope it's true, for her sake."

"And ours," Dalton added, with uncertainty. "It looks like Kayla's been honest with you. You seem to know a lot about what's going on."

"Not really. She came to tell me that she's joining Lev Shalom as a single member. That's when she told me about Daniel."

Dalton decided to offer some unsolicited advice. "Josh, I like you, but I'm afraid that you're still wet behind the ears when it comes to delicate counseling situations. It's crucial to keep a professional distance from troubled members. Kayla Morales is one of my best teachers, a devout Jewish woman, and a strong person. But, the fact that she was able to love Daniel Lewisohn is a red flag. I'm not sure it's completely over. So be careful!"

Josh knew that Dalton was speaking from experience. He thanked him and as he shook hands with Rabbi Dalton, he said, "On a more pleasant subject, let's talk about your Shabbat visit soon."

It was late when the rabbis walked out, and Sarah Bright was putting on her jacket. "Rabbi Dalton, I'm about to head home, but I left a few messages that seem important and only you can handle. Rabbi Stein, I hope to see you again soon."

"God willing."

Dalton smiled at Josh, "I'm looking forward to praying with you at your *shul*. I hope your congregants like to sing."

"That all depends on what you call singing!" Josh laughed. Then he added, "Shalom, shalom!"

CHAPTER 34

Josh was tired of waiting to hear from Rachel. Since Rosh Hashana, he had focused on hospital visits, the youth group, and getting to know new and old members. He had intended to have a serious conversation with her, but there hadn't been any time. Even his desire to bring closure to his complicated relationship with the Halperins had moved to the sidelines. Now, their daughter Leora had unexpectedly appeared, and he didn't have time for her either.

Overwhelmed as he was with obligations, Josh missed Rachel. She played such an important role in his life in Chicago. He decided to try again.

Rachel's cell phone rang as she was getting ready for bed. Recognizing that it was Josh, she let it ring a couple of times before she answered it..

"I guess it's time to talk, but it's late," she said.

Josh was apologetic, "I just got home. I've been meaning to call you all day, and this the first chance I've had. I've left messages for you, you know."

"I know, Josh, but I've been thinking about your inability to maintain a steady relationship. Messages late at night don't impress me. This problem of yours to find two minutes to call me during your busy day is perfect proof that you're not even trying to fit me in. Plenty of other people text me with all kinds of foolishness, but from you, nothing."

"OK, Rachel, you made your point," Josh affirmed. "I've been inconsiderate, and I'm sorry. Anyway, I don't want to talk on the phone. I want to see you in person."

"Prove it."

"Let me come over tomorrow night and I'll bring dinner. I'll be there at eight o'clock."

"I'm too tired to argue," Rachel yawned. "Good night."

Josh realized that it was the best he could do under the circumstances. On the one hand, he didn't want to lose Rachel. On the other hand, he was only too aware that she expected more of him than he could offer, at least for now, and she held a grudge. The kind of woman he wanted by his side had to share him and not control him. Rachel was beautiful and smart, but if he was honest with himself, he knew she didn't really get him.

Josh had a hard time falling asleep and an even harder time waking up in time for morning services. Part of the reason for his lethargy was the disturbing dream he'd had. In it, he was knocking at Rachel's door with two shopping bags of food. Serena answered the door with a scowl on her face. She was angry that Josh didn't know that Rachel had moved, and that Leora had taken over Rachel's job at the law office. Not only that, Leora's husband, Aaron, was running their landscaping business with Elijah Dalton as their consultant.

Josh woke up with a start, and wished that he had taken a dream interpretation class like some of his colleagues, but he had an idea that his life was going to get even more complicated and his dreams even more troubling. He spent the day in meetings with a recent widow who was in dire financial straits, followed by a group of senior citizens complaining that the synagogue was no longer responsive to their needs, and finally, with the preschool director asking him to greet parents on the carpool line. Even though he was worn out, he gathered his strength for the evening ahead. He knew it was going to be a challenge.

As promised, Josh rang Rachel's doorbell at eight sharp. Rachel greeted him with a big smile and helped him bring in the take-out Chinese from Chai Chopstix, beer, and flowers. She had decided that they would have a pleasant dinner before they had the serious talk they both anticipated. The food was delicious, and they consciously kept the conversation light.

By nine o'clock, Rachel was tired of controlling her emotions. "You hurt me, Josh."

Even though he didn't want to, Josh became defensive. "How long are you going to obsess about my fatigue at your parent's house? I was exhausted and I felt sick. And another thing, Rachel, how obvious did you intend to be when I was with Rabbi Dalton at Kalman's? I know you're angry, but I don't know how to deal with that. That's my life as a congregational rabbi. I get tired after two solid days of sermons and shaking hands. I want to nurture professional relationships with other friendly Chicago leaders. I'm in constant meetings with people who have serious problems. And I'm just getting started."

Rather than being mollified, Rachel was more incensed, "And what about me? If you really care about me, as you claim to, I'd be at least as important as everybody else. Who else solved the Holocaust Memorial mystery with you? You couldn't have done that without me, and you know it. I'm no Bunny Halperin, the dutiful spouse who exists mainly to help her husband succeed. I know myself well. I need to be more than my husband's support; I need to be his partner. I need attention as much as you do."

The conversation had moved way beyond Josh's anticipation, and he blurted out, "You're talking about a married, rabbinic couple, Rachel. We're not there, and I'm not ready to talk about it. You know how I feel about you, and I want to continue to be with you, but I need much more time."

Rachel had a flash of recognition, and she realized it wasn't going to work, at least according to her fantasy. And it was a fantasy.

"Josh, it's so clear and so sad. I've had plenty of years to practice law and have boyfriends. I'm ready to get married and have a family, and you're the kind of man I'd like to grow old with. But I'm not going to wait until you're able to have the conversation I want to have right now. You had time to have dinner with Rabbi Dalton, and yet, not with me. If you love me, you have to put me first."

"Love? I can't allow myself to think like that right now. I think I love you, but I'm not ready to marry you just to prove it. What now?"

Tears welled in Rachel's eyes, but she wanted to shake Josh up. "There's a man I work with, a Jewish guy, who's taken me out a couple of times. I know he'd like to get serious. There's another man, a lawyer in another firm, who calls me at least once a week. Other men would do anything to capture my attention and they want to spend as much time with me as they can. I wish I wouldn't have to say this, but it's time for me to pursue my other options."

Josh was struck with the reality that he was about to lose Rachel. He stood up and went to her.

They instinctively held each other and kissed. But it wasn't the same. They both knew that it was over. Rachel walked Josh to the door. Interestingly enough, neither of them said 'maybe we can give it a little more time'.

CHAPTER 35

Last week, when Serena and Rachel had bumped into Josh and Rabbi Dalton at Kalman's, Rachel's antipathy toward Josh was obvious, and even Dalton noticed it.

Serena, unaware that Rachel and Josh had already had a decisive discussion, was determined to rekindle the sparks between them. She hated playing the role of 'interfering mother', and yet, she couldn't help it. She planned to bring their relationship up at their weekly Monday night dinner.

The Berg women sat silently at Kalman's. Rachel busied herself checking her cell phone messages, and Serena studied the menu which, of course, she knew by heart. Kalman came over to greet them, sensed the iciness at their table, said a brief hello, and wisely walked away.

When the waitress came to take their order, Serena responded crisply, "Veggie lasagna," and Rachel, her eyes still fixed on her phone, said, "Salmon plate--medium." The waitress wisely made a hasty retreat.

Millie Morris, one of the *shul* office support staff, approached the Berg duo with a big smile on her face. "Guess what, Serena? My daughter's engaged! Isn't that great?"

Serena composed herself and glanced quickly at Rachel, "*Mazel tov*, Millie! Is that her on-and-off boyfriend? How old is Julie now? I'm so happy to hear good news."

"Julie and Rob have been dating ever since they were in college. I never thought they'd finally make a commitment. Julie just turned twenty-nine. That's how long it took for them to come to their senses. She finally gave Rob an ultimatum and, obviously, he didn't want to lose her."

Making sure that Rachel was listening, Serena stated, "That works sometimes, I know, and it never hurts for a woman to put her cards on the table."

Rachel put her phone into her purse and took a deep breath, "What if Rob had walked away? What then?"

Millie realized that the conversation had taken an uncomfortable turn she did not wish to pursue. "Thank God it all worked out!"

Millie would have been interested in asking Rachel about her love life, but it was clear that the conversation was over. "Well, you're the first to know our good news, and now I'm going to move on and spread the word."

Rachel mumbled a weak '*mazel tov*', retrieved her cell phone and resumed texting.

The meal was served and consumed quickly and uncomfortably. Rachel was furious. "I can't believe that you purposely used Millie's announcement to make a point with me. How transparent can you be! If this is how our weekly dinners are going to go, should we just decide right now to stop? Do you think that Josh and I haven't had conversations about our future? And how do you think those conversations have gone? Well, I'll tell you. They've been crappy. It's over. There's nothing between Josh and me except anger on my part and hesitation on his. Are you satisfied, now?"

Serena reached over and took both her daughter's hands. "I was hoping that the two of you would realize how much you could help and strengthen each other. Thank you for telling me the truth. As for our weekly get-togethers, they mean too much to me to give up. I love you, Rachel, and I want the best for you, whatever that is."

Rachel was moved by her mother's compassionate reaction. She had expected an emotional outburst when she told Serena about the breakup with Josh. There was more depth to her mother than she realized, and she, too, wanted to maintain their Monday dinners.

Rachel summed it up, "I love you, too, Mom."

They paid the bill and walked to their own cars. Driving home alone, Serena began to cry. *Rachel thinks I have it together, but wait until I get home and tell Herb. I know I won't sleep at all tonight, thinking about this.*

CHAPTER 36

No one was home when Rabbi Elijah Dalton's phone rang. Returning from a *shiva* visit, they were worried and exhausted. The woman who had died left three small children and a husband who was too devastated to pick up the pieces. Congregation Bet Hillel's members would take care of the family's physical needs, but the Daltons knew the emotional piece of grieving would take much more time.

They saw the flashing phone recorder and looked at each other. Dalton said, "I can't bear any more bad news tonight. You can listen if you want to, but I'm going to bed."

Ruth came into the bedroom a few minutes later with a strange look on her face. "I think you have to listen to the message yourself. This is serious."

Dalton got up and retrieved the message:

This is Kayla Morales. I'm calling to let you know that I have to leave town for a few days. Something happened and it looks like I'm the only person who can take care of it. I have a substitute teacher covering my class for the rest of the week. I'll explain everything when I get back.

Elijah and Ruth looked at each other. "It must be her mother," Ruth declared.

Elijah answered, "As bad as that might be, it's a whole lot better than some other possibilities."

"Like what?

"Obviously, I'm letting my imagination get the best of me because I'm so tired. I know her mother's been sick, but I always have Daniel Lewisohn in the back of my mind. I'll try to call Kayla on her cell tomorrow."

It was late, but Josh decided to stop in his office for a minute after the monthly Lev Shalom board meeting. He listened to the only message on his answering machine:

This is Kayla Morales. If I sound out of breath, it's because I'm rushing out of town. I got a call that needs my attention. I have to cancel the appointment we scheduled and I left a message for Serena. I should be back by the end of the week, and I'll tell you everything when I return.

Josh's mind raced, *What was that about? She told me her mother's been sick and Kayla's probably the only responsible sibling. I hope it's nothing else. Kayla's a push-over for someone in trouble.*

CHAPTER 37

Kayla pulled up at Daniel's brothers' house in Racine. She had driven for hours. She was furious and beyond exhausted. Bobby and Will Lewisohn, who had been waiting for her on their front porch, ran to the car.

"We were up all night looking for Dan," Bobby shouted.

"We drank a lot last night, and all of a sudden Dan left the house and drove away," Will explained. "We don't know where he went, and that's why we called you. We thought he was back in Chicago."

Kayla could just imagine the scene last night that precipitated the hysterical phone call that she had received. Kayla groaned, "I'm too tired to figure this out right now. I don't think he's in Chicago, but somebody better find him fast."

"You're damn right about that!" Will exclaimed. "He can get real crazy when he drinks."

"I've had enough. After this, the two of you...and only the two of you... can deal with your brother," Kayla said, flatly.

"You gotta help us," Bobby pleaded. "We need you. We figured you'd know what to do."

Kayla had no desire to explain anything to Daniel's brothers, but she said, "Daniel and I just broke up. I have no idea what's going on with him, except that he said he was leaving Chicago to spend time with you guys."

"Yeah, Dan told us you got all religious on him and now you want him to go through all these changes. Kayla, honey, Dan isn't gonna change for anybody, not even you."

Kayla shrugged, "OK, now that I'm here, let's figure out what to do before Daniel self-destructs. But first, I have to eat something and sit a minute."

The three of them went into the kitchen, where empty beer and liquor bottles covered the counter and table. There was an overflowing garbage can and a sink full of dirty dishes. Kayla went to the refrigerator where she found two apples. They didn't have too many brown spots, so she ate them both.

"Is there an unused glass around?" she asked.

When she received one that looked practically clean, she filled it with tap water, drank it, and sat down at the kitchen table.

Just then the phone rang, and Will grabbed it.

"It's Dan!" Will announced. "He was picked up for DUI."

"Let's go! We gotta get him out," Bobby decided. "You coming, Kayla?"

"Are you kidding? He was lost and now he's found, and the mystery's solved. I'm leaving before you bring him anywhere near me."

"Aw, Kayla, honey, don't be that way. You know you love him. Stick around and give him another chance. He wouldn't be so messed up if he was still with you," Will said, desperately. He knew that she was the only person who could influence their brother.

"I won't be here when you get back," Kayla stated, calmly. "I have to rest a little bit, and then I'm leaving."

Bobby and Will headed to the police station, sure that Kayla would change her mind after she had time to think. It didn't occur to them that she would have the guts to leave their brother like that.

As they drove into town, Will predicted, "That woman's gonna be there when we get home. She's never gonna leave Dan. They've been through worse than this before, and she always takes him back."

"Not like our wives," Bobby snickered. "That Kayla stands by her man. The next time we get married, we gotta find chicks like her."

"But not religious ones! That ruins everything. A guy still has to have some fun, and those high-falutin women really mess up the good times."

Bobby laughed, "You got that right! Good thing Kayla wasn't here last night."

Kayla fell asleep while the brothers went to get Daniel at the police station. When she woke up, nearly two hours had passed. She opened a kitchen cabinet and found a box of Ritz crackers, a treasure. She was determined to leave before they came back, with or without Daniel. She took the box with her and headed out the door for home.

CHAPTER 38

Kayla had plenty of time to think as she drove back to Chicago. First, she had to change the locks to her apartment. When she got home, before hopping directly into bed out of pure exhaustion, she called a locksmith.

She decided to take one more day off from teaching in order to prepare for her newly independent life. In addition to her locks, she changed her email address and her phone numbers. Along with her new contact information she informed her friends and family about leaving Daniel and, with fortitude, starting over. She was sure no one who cared about her would try to change her mind. She couldn't count the many times people had begged her to dump her fiance.

Two important phone calls remained. First, she contacted Rabbi Dalton, who was not only her boss but her beloved mentor. She wouldn't be the person she had become without his guidance and support. His wife, Ruth, was like a mother to her.

"Rabbi Dalton, I have some news for you, which you will probably welcome."

"Let me guess," Dalton admitted. "When you left that emotional message, I was pretty sure that it had something to do with Daniel. I feared that you were going to meet him someplace, and then I began considering the possibilities. Either the two of you were eloping or you were going to leave him. However, I soon realized that you would never get married without telling my wife. Am I correct?"

"I don't know whether to laugh or cry," Kayla answered. "You were right. I got a call from Daniel's brothers begging me to come help them. Daniel had shown up at their place, totally unexpected, and told them a bunch of lies."

"So you went there? Did you really think you could convince him to come back with you?"

"Of course not. I went there because I was afraid that Daniel would do something really dangerous, either to himself or somebody else. And he did."

Dalton was used to the role of counselor. "Kayla, did you really think that you could stop Daniel if he was determined to do something frightening? Surely, you've had enough of that, or have you? I'm not sure you're ready to give up. I know I'm being blunt, but I, too, have had enough of Daniel Lewisohn's demons. His problems are way beyond our abilities to help."

Kayla sighed deeply, "That's why I left Daniel with his brothers. But it's not going to work because they're incapable of doing anything more than keeping their own heads above water."

"Do Daniel's brothers have any connections to other Jewish people? Is there a rabbi who could step in? Do they ever get to St. Louis or Chicago? I know they were married to Jewish women; what happened? Do they have children?"

"Let's not get started with reviewing the dysfunction in that family." Kayla insisted. "They're both lazy, divorced, never see their kids, are disconnected from other Jews, and they're alcoholics, to boot!"

"So, Daniel's brothers can't help him either. Just promise me that you'll stay here where you have a job, friends, and the possibility of a good life. I'm positive that Daniel will come back looking for you. When he does, don't feel sorry for him. I refuse to be sympathetic or even passive if you take him back. This has escalated too far for either of us."

"Daniel's not interested in help. You know that he's always sure that everyone else is wrong, and he has it all figured out. It's frightening, I'll admit."

"Let's do this," Dalton suggested. "My wife and I will be happy for you to stay with us for a while. We have to make sure you're safe."

Dalton heard the conviction in Kayla's voice. "For now I'm comfortable in my own place, and I already changed the locks. I'm through with Daniel. I just called to tell you the situation and explain why I left so unexpectedly."

"I'll see you tomorrow, Kayla. Why don't you stop by my office after school. I urge you to stay with us."

Kayla had one more difficult phone call to make. She hoped Rabbi Stein was still in his office, even though it was late in the afternoon. If he wasn't there, she was reluctant to reveal too much in a voice message on his machine.

The phone rang as Josh was about to leave. He was surprised and re-lieved to hear from Kayla so soon after he had received her emotional message the day before.

"Kayla, I hope everything's OK. At first I thought that your mother needed you, but then I imagined that you left town suddenly because it had something to do with Daniel. Am I right?"

"I just got off the phone with Rabbi Dalton, so I'll spare you having to ask me any questions. I'll get right to the answers."

Josh sat down and listened carefully as Kayla told him the whole story. Her matter-of-fact presentation was succinct, yet he knew that she wouldn't have called him if she didn't want his reaction. His response was honest.

"I'm sure you have mixed emotions about Daniel, even though you say it's over. You didn't ask for my advice, and of course you may decide to disregard it, but here goes.

First, I think you should change all your locks."

"Done."

"Good for you. I also suggest that you get all new contact information, including phone numbers and email addresses."

"Done and done!"

"I do have another concern," Josh cautioned. "You may be through with Daniel, but I guarantee he's not through with you. Is there anywhere else you can stay?"

"Rabbi Dalton said the same thing. Since you agree with him, I may actually accept the Daltons' invitation to stay with them until I can figure out my next move."

Josh was relieved. "Will you need a place to stay over Shabbat this week? Obviously, you can't walk here from the Daltons' home. It's miles away."

"For the time being, I'll stay with them over Shabbat and walk to Bet Hillel. Hopefully, I'll be back at Lev Shalom soon."

After the call, Josh decided to remain in his office and catch up on some work since it was almost time for evening services. As he went into the main office to review a new member application that Serena had told him about, the synagogue front door buzzer sounded. He looked at the outdoor surveillance camera above Serena's desk and was surprised to see Leora Halperin standing there. He buzzed her in.

Leora was equally surprised to see Josh where Serena was supposed to be. She felt the necessity to explain her late arrival.

"*Baruch Hashem*! I'm so glad you're here. I got stuck in traffic and wondered if Serena would wait for me. I told her I'd be here by five, the latest. I guess she gave up on me and left."

"Leora, it's almost six o'clock. Are you sure that you didn't want to see me instead? I do have a habit of losing track of time, and I'll bet you knew that," Josh joked.

"Busted!" Leora laughed. "You got me."

Josh sat down at Serena's desk, straightened his glasses, and asked, "How may I help you, Ms Halperin? Are you new to town? May I offer you one of our carefully crafted, high quality, slick Lev Shalom brochures? And, if I may be so bold, may I ask if you have a husband and children who might avail themselves of our extensive family programming?"

Leora decided to play along, "No, Rabbi, I remain unmarried, to the disappointment of my parents. Perhaps you know them? Rabbi Ephraim and Sondra, aka Bunny, Halperin. In fact, my father served as spiritual leader here for almost fifty years."

Josh was enjoying their flirtation, but he knew better than to take it further. He looked at his watch. Services would begin in fifteen minutes. "I hope we can continue our conversation at another time and another place. But I really do want to know why you're here."

"To get an application for membership, of course. Serena said it would be on her desk if I got here after she left for the day."

Sure enough, Josh noticed the application. He quickly read and removed the yellow post-it note that Serena had attached to the form that was meant for Josh's eyes only: '*Rabbi, what's this about? Doesn't she live in NY?*'

Josh was confused. Why was Leora applying here? She must have been serious about moving back to Chicago. Even more interesting, did her parents know about this? From his enjoyable, yet admittedly limited, experiences with Leora Halperin, he was sure that she always made up her own mind.

"So, you're definitely moving here?"

"I believe that's my application right there in your hand!"

They both laughed as he handed it to her.

Josh wanted to delay her departure a little longer. He assumed his light-hearted manner again. "You realize, of course, that you're no longer a ward of the previous rabbi. Your membership is going to cost you big bucks. This is no shoestring operation. We're a full service, high class establishment. If, and I emphasize, if your application is approved by our highly selective membership committee, your dues as a single person will be astronomical."

"Duly noted. I must tell you that money is no object to a woman of my considerable accomplishments. I'm more concerned about the rabbinic leadership here. I've heard that the interim rabbi is young, handsome, and unmarried himself."

Leora blushed. She couldn't believe she'd said that, but it wasn't the first time she'd said exactly what was on her mind. It had served her well in her work, but not always with the men in her life.

Josh was embarrassed, too, but he didn't have a chance to ease the sudden tension. Leora grabbed the application, and with a speedy goodbye, started to make a hasty exit.

"Will I see you at the farewell *kiddush* for your parents?" Josh called after her.

Leora stopped and turned back to face Josh. "Of course! My brothers and their families will be here, too. I'm looking forward to hearing your sermon and all the wonderful things you're going to say about my parents."

Reluctant to end the conversation, Josh walked Leora to the door. He had a sudden impulse to hug her, but he was able to resist that urge. Leora sensed his closeness, hoping that he'd do something physical. Well, if the Orthodox rabbi was able to control himself, she could wait.

CHAPTER 39

Rachel Berg was getting ready for her third date with Glen Stempler, a partner in her law firm. He had been trying to date her for a long time, but her fixation on Andy Meyers and then Josh Stein kept her from taking Glen seriously. After accepting his first invitation to the symphony, and having a wonderful time together, she realized that there were other interesting Jewish men in the world.

On their second date, Rachel was surprised that Glen made dinner reservations at the most upscale kosher restaurant in town. She knew that he was not religiously observant; therefore, she was touched by his sensitivity. He knew she would not eat meat at a non-kosher place because they had had many conversations at work about her traditional lifestyle. In fact, the first time they talked about anything personal was when Glen had invited her to accompany him to a Friday night concert. She explained that she was a Sabbath observer and hoped they could go out another time.

Glen had been married to the daughter of a family friend, but the marriage lasted less than two years. His wife wanted to start a family before Glen was ready to assume more responsibility than he already had in completing his law degree. They parted as friends, probably because they had known each other their entire lives. After the divorce, his ex moved to Florida and remarried.

It took years of hard work before Glen made partner in the firm. Now, at the age of forty-three he was ready to meet the right woman, buy a house in the suburbs, and fill it with intelligent, fun-loving children. Over the years he dated other women, but for some reason, from the day she started at the firm, he was fascinated with Rachel Berg. Not only was she beautiful and dignified, but she was also smart and tough, just the type of woman he liked. But at first, she rebuffed his advances.

Rachel saw in Glen qualities that she respected, and he was really good looking. His hair was beginning to gray in all the right places. The fact that he was an early morning jogger and played racquetball showed on his trim physique. It didn't bother her that he and she were the same height or that he left kitchy surprises on her desk. She was charmed by his attention; however, it took her a while to go out with him. Now, things were not moving forward with Josh, and she was tired of her mother's questions.

On this, their third date, Glen was taking her to a play at the Goodman. She had no idea how he was able to get tickets at the last minute. They must have cost a fortune, and she appreciated it. In a million years, Josh would never have thought to do such an extravagant thing. It was just one more reason to move on. She worked on a mental list of Josh's good and bad qualities. It was becoming clear that Josh was not the right man for her.

After the play, Rachel planned to have a serious conversation with Glen. Before it got hot and heavy with them, and she knew it soon would, there were important things to discuss. There was no way Rachel would give up Shabbat observance or a kosher home. Her children would definitely attend Jewish day schools. There were other things, too, that had to do with her upbringing and beliefs, so tonight's talk would be crucial.

Glen sensed Rachel's anxiety at work all day. The first two dates had been close to perfect. He and Rachel had a lot in common and enjoyed sharing attorney anecdotes. On the second date he found out she was a great kisser. He was sure she wasn't going to stop seeing him, and he wondered if she was ready to talk about moving their relationship to the next level, sex. Rachel was the kind of person who spoke her mind, but would she bring up the subject of intimacy or just let it takes its course? What else could be making her uncomfortable? He'd find out soon enough.

They thoroughly enjoyed the play, and Rachel suggested they go back to her apartment to talk. She had planned ahead. There was expensive red wine and plates of dips and gourmet crackers. After sampling the food, they sat side by side on the sofa. Before any amorous event could commence, Rachel made it clear she had something to discuss.

"I don't know where this is going, but you know that I really like you," Rachel began.

"Well, that's a good start," Glen smiled. "I'm sure you know how I feel about you."

"So before this goes any further, I have to make a few things about me clear."

"Like what? You hate being an attorney? You hate your parents? But wait, I happen to know that you like practicing law and you love your parents. Oh no, do you have a secret love child or an embarrassing tattoo?" Confused, he leaned back and waited.

"Nothing like that. It's about being Jewish."

"I'm Jewish! No problem. In fact, I'd be only too happy to prove it!"

"No need for that," Rachel laughed, "I have a feeling that I'll find out soon enough. I want to restate things you already know about me. I'm traditional. I eat kosher food, I belong to an Orthodox *shul,* I attend services, and I'm going to send my children to Jewish schools. Because I want to keep seeing you, I have to know how you feel about my life-style. I've thought about this a lot, and I'm committed to it."

"I'll do whatever it takes to be with you. At least I'll try," Glen answered. "Let me tell you about my Jewish experiences. I became a Bar Mitzvah at my parents' synagogue in Highland Park and was active in the youth group. I even went with them to Israel. I can read Hebrew, but of course, I don't understand a word. I love Passover and do not eat bread for eight full days. On Chanukah, my family always has a big party and we light candles every night. And let me just add that I eagerly await the moment that our relationship goes further."

Rachel stopped him. Here was a man who wanted nothing more than to be with her and make her happy. Why wait around for Josh Stein to get his act together? Glen had been trying to date her ever since they met. He had even found out when her birthday was and sent two dozen long-stemmed roses to her desk.

She vividly recalled their first date. It was the most lavish she had ever been on, and she had dated wealthy men before. It began in a limou-sine, then moved to great seats at the symphony, and ended up with champagne and chocolate truffles on the beach at Lake Michigan, bun-dled under designer wool blankets. Glen made it clear that he had dated enough women to know that she was the right one for him. Rachel's fixation on Josh had kept her from making room for this wonderful man. Only now, with her disappointment and anger at Josh, was she ready to give Glen a chance.

There in Rachel's apartment after the play at the Goodman, Glen wasn't shy. He hadn't become a powerful lawyer at a prestigious firm without learning how to maneuver a case in the desired direction. His skills and ardor for Rachel surfaced.

"A minute ago, I offered to display my Hebraic symbol. I want you to know that I wasn't joking. In fact, I think I'll begin by removing my jacket and tie and make myself comfortable. Is that OK?"

Rachel nodded solemnly, "Counselor, proceed..."

Glen took off his shirt and draped it over the sofa. Then came his shoes and socks. Next his belt. He looked expectantly to his hostess for a sign.

Rachel nodded her approval, "Well, it looks like you're getting ready for bed."

She headed to the bedroom and Glen followed.

As they slowly undressed each other, Rachel couldn't help comparing Glen to Andy Meyers, the only man with whom she'd ever been intimate. While that lovemaking was intense, the relationship was never fulfilling. As for Josh, who even knew what he was capable of? And she was in no mood to wait around forever in order to find out. With Glen, there was no question; she knew it was going to be fun.

It started innocently enough with a good many passionate kisses, then moved quickly to a satisfying evening of lovemaking, interspersed with romantic off-key singing by Glen. Rachel enjoyed herself immensely. She doubted that Josh could muster such energetic seduction. It was inconceivable that Josh could make a joke about his circumcision, and even more far-fetched for an Orthodox rabbi to follow her into the bedroom on the third date. True, she identified with the Orthodox movement; at the same time, it was such a relief to be pursued by a red-blooded, sexually-assertive male.

Rachel was satisfied. During the night and next day in her apartment, she and Glen talked about many things. It was a decisive weekend for her. There was no way to know what Josh was thinking, but Glen's intentions were clear.

Before he left Sunday night, Glen stated his case. "You're the right woman for me. You're beautiful and smart. I want you to be the mother of my children. I'm over forty years old and more than ready to settle down."

Rachel knew better than to react to his impulsive words. She also knew better than to discount them. "Glen, there's a lot more to it than admiration and chemistry."

Glen laughed, "OK, let's say that you're right. In the meantime, what are we doing next weekend?"

Rachel challenged, "Are you planning to spend a traditional Shabbat with me?"

"Remember what I said? Of course I am. Any kind of Shabbat that you want."

CHAPTER 40

Kayla Morales was just about to dismiss her sixth grade art class when she heard a loud disturbance in the hall. She cautioned her students to return to their chairs and stay in the room. She locked the art room door and pressed the intercom button to the front office to alert them and ask for help.

Her door was suddenly kicked open and Daniel Lewisohn was in her face. The students sat in terrified silence as they watched Kayla take Daniel by the arm and move him into the art storeroom. "Stay seated and don't worry," Kayla firmly instructed her class.

Kayla shook her head in disbelief. She had foolishly convinced herself that she could be rid of Daniel and his problems. *Why didn't he just stay with his brothers? Obviously, they couldn't handle him either. Now what?*

Within minutes the police had been called, and the school principal and Rabbi Dalton ran into the art room. One of the students pointed to the storeroom and blurted out, "There's a mean-looking white guy in there with Ms. Morales!"

Dalton knew that the 'mean-looking white guy' had to be Daniel. He asked the principal to escort the students out of the room and into the lunchroom. He pounded on the storeroom door and demanded, "Kayla, is everything OK in there?"

"We're fine, but don't leave," Kayla called back to him.

"It's not going to be fine unless you get the hell out of here, and I mean now!" Daniel yelled.

Dalton knew better than to leave them alone. "I'm not going anywhere until you both come out of there. Daniel, this is a warning. Don't do anything stupid!"

"Fuck you, Dalton! Know what? You're the one who's stupid. Here's *my* advice--leave Kayla and me alone. This is none of your business."

Two police officers rushed in, forced the storeroom door open and pulled the occupants out. Kayla told the officers that it was a misunderstanding and no one was hurt. Rabbi Dalton calmly asked the police to wait in the corridor, after they were assured that no one was in danger. Then he turned to the couple, noting Daniel's tight grip on Kayla's wrist.

Dalton faced Daniel squarely, but his words were for Kayla, "Ms. Morales, you're endangering the children in our school as well as yourself by continuing to have anything to do with this man" Then he turned, "Daniel, one of these days something bad is going to happen, and you're the only person who can prevent that. I wish you no harm, but for your own good you have to move on. Stay away from here!"

Daniel dropped his hold on Kayla, stepped back, and pointed his index finger at the Rabbi. "Dalton, you better learn to mind your own business. Kayla, we're not finished yet."

With that, he stormed out and drove off, as the police followed him.

Kayla collapsed into a chair and Dalton sat down beside her. It took both of them a while to calm down enough to talk. Kayla decided to ask the Rabbi if she could continue staying with him and his wife until the situation with Daniel resolved, but she knew she was fantasizing. That relationship was never going to get better. In fact, it was clear that everything between them was worse. She didn't know what to do.

Dalton assured her that she had a safe place with him and his wife, but without a restraining order, Daniel would continue to menace her.

"Kayla, if you plan to keep your job, deepen your Jewish experience, and stay in Chicago, Daniel has to be completely out of your life. By now, it should be clear to you that you can't help or change him. Tomorrow morning, I want you to get that restraining order, and if Daniel tries to see you, I expect you to have him jailed. Those are my terms. That's the only way Ruth and I can help you."

"I wish it were that simple. No piece of paper and no official authorities can control him. You know what terrifies me? I'm afraid he will get so crazy, he'll end up killing himself."

"That's not what I'm afraid of," Dalton responded. "I'm worried about you. In order to control you, God knows what he could do."

Kayla began to think out loud, "His brothers believe that I have a certain ability to manage him. Once Daniel gets back to work and into a familiar routine, he'll be his old self again. That's when I'll be able to separate myself from him. Things were going OK until I got serious about being Jewish. He didn't want me to change in any way. I was in love with him, and he knew it. When I started to love Judaism, he couldn't compete and he didn't want to join me as I became more committed to this life."

Dalton shook his head. "Kayla, your story's classic; it could be in a case study in a psychology textbook. You're the enabler in a codependent relationship that will not change without you understanding and changing the role you've been playing."

Dalton stood up and walked purposefully to the door. "Kayla, wise up, girl. You're playing with fire. Protect yourself and make an appointment with a therapist. There's nothing more I can say or do."

Sitting alone, Kayla put her head in her hands and began to cry.

CHAPTER 41

Serena and Rachel met for their weekly dinner at Kalman's. Serena had been plagued by calls from James Traub, who was hounding her about Rabbi Halperin's departure. Even though Serena refused to gossip about *shul* business with anyone, Traub's badgering worried her, and she wanted to talk to her daughter about it.

As they waited for their orders of wild mushroom soup and grilled salmon, Serena sought Rachel's counsel.

"I'm worried about Rabbi Stein," Serena began.

"You're assuming that I care about him." Rachel responded cooly.

"Rachel, what's that supposed to mean?"

"Never mind. I'll get to that in a minute. What do you want to talk about?"

"This reporter, James Traub, won't stop trying to pull all of us into talking about Rabbi Halperin's reasons for leaving Lev Shalom. And he'll concentrate on Rabbi Stein."

"So what's wrong with that? He's a reporter and that's his job. Do you think I drop a case because it's hard getting witnesses? Of course not. And while we're on the subject, I may as well tell you that you can stop hoping that Rabbi Stein will be your son-in-law."

"When did I ever say that?" Serena asked, nervously.

"Mom, cut it out! From the very beginning, when you first set eyes on an eligible, religious, good-looking male, you began to dream about the two of us."

"At the risk of sounding like a broken record, let me remind you that it was your idea to invite his family to join us on Rosh Hashanah!" Serena countered. "What happened to all the time you two spent together? Rabbi Stein's a busy man. I know you want more attention from him, so be patient. His job is about taking care of *shul* business and attending to congregants' needs."

Rachel opened up. "I'm not a kid, and I thought that Josh would jump at the chance to settle down with someone as suitable as me. And let me just add, there was plenty of chemistry, too. I realize now that Josh still has a lot of maturing to do before he knows what's good for him. I won't wait around for him to decide if we're meant to be together. You and I both know that I would be the ideal partner for him, but he's too confused and slow-moving for me."

Serena was taken by surprise. "Have you and Josh discussed all of this?"

"He left messages, and we got together at my apartment to talk. It was awful. He should have been knocking down my door if he loved me. Obviously, Josh Stein has all the time in the world to figure out what he wants, but I don't."

"Rachel, are you ever going to find the perfect man? Give Rabbi Stein a chance to settle down, and then he'll have plenty of time to work on a relationship with you."

"If Josh wants to pursue me he's going to have some serious competition because I'm dating a lawyer in the firm."

Serena gasped, "When did this begin?"

Catching Serena's agitation from across the room, Kalman decided to personally serve their soup orders.

"I had to greet the beautiful Berg women myself! The two of you seem deep in conversation, a rarity among the mothers and daughters around here. I only wish my own wife and daughters were as close as the two of you. I'll bet something's brewing...anything you'd care to share?"

Serena and Rachel couldn't help acknowledging Kalman's overt attempt to elicit any possible news.

"If you're inquiring about me and Rabbi Stein, I hate to disappoint you. My mother and I are just talking about a journalist who's interested in Lev Shalom. Sorry, Kalman."

With his hands on his hips, Kalman faced the women with a big smile, "I'm sure that if there were anything exciting happening in the Berg household, you'd be sure to let me know. After all, I'm the best caterer for all *simchas*." Smiling, he backed away.

Making sure that Kalman was out of earshot, Serena resumed questioning her daughter. "You're dating somebody new? Who's this lawyer? How old is he? Is he Jewish? Is he religious?"

Rachel put her spoon down. "Here's the dossier on the man I'm dating. His name is Glen Stempler. He's a bit older than I am and a partner in my office. He's not as religious as Josh Stein, but he wants to do anything that will support my choices. He's very smart and funny, and

Mom, here's the bottom line: He's crazy about me. Anything else you want to know?"

"How long has this been going on?"

"We started seeing each other after Rosh Hashanah. You know very well that things went downhill between Josh and me at that time. Glen's been trying to date me since we met. He used to bring me souvenirs from some of his trips and whenever he went out for lunch, he invited me to join him. Finally, I took a good look at him. Unlike Josh, he's never moody or exhausted. He's upbeat and a lot of fun. Did I mention that he adores me?"

"But, do you adore him?"

"Enough to bring him to services with me next week."

"Next week? Are you sure you want to do that? It's the big *kiddush* in honor of the Halperins. Everybody in the *shul* will be there, Rachel. That's all I need. Questions from all the gossips. Let me ask you something: Does Rabbi Stein know you're dating this Glen somebody?"

"Do you think that I have to report my romantic interests to a man who's too busy to care? No, I haven't discussed Glen with Josh."

They had hardly touched their soup when Kalman appeared with their entrees. "Something wrong with the soup? Or too much to talk about?"

Rachel smiled, "You have my word, Kalman, if there's any information we want to disseminate, you'll be the first to know."

"I'll hold you to that, ladies."

They started eating, but Serena still had more questions. "If Rabbi Stein wants to get you back, would you consider it? I mean, are you just dating Glen on the rebound? It's cruel to use Glen to make Rabbi Stein jealous."

"I really like Glen Stempler. He's much more my type than Josh and he's ready to make a commitment. And, yes, I welcome the stares and comments from nosy congregants at the *kiddush* next Shabbat."

CHAPTER 42

The phone on Serena's desk was ringing as she walked into the *shul* office. It was James Traub still hoping to interrogate her.

Serena assumed a strict teacher voice, "Mr. Traub, there will be no time to talk to you between now and the synagogue farewell *kiddush* for the Halperins next Shabbat. In fact, there's no reason for us to talk at all. I've worked here for more than thirty years, and everything that needs to be said is already well known."

"When exactly is that *kiddush*?"

Serena answered curtly, "Next Saturday after services. Now I have to get back to work."

"Just one more question. Is the *kiddush* open to everyone? If so, and I'm sure it is, I'll see you there! I don't want to miss something so important."

"Mr. Traub, let me give you a tiny piece of advice, since you seem intent on joining us next week. Wear a suit and leave your camera and recording device home. I'm a peace-loving woman, but I'm warning you, don't test me. I'll be watching you the whole time. And if I catch you doing anything I don't like, I'll have you escorted out."

Wanting to establish his Jewish roots, if only gastronomically, James tried a new tack. "Thank you, Mrs. Berg. I appreciate your assistance. Is it OK for me to sample the *kiddush* food? You may be interested to know that I'm not a *kiddush* novice. I'm a pushover for herring and kugel. I'm looking forward to seeing you next week."

As soon as Serena hung up from Traub's annoying call, the phone rang again. This time it was Leora Halperin asking if Serena could use her help with her parents' *kiddush*. Serena wondered if Leora was ever going back to New York, but she didn't feel comfortable asking.

Serena answered, "That's very kind of you. Your oldest brother will be speaking from the *bimah* after Rabbi Stein's message, and I expect he'll represent your family. Your father will deliver the sermon, and we're all looking forward to that. If you have any suggestions, I'm happy to hear them, but I think we're in good shape."

Leora answered the unasked question. "At the last minute I decided to stay in Chicago to help my parents until they leave. Feel free to call me if you need me."

Serena was sure that she knew the reason for Leora's extending her stay. Everything Serena had prayed for and optimistically planned was changing. Nothing was happening with Rachel and Rabbi Stein, and something was definitely happening with Rachel and that lawyer. And now Leora Halperin and Josh Stein seemed to be a couple. Serena would never have imagined any of these scenarios. To make matters even more uncertain, Bob Small, as the *shul* president, would speak at the service on Saturday. Would his animosity toward Rabbi Halperin show? And now, that obnoxious reporter would be present and on alert, probably catching any of Bob's innuendos.

Across town, driving home from work, Bob Small thought about the words he would deliver at the farewell service for the Halperins. He wondered how to say good-bye to the man for whom he had lost all respect. He decided to make it short, if not sweet. Reaching back in his memory of all the years in which he had been connected to the Halperins, his thoughts were clouded by personal indignities and disappointments, and it was impossible to conjure up anything truly nice to say. He had to talk it over with Sheila.

Sheila was in the kitchen making a pot of chicken noodle soup for a sick neighbor. Energized by the delicious aroma wafting toward him, Bob draped his jacket on a kitchen chair, sat down, and waited to be served.

"Hello to you, too, Sweetie!" Sheila laughed. "What makes you think this is for you?"

"I gotta talk to you about something. It'll be easier with a bowl of soup in front of me."

"OK, just one bowl. It's for Sonia Kesselman next door. She's got the flu."

Sheila placed a bowl of the soup in front of Bob and sat down next to him.

Between heaping spoonfuls, Bob expressed his inability to find anything good to say about the Halperins at the service honoring them.

"Well, Bob, you could just mention that they've been here a really long time and the *shul* has grown a lot, and he's written some popular books, and you hope they'll be very happy in their gorgeous penthouse apartment in Jerusalem. Things won't be the same without them leading the *shul*. How's that?"

Bob winked as he picked up the bowl to drink the last drops of soup.

"Well, that just about sums up that man's career." Bob hadn't entirely lost his sense of irony. "You're sure I shouldn't mention Bunny's fancy clothes and jewelry?"

Even though Sheila knew he was joking, she gave him one of those looks, and turned back to the stove.

"I know what!" Bob exclaimed, slapping his thigh, "I'll call Rabbi Stein and put him to the test. He better have some good Jewish quotes or stories for me to use. He's not gonna cross me. Not now, when he has to stay on my good side."

Josh passed Bob's 'quote and anecdote test' with flying colors. That was the easy part. He was working on his own tribute and had plenty of source material lying on his desk when Bob called. Josh wanted to praise the Halperins for everything they had done to build Lev Shalom, but when he asked Bob for information about the *shul* in its early days, Bob had nothing good to offer because of his long-held antipathy toward Rabbi Halperin.

Josh decided to call Leora for memorable stories about her parents in the old days when Lev Shalom was beginning to grow. Not only was Leora thrilled to get a call from Josh, but she offered to come to his office with photographs and memorabilia that she hoped could be displayed in the synagogue foyer over the weekend.

That afternoon, Bunny saw her daughter going through boxes of albums that had been packed for the move. Leora explained that she and Rabbi Stein were arranging a 'memory wall' depicting the Halperin family history at Lev Shalom. Bunny refused to get involved and admonished her daughter.

"Leora, I know why you're doing this, and this flirtation with Rabbi

Stein isn't going to help anybody, not even you. Can't we just cut our ties with this community and say good-bye once and for all?"

"I've always considered Chicago my real home," Leora claimed. "In fact, when Aaron and I thought we had a future together, we talked about moving the business here. It's entirely possible that I'll be leaving New York permanently, and I may as well tell you that I've definitely decided to sell my half to Aaron. If anybody could understand my desire to start over it should be you. What do you have against Josh Stein, anyway?"

"Let me put it this way, Leora, Rabbi Stein came here to learn from your father. Now, he's taking his place, at least until he infuriates Bob Small so much that he will be unceremoniously dismissed. I don't think that Rabbi Stein will be here forever, so if you're counting on moving here in order to be with him, that seems foolish, doesn't it? You ask what I have against him? I see an undeveloped, out-of-place novice."

"You mean like Daddy was when he came here?"

Bunny was caught off guard, but she rallied, "Daddy had me by his side, and we built this community together. And, let me just add, Ephraim Halperin's intellect and maturity were in place from the beginning. I don't see those qualities in Joshua Stein."

"Maybe not yet, but I believe you're wrong. As long as we're being honest, I have to say that Josh's caring nature and love of Judaism will carry him through as he gains the experience and wisdom that Daddy has. Yes, it's true that Daddy's the best, and you're the best. I want to give Josh a chance, and I believe I can help him."

Bunny had no response, except to put her arms around her daughter and kiss her. Leora was deeply moved by her mother's unexpected gesture, and they held each other. Leora then got back to selecting memorabilia from the boxes.

The next morning, Leora brought a few favorite photographs to Lev Shalom. There were pictures of Bunny and Rabbi Halperin in their first makeshift synagogue social hall across town. Leora wanted Josh to appreciate the circumstances under which her father had begun.There was another photo of her mother and father at a *brit milah* ceremony. The Holocaust survivors were determined to have children who could live as Jews, and her father made sure that any newborn son received a proper circumcision, even if the new immigrants couldn't afford it. It was Rabbi Ephraim Halperin, in his twenties at the time, who arranged to pay the *mohel* and to provide a celebratory meal in the *shul*. In one photo, Bunny, wearing an apron, led a committed group of women who cooked and baked for the joyous families.

As Leora spread the group of pictures on Serena's desk, both women responded with a mixture of audible sighs and loud laughter. Josh came out of his office to see what was happening. He had never experienced that side of Serena.

Leaning on her desk, Josh listened to them talk about the old days, even before Leora was born and before Serena began to work at Lev Shalom. As Leora identified people and places, Serena noted the easy rapport between the two young people standing shoulder to shoulder.

Leora asked Serena to look over the pictures at her leisure and to add them to the growing Lev Shalom archive displayed in the hall.

"I have something for you," Leora said to Josh, pulling a bag from a nearby chair. "It's for your office."

Leora and Josh headed into his office. Mindfully, Josh left his door slightly open, then asked, "So what's in that bag?"

"My father had this on his desk in the original *shul*, and it's been in our house for years. It never made its way into this building, and we found it while we were packing."

"Why is your father giving it to me? Are you sure this isn't your idea?"

"I admit that it's my idea. I want it to be here every time I come to visit you. When I discovered it, I had a feeling that you would treasure it. For some reason, it's always been a favorite of mine."

Leora lifted a block of wood from the bag. It bore a rare exact replica of the 1948 gold Israel Medal, depicting the famous profile of Theodore Herzl, the father of modern Zionism, a unique collectible.

Josh was overwhelmed. He placed the treasure on his desk and stared at it. "I'll keep it right here. Whenever you visit Lev Shalom, you'll always know where it is."

Leora asked pointedly, "And what exactly is your office visitation schedule? You see, I really like that commemorative medal and I might want to check on it a lot."

"I have an even better idea," he said, lifting the object. "If you're in Chicago, and you desire to see this on a regular basis, I can bring it to you anytime."

"What if I start to miss it tonight? What if I'm taking a walk and I get an urge to see that medal? What then?"

"I guess I better give you my personal cell phone number. You seem like the kind of woman who doesn't beat around the bush when you want to see something important."

"You're right about that, Rabbi Stein. I have a tendency to speak my mind, for better or worse. In fact, I'm going to start right now. Would an Orthodox rabbi of your generation meet a friend at a bar for a beer?"

"Absolutely! How about tonight?"

"It's a date!"

"Do I bring the commemorative medal with me?"

"Well, I guess, if I have an overriding desire to see it, we can stop by your office afterward, can't we?"

"What If I have an overriding desire of my own?" Josh laughed.

"Such as?"

"You'll have to wait and see!"

Leora realized that she had set into motion something of which she was no longer in total control. It was exciting. She didn't understand her attraction to pale, dark-haired Josh Stein, whose glasses somehow enhanced his amused face, but the feeling was overpowering.

"It's easier for everybody if you don't pick me up at my parents' house. I'll meet you at Casey Mulligan's Tavern downtown at 9:00. Do you know where it is?"

"Trust me, I'll find it."

"I know you will," Leora whispered as she leaned over his desk and almost kissed him. She tried again, and succeeded.

Leora backed slowly toward the door, encouraged by Josh's broad smile.

Serena was returning to her desk from the social hall. From the look on Leora's face as she left Josh's office, Serena knew that things were heating up.

CHAPTER 43

Uncertain of the exact location of Mulligan's Tavern, Josh left himself plenty of time to get there. As a result, he was already seated at a small table when Leora came in. It took her a minute to identify her date because of Josh's unexpected attire.

"Rabbi Stein, your Cubs hat, tieless shirt and khakis could have fooled me! Fortunately, those bookish glasses give you away. You look great!"

"You do too, Leora. Josh is my name from now on, except in the office when Serena's on guard. And I'm pleased that you noticed my Cubs hat; it was with great effort that I left my Red Sox one at the bottom of my closet right on top of my Celtics jersey."

"Are we ready to order or do you want me to tell you my life story first?" Leora asked.

"I bet we're clever enough to drink and talk at the same time," Josh laughed. "What do you want to drink?"

"Any dark beer you choose will be OK."

Josh came back with two Heinekens. Leora nodded her approval. "In my opinion, this is the perfect time and place to tell you something about myself. I'll make it fast."

Josh didn't want her to go fast. As far as he was concerned, the longer the better. "Since my mother is back in Boston, I don't have a curfew. Take all the time you want. I have a feeling that this will be entertaining."

It took Leora and Josh two beers each to get their stories told. Leora left out the part about her parents' advice to stay in New York, and Josh left out his college love affair with the non-Jewish Miri Soto, but he did tell her about his broken engagement to Debbie Kahn. Other than those deletions, they did a good job of revealing their backgrounds and circuitous paths to the present.

Josh decided a summary was in order. "It's pretty clear that we're both unsettled. I have no idea what my future will be at Lev Shalom; I think I'd like to stay. I'm now sure that Rachel and I have no future together, and I'm relieved. You, Leora, are possibly moving back to Chicago, yet you have to finalize your exit from your business and relationship with Aaron."

Leora hadn't expected such a serious conversation, but she'd had her fill of bantering and was more than ready to talk about important things.

"For some inexplicable reason I've been attracted to you ever since our first conversation," Leora admitted. "I've shamelessly pursued you and found every excuse to stay in Chicago, to my mother's extreme displeasure. She wants to leave here and never look back."

"What about your father?"

"My father doesn't know that I'm determined to move here and be near you. At the same time, he'll be thrilled to return as a scholar-in-residence at Lev Shalom and other venues any time he's invited. As you've learned, he's pretty famous, no matter what Bob Small would say."

Josh relished Leora's honesty and hoped there would be none of the drama he experienced with Rachel Berg. It would be a relief that Leora's parents wouldn't be there to affect their relationship, wherever it might go.

"I have to ask you," Josh jumped in, "and I have to ask it now. It's obvious that we're attracted to each other. My past experiences with women haven't gone well because the kind of women I fall for are strong and independent, like you. In that way, you're my type. But I don't want to repeat past problems. When you move back to Chicago, what happens if this doesn't work out? I don't want to lead you on, and at the same time, I definitely don't want to push you away."

Leora understood Josh's confusion, and responded easily, "I'm in no hurry. I fell into an engagement with Aaron, just as you said you did with Debbie. Neither one of us wants to make that kind of mistake again, and that's fine. I like you, you like me, and that's great. And while we get to know each other, I've got to make sure the Holocaust Garden is properly completed. You and Lev Shalom still have to discover if you're a match. There's plenty of time and lots of opportunities for us. I don't see any of it as a problem."

A sense of relief erased Josh's anxiety. The pressure that had accompanied his relationships with other women was absent here. He was grateful that Leora was a woman who wasn't going to push him into anything.

Instead of ordering another beer, Josh and Leora decided to take a walk to try to find a grocery store that was still open. They happened upon a little neighborhood spot where they bought six small bags of chips, two bottles of water, and a pack of napkins. Even though it was windy, they had their 'meal' on a bench across the street and talked until Leora asked, "It's pretty late. Don't you have to get up for *minyan* in the morning?"

None of Josh's other girlfriends would have asked that question, but Leora's upbringing had conditioned her to be aware of it. Her father went to morning services every day, no matter how late he had stayed up the night before. Leora didn't even realize that her question was significant.

Josh was disappointed when he looked at his watch. He was enjoying eating chips and talking about the *shul* with somebody who was an insider. He finally had a way to express his frustration with Bob Small and his uncertainties about depending heavily on Serena because of his chaotic relationship with her daughter, Rachel.

Leora popped the last chip in her mouth, took a gulp of water and stood up. "This is what I have to say about Bob and Sheila Small. Don't cross them, but on the other hand, it's essential to stand up to Bob. He always shoots from the hip, and Sheila loves the fact that he's the boss. In return, he treats her like a queen; so they are the de facto king and queen of Lev Shalom right now. My father knew how to handle Bob, and because they were able to keep their mutual distrust of each other in check, things worked out. My point is, don't let personalities keep you from maintaining your self-respect and self control. Bob and the board will soon learn what you stand for."

Josh knew better than to reveal the real circumstances that led to Halperin's departure.There was no reason to give Leora information about her father that would hurt her. He decided that she should believe it was Halperin's heart condition and her parents' desire to make *aliyah* that forced their decision to move.

Josh walked Leora to her car and suggested, "Let's do this again soon. The combination of beer, junk food, and you is already my favorite steady diet."

"I had a great time, too," Leora agreed. This time she left Josh without so much as a hug, but she had received something better.

Josh was hopeful, too. Maybe this would work out.

CHAPTER 44

In the law office, Glen stopped by Rachel's desk to show her two tickets to the opening of an Andy Warhol retrospective at the Art Institute.

"I've been wanting to talk to you, too, but not here," Rachel whispered.

"If you're going to propose, I accept."

Rachel laughed, "It's crossed my mind, but I'm still saving for the ring."

"I have a lot of money. I'll give you some."

Rachel didn't have time to continue the repartee. "I want to talk about this weekend. I'll see you later."

After work, Glen and Rachel met for a salad, and Rachel gave him an overview and orientation about the upcoming Shabbat at Lev Shalom.

"You and my parents have never met. You and Rabbi Stein, my former 'man of interest', have never met. You and Bob Small, the synagogue president, and his unforgettable wife, Sheila, have never met. In fact, you've never met the Halperins, whom they're honoring."

"And…?"

Rachel continued, "What I'm trying to say, Glen, is that you don't know them, but more importantly, they don't know you."

"And...?"

"Once everyone meets you at services with me, we'll become the topic of discussion for weeks."

Glen beamed, "Bring it on! I'll wear my lucky socks which should protect me from harm. I'm actually looking forward to it. I'm sure you'll be proud of me, and I know I'll feel comfortable as long as I'm with you."

Rachel had to admit that Glen was a prize.

As they left the restaurant hand in hand, Glen had an idea. "It's my turn to invite you to my apartment. Another of my talents is ordering meals, and I'm totally ready for your visit with disposable paper and plastic, and a menu for gourmet kosher takeout."

Rachel was happy to seize the moment. "I'd love to come for dinner as long as your feelings won't be hurt if I check the ingredients."

"Rachel, I'm a smart guy, remember? I'm totally prepared to fulfill all your needs. Right now, I'm thinking about tonight, after dinner, when I'll have a chance to prove it once again."

"I *am* feeling pretty hungry. Let's see how competent you are with food and anything else you provide tonight."

When Rachel arrived, she was delighted that Glen had purchased such wonderful food. The Spaghetti Primavera and green salad with vinaigrette dressing were outstanding, and they lingered at the table until they had drained the bottle of Pinot Noir. There was almond biscotti too, but that could wait until later.

After a most satisfying sexual interlude, Glen announced, "I've waited my entire life for a woman like you, Rachel. I love you, and I mean it. I'm used to trusting my instincts, and I know we make a great couple."

Rachel stopped him. "Glen, your instincts may have served you well, but mine have caused me pain and confusion. Let me tell you a couple of facts about me before you continue. The only man I ever slept with was married. I believed him when he assured me that he was going to leave his wife and marry me. Then, one evening using the key to my apartment that I had given him, he showed up to announce that his wife was pregnant, but he still wanted to continue our relationship. Because of my friendship with Rabbi Josh Stein, I was able to end my relationship with the married guy. I immediately transferred my romantic fantasies to Josh. Fortunately, I realized that even though we both had strong feelings for each other, I was miles ahead of him in my expectations. So, Glen, you might trust your instincts, but I don't trust mine."

Glen gently took Rachel's face in his hands. "After what you just told me, it makes perfect sense for you to rely on my instincts, doesn't it?"

Things were getting too serious for Rachel. She wasn't sorry that she had told Glen about married Andy and reluctant Josh, but she and Glen needed more shared experiences. The sex was great, and it had been a long time since she had let herself relax in a man's arms. But that wasn't enough. On the other hand, she couldn't find anything wrong with Glen. He even supported her style of traditional Judaism, and she was sure that he was the kind of man who could become comfortable in her world. And, to top it all off, her mother would adore him.

As a matter of fact, it wouldn't just be her mother. Rachel adored Glen, too, but she wasn't ready to admit it because that would mean she was vulnerable, and she refused to be weak. In the meantime, she was more than happy to express her appreciation of Glen's many talents. He certainly knew how to please her.

CHAPTER 45

Kayla Morales had been staying with Rabbi Elijah and Ruth Dalton for several days. It was late Friday afternoon, and she was helping in the kitchen as Ruth prepared for Shabbat.

"I'm really looking forward to spending Shabbat here, Ruth. It would be perfect, except for one thing. I had planned to be at Lev Shalom this weekend because it's the farewell *kiddush* for Rabbi and Mrs. Halperin, and Rabbi Stein has probably prepared a special tribute to them."

"Kayla, honey, I was under the impression that you weren't fond of Rabbi Halperin."

"I've been thinking about that. Now I realize that he correctly understood Daniel's nature. I hoped that Daniel would make an effort to get along with him, if only for my sake. But that wasn't the end of it. Subsequently, he was also belligerent with Rabbi Stein who tried to welcome us as a couple."

"I've heard good things about Rabbi Stein. In fact, he and my husband have gotten together a couple of times. Elijah and I discussed having the rabbi over for dinner soon."

This was new information for Kayla. "My two favorite rabbis already know each other? Well, I'm not surprised that they get along."

"Smells like Shabbat in here!" Rabbi Dalton declared as he came into the kitchen. He grabbed a teaspoon and took a taste of spicy baba ganoush from a bowl on the counter. He nodded his approval and left the cooking to the experts.

The next morning, as Elijah Dalton rose to deliver a sermon to his congregation at Bet Hillel, Josh Stein at Lev Shalom stepped up to the lectern to praise the Halperins. He carefully avoided looking at the *shul* president, Bob Small, who was sitting near him on the *bimah*. With great effort, he kept himself from focusing on the beaming face of Rachel Berg who was making eyes at a man across the *mechitzah*, whom Josh had never seen before. At the same time, Josh was pleased to be the recipient of Leora Halperin's total attention.

Josh delivered a short sermon based on the weekly Torah portion, after which he honored the Halperins by comparing them to the biblical Abraham and Sarah, whose exemplary acts of kindness and faith spread the belief in God to the nations of the world. Josh likened the lives and beliefs of Jewish ancestors to the welcoming atmosphere the Halperins created, both in their home and in the early days of the synagogue, when it was a haven for Holocaust survivors. Josh lauded Ephraim Halperin for spreading the word of Torah throughout Chicago and to the nation, with his popular books and appearances in the media. The Halperins had built Lev Shalom into a large, thriving synagogue, famous for its retention of traditional Jewish values, enriching classes, and strong youth programming.

Just like the matriarch Sarah, Bunny Halperin's beauty and graciousness were legendary, while Ephraim Halperin's tenacity and spiritual strength were easily comparable to the patriarch Abraham. In the early years, while raising a family of her own, Bunny assumed the responsibility to teach the women of her congregation how to manage a kosher kitchen and observe the laws of family purity. She also founded the sisterhood and led a Sunday morning study group.

Ephraim Halperin, although American-born, delivered his early sermons in both Yiddish and English, slowly guiding the congregation into
a community of Jewish observance and leadership in many Chicago
organizations.

Rabbi Halperin's oldest son, representing the family, charmed the congregation with family anecdotes. Then, Bob Small, on behalf of the synagogue, presented the Halperins with a sterling silver Cup of Elijah and
kept his remarks brief. Josh was amused by the look of relief on Bunny
and Sheila's faces as Bob returned to his seat on the *bimah*.

The last speaker was Rabbi Halperin himself. His dignity, intelligence,
and scholarship were perfectly united in his last words to the congregation he had built. It was clear to many of those in attendance that the
Halperins' lifelong desire to make a permanent home in Israel was at
last being realized. They had done what they had been meant to do in
Chicago, and were now beginning a new life in the Holy Land. Ephraim
Halperin was uncharacteristically sentimental as he thanked his Lev
Shalom 'family' for almost fifty years of exciting challenges and personal fulfillment. With a few poignant anecdotes, he brought tears to
many eyes, including his own.

Two of the Halperins' grandchildren led the closing prayers. After singing the final prayer, *Adon Olam,* the entire Halperin family, their sons
and daughters-in-law and all their grandchildren led the congregation
into the social hall for the *kiddush*. Their daughter, Leora, lingered a
minute or two and walked into the *kiddush* with Rabbi Stein. The Halperins were stopped along the way to greet well-wishers and to talk about
the photographs and memorabilia on display.

Bunny searched the room for her daughter and spotted her walking with

Josh. A morning which, until that moment, was filled with joy, suddenly lost some of its glow for her.

Why is Lee-Lee doing this to me? Does she have to be so obvious? She should be standing with us and her brothers, but no, she's openly attaching herself to Stein. Our daughter has lost her mind, as well as her sense of responsibility. I hope Fred doesn't notice. Is she serious about moving back to Chicago? We're never coming back here, no matter what happens with her and Stein.

Bunny stifled her thoughts and joined her husband to make the rounds in the social hall. As they mingled, Bunny caught Leora's eye and gave her 'the look'. Leora knew what she had to do and left Josh's side to join her family.

CHAPTER 46

"I want you to meet my friend, Glen Stempler," Rachel beamed, as she introduced him to Josh.

Josh extended his hand to the stranger he had wondered about during the service and said, "Good *Shabbos*. Welcome to Lev Shalom. I'm always happy to meet Rachel Berg's friends."

Glen wanted to establish his connection with Rachel to her former boyfriend. At the same time, he had to tread carefully because he wasn't quite sure what Rachel wanted Josh to assume about him.

"I'm definitely a great friend of Rachel's," Glen affirmed. "I'd like to think that I'm her closest friend. We met at the office and have formed a meaningful relationship."

Glen thought, *Josh Stein isn't what I expected. He looks kind of underweight. And those uncool glasses? That clean-cut, studious persona doesn't convey much machismo. What did Rachel ever see in this guy?*

Simultaneously, Josh thought: *Glen is pretty full of himself. And what's Rachel doing with a guy who's just barely as tall as she is? I bet he's already her obedient servant.*

Glen sensed Rachel's support, so he continued, "Because you're Rachel's rabbi, it's only fair for me to let you in on something."

Rachel could hardly contain her pleasure at Josh's growing discomfort. She knew that Glen was on a roll, and she looked forward to Josh's response. She linked her arm through Glen's and waited.

But Glen didn't get to finish his comments. Reaching deep into his rabbinic storehouse of self-control, Josh smiled. "I know that any man who's able to sustain Rachel's interest has to be special. She has high standards, as I'm sure you know."

People were waiting to speak with him, so Josh excused himself by adding, "Mr. Stempler, I hope we get another chance to meet. I'm counting on Rachel to arrange it. Good *Shabbos* again."

Buoyed by their successful interchange with Josh, Rachel steered Glen over to Leora Halperin who was standing alone, taking in the scene. With her hand in Glen's, Rachel introduced them.

"Leora, I'd like you to meet Glen Stempler, the most important man in my life. We work together and play together."

This unexpected bit of good news took Leora by surprise. Could it be that there was no longer any attachment between Rachel and Josh? Did Josh know about Glen? Would this be a relief for him or would he be devastated? Leora spotted Josh, who seemed to be in fine spirits. She wondered what he thought about Rachel and Glen being together at such a public gathering.

Leora smiled warmly, "The two of you look so happy! Imagine finding a kindred spirit right where you work! Glen, are you as high-powered an attorney as my friend Rachel?"

Glen smirked, "You better ask Rachel about the extent of my power." Turning toward his girlfriend, Glen asked, "Rachel, would you say that

I'm high-powered?"

Squarely facing Leora, Rachel affirmed, "Glen is just about as high-powered as they come!"

Leora assessed the situation accurately, "I can see that you two are perfect for each other. Glen, I'm happy that Rachel brought you here. I know we'll meet again."

Rachel's spirits were soaring to the extent that she hurried to introduce Glen to her parents. As they reached Serena and Herb Berg, Rachel saw Bob Small rush toward Josh.

"Rabbi!" Bob brusquely interrupted Josh who was chatting with a group of Lev Shalom regulars., "You gotta come with me now! There's this weird guy out in the lobby who's trying to get into the *kiddush,* but the guard won't let him."

"What's going on? Let's welcome him in. He's probably here for the Halperins."

"Are you kidding?" Bob barked. "The guy's wearing sneakers and a T-shirt. I think I saw him in the *shul* office with that black girl. I didn't like him then, and I don't like him now. Are you coming, or not?"

Josh knew who Bob was referring to. *What's Daniel Lewishon doing at Lev Shalom? Kayla's not here, and I know Daniel didn't come to honor the Halperins.*

Bob hustled Josh to the lobby where Daniel was leaning against the wall, far away from other people who were standing around enjoying the photographs. Once Josh saw Daniel, Bob inched slowly back toward the social hall, keeping the two of them in sight. He sensed trouble.

Josh assured the security guard that he knew Daniel, and there was no problem. The guard stepped back a bit, but remained close. Smiling, Josh began, "Good *Shabbos,* Daniel. I haven't seen you for a long time. Is everything OK?"

"I came to get Kayla. Where is she?" Daniel demanded. "If anybody knows where she is, you do. So you better tell her I'm looking for her, and, Stein, do it fast. I mean business, so don't mess with me."

Josh wasn't going to be bullied, and he certainly wasn't going to reveal that Kayla was staying with the Daltons across town. "I'm not Kayla's keeper," Josh replied, calmly. "I'm under the impression that the two of you broke your engagement, and that Kayla became a member here on her own."

"Last chance, Stein," Daniel sneered, menacingly. "Get me to Kayla, or you'll be sorry."

"I can't do that," Josh stated, slowly turning away. For a few seconds, Daniel watched him walk back toward crowd in the social hall.

Bob Small had been carefully observing the interchange between Josh and Daniel. Suddenly, he saw Daniel pull a gun from his pocket and aim it at Josh's back.

"He's got a gun!" Bob yelled across the foyer, but he was too late.

After a single shot, Daniel shoved the guard to the ground, fled the building, and raced to his car that was idling on the street nearby.

Gasping for breath and bleeding, Josh collapsed to the floor. Confused, screaming men and women and terrified children scattered at the sound of the gunshot, and Bob hollered at the top of his voice, "We need a doctor, quick!"

Among the many congregant physicians who rushed to Josh's aid, an ER doctor pushed forward, and someone called 911. They attended to Josh until the ambulance arrived. By that time, parents had grabbed their children from the social hall and playground, and the guard had called for back-up.

Bob took charge as people were ushered back into the social hall. "We don't know where the shooter is, and we have to stick together and be very careful. For the time being, we're locking the *shul* doors. Make sure you have your children with you, and stay inside until we get an all-clear from the police." Then Bob raced to the ambulance where the EMT's were working on Josh.

Rabbi Halperin got everyone's attention. "Thank God, Rabbi Stein's being cared for and is on his way to the hospital. We've already identified the man who shot him, and it's just a matter of time until he's apprehended. We should all be grateful that Mr. Small acted so quickly and prudently. He went along in the ambulance and is going to stay with Rabbi Stein."

Sheila appreciated Rabbi Halperin's comment about Bob's quick thinking. It was about time her husband was recognized for being a great leader. *All these years, Bob's been doing the heavy lifting around here. The shul couldn't function without his fast thinking. Finally, now that they're leaving, Halperin gives Bob some credit*, she thought.

Rabbi Halperin didn't miss a beat. He stopped for a moment; now it was his place to take over. He gestured toward his wife and family standing nearby and assumed the voice for which he had become famous. He got everyone's attention. "In my wildest dreams I never imagined that my final Shabbat here as Lev Shalom's Rabbi would be anything less than perfect. But, let me tell you, being with all of you and my family, and having just shared a traumatic moment together underscores the closeness I feel to each of you."

Bunny moved to his side and took his hand. Halperin continued, "Please join me in the sanctuary, and we'll recite select psalms for Rabbi Stein's *refuah shelemah,* a speedy and full recovery."

Most congregants followed the Halperins into the sanctuary, and the rabbi asked his younger son to lead the prayers. The recitation began, but Bunny had a hard time concentrating because she didn't see her daughter anywhere among the group.

As the ambulance pulled away with Bob accompanying Josh, Rachel and Leora found themselves standing side by side. Rachel noticed tears in Leora's eyes, and she realized that Leora cared more deeply about Josh than she did. Rachel instinctively put her arm around Leora, and Glen took Rachel's hand.

Satisfied that her husband was with Rabbi Stein, Sheila Small headed slowly to the foyer. She looked around and spotted a man surreptitiously speaking into his cell phone. As soon as he saw her, he slid his phone into his pocket. Sheila recognized James Traub, the reporter who had interviewed her husband. He had just been an eyewitness to the event that would put his story on the front page of *The Chicago Journal.*

CHAPTER 47

Customarily, Rabbi Dalton went into his study immediately after *havdalah* at the end of Shabbat to check the news on his computer. Stunned by what he read, he called out to his wife and Kayla, "Rabbi Joshua Stein of Congregation Lev Shalom was shot!"

Kayla had a sinking feeling in the pit of her stomach. "I know who did it!" she cried.

Kayla had kept Will and Bobby Lewisohn's number, but she wanted to use the Dalton's phone to contact them.

Will answered."It's about time you called about Dan. We're on our way to try to get him out on bail, so we can beat the crap out of him. The dumb-ass shot a rabbi, and Kayla, you gotta fix this. We've been trying to call you all afternoon, but your number's out of service. Why'd you change it?"

"I changed my number for this very reason, and I'm not calling you from my new number now, so don't bother trying to get me here. Your brother's invented an evil fantasy about the rabbis at Lev Shalom. I even warned one of them that Daniel could be dangerous, and he blew it off. I'm calling you to make my position clear. Don't try to reach me anymore because there's nothing I can do." Then she hung up.

Dalton called Rabbi Stein's number, but was only able to leave a message. Then he dialed Rabbi Halperin's home number.

Bunny answered, but it took her a minute to figure out exactly who Rabbi Elijah Dalton was. "Even though it's late, my husband just left for the hospital to check on Rabbi Stein. He promised to call me as soon has he has some information. But I have to ask, how did you know about the shooting? Did somebody call you from Lev Shalom?"

Rabbi Dalton answered with a question of his own. "Does the name Kayla Morales mean anything to you?"

"No, who's Kayla Morales?"

"Miss Morales is the former fiancee of Daniel Lewisohn, the man who shot Rabbi Stein. She's standing right here with my wife and me. We insisted that she stay with us after Daniel began exhibiting some problematic behaviors. We found out about the shooting this evening, after Shabbat.

Bunny was confused. "Why is the shooter's fiance with you? What do you have to do with all this?"

"Mrs. Halperin, thank God your husband wasn't harmed. He and Rabbi Stein know all about Daniel Lewisohn and Kayla Morales. Ms. Morales is now a member of Lev Shalom, but our Bet Hillel was her first synagogue in Chicago, and she teaches at our school. My wife and I are close with her, and we're determined to protect her from her former fiance."

Still confused, Bunny assured Dalton that they'd keep him apprised of the situation. After she ended the conversation, she returned to the concerns that had preoccupied her all day. Her husband had been in a state of perpetual motion, unable to concentrate on anything except the clock on the wall. As soon as Shabbat was over, he rushed to the hospital to see Josh.

Their daughter, Leora, had not come home after the shooting, but Bunny knew where she was. She was sure that her daughter had walked all the way to the hospital in Evanston to be with Josh Stein. That relationship was already beyond Bunny's control. What Bunny didn't know was that as soon as her husband entered Josh's hospital room, everything about Leora and Josh would become clear to him, too.

It had become clear to Bob when Leora walked into the hospital waiting area earlier that day.

CHAPTER 48

At first, Leora and Bob sat uncomfortably in the hospital lounge, waiting for Josh to be admitted to a room where they could stay with him. Bob wasn't the type to remain idle for long, and he paced back and forth along the hallway, itching to know what was going on with his unexpected companion. Obviously, there was some significant connection between Halperin's daughter and Halperin's assistant rabbi, and Bob's curiosity got the best of him.

He settled himself into a chair next to Leora and asked, "Funny that we're the two people who are here, isn't it? I mean, I know why I'm here, but why you? Are you a nurse or something?"

Leora had to laugh. "Mr. Small, you know very well that I have a business in New York, and I'm not at all involved in the medical profession. What you really want to know is my relationship with Rabbi Stein, right?"

Bob leaned forward in his chair, "You were always a smart cookie! There's no beating around the bush with you, so let me just come right out and ask. You and Stein have something going? I kinda thought that he was with Rachel Berg. I musta missed a coupla beats."

Leora had no desire to be cagey, "Let me put it this way, I care about Rabbi Stein, and I find him to be very attractive, polite, and intelligent. You might be surprised that I also feel that he's interested in me. As for

Rachel Berg, who happens to be a friend of mine, I don't think that she's still in the picture. Any other questions?"

In spite of the circumstances, Bob was beginning to enjoy himself. He liked Leora's straightforward style, and he decided to tell her what he had been considering during the hours they had been waiting.

"Let me run something by you. I don't know how much you know about problems between your father and me, but that's beside the point. What I've been thinking is that we're gonna need your father to stay in Chicago a little while longer to help out until we find out what's gonna be with Stein."

Leora read between the lines and had a question, "Is Lev Shalom planning to hire Rabbi Stein permanently?"

Bob had to hedge, "Let's just get over this hump. Stein still has to prove that he's got what it takes."

"What if my father won't stay?"

Bob winked, "I'm pretty sure he'll help us out. After all, he'll be a big hero if he does."

"What did you mean about problems between you and my father?"

"That's old news. It had something to do with the Holocaust Memorial Garden, and I'm not gonna go into that now."

Just then, a doctor came into the lounge and told Bob and Leora that Josh had been transferred into a room and was sedated, but they could sit with him. They hurried to the room. The rest of the afternoon went by slowly, with Bob intermittently pacing back and forth in the hallway.

Leora pulled a chair next to the patient, and waited contentedly by his side.

Finally, Bob looked at his watch and told Leora that Shabbat was over. He expected her father to arrive any minute. He was right.

Ephraim Halperin was completely unprepared for the scene before him as he entered the hospital room where Josh lay sleeping. The patient was the center of a strange tableau, consisting of Bob Small seated on the left side of the bed and Leora seated on the right, with her hand resting on Josh's arm, carefully avoiding the IV. A nurse was there, too, checking the patient's vital signs.

Bob, looking weary and at the same time agitated, jumped up, eager to talk to Halperin.

"I've been thinking about this all day, and I've got something important to offer you," Bob announced.

Halperin had not raced to the hospital to hear anything but news about Josh Stein. "Is it about Rabbi Stein?"

"In a way it is, but it's mostly about what I have to do now."

"Hi, Daddy!" Leora interrupted. "Mom must be pretty upset that I didn't come home this afternoon, right?"

Halperin was aggravated that the two people who had been with Josh all afternoon had nothing to report about the patient. "Would either of you care to focus on Rabbi Stein? Is he out of danger? Did he lose a lot of blood? Did anyone call his parents?"

Leora smiled. "You're right," she admitted, "It looks like Josh will be all right, but it was much more than a flesh wound, and it'll take time to heal completely. He'll need physical therapy. He had to have a transfusion because he lost a lot of blood, but thank God the bullet missed the major arteries and didn't shatter any bones. The surgeon said that it'll be at least a month until Josh can get back to work full time."

"That's what I gotta talk to you about," Bob interjected, getting back to his subject. "I'm eating humble pie, Rabbi. We need you to cover for Stein until he can come back. Whaddya say?"

Even though Bob had broached the subject with her, Leora exclaimed. "I assume you realize that my parents are completely packed and ready to move. Slow down, Mr. Small; this is a complete surprise to my father."

Halperin disregarded Bob's question. There were more pressing things to attend to. "Bob, take my phone and ask Serena to send an email to the members of the congregation, ASAP. Then, I'll contact Rabbi Stein's family myself."

Leora interrupted again, "And I'm going to stay here with Josh. Daddy, before Bob uses your phone, let me call Mom. I know you won't be able to convince her about anything that has to do with Josh and me, but I'm going home with you to get some stuff, and then I'm coming back here."

Bob and Halperin were both taken aback at Leora's statement. Neither one of them was prepared for her apparent commitment to the well-being of Josh Stein. They remained speechless as Halperin handed his phone to Leora.

While Leora spoke with Bunny, Josh opened his eyes, assessed his surroundings and tightened his fingers around Leora's hand. Without a word, he closed his eyes once again, the better to hear the conversation between the *shul* president and the former rabbi. He wasn't disappointed. In fact, it was entertaining.

Bob began, "Rabbi, we're just starting our search for a senior rabbi. We were taking our time because Stein's in place. But, we're stuck. We need somebody who knows the ropes to handle the *shul* until Stein comes back. Frankly, I don't think Stein's as sick as they claim, so it shouldn't be more than a coupla weeks. You're the man for the job, and I'm asking you to stay, even though you're probably pissed as hell at me. Are you gonna help us?"

Halperin took Bob's vacated chair and assumed a thoughtful pose. He had often fantasized that the tables would turn, and one day Bob Small would beg him to come back. Naturally, he should refuse Bob's fumbling, inappropriate request, but Halperin loved being the rabbi of Lev Shalom. He knew, in spite of the board's decision and the rumors floating around, that his congregation would welcome him back, like the knight in shining armor who saves an entire city with one brave act.

"Bob, I understand the synagogue's current predicament, and I'll give it some thought. Of course, I have to discuss your request with Bunny. I assume you're speaking without consulting your board of directors. So you see, I'm not sure you have the authority to make that proposal. Not that you would ever do anything without proper process, but I think you're getting ahead of yourself. Why don't you call one of your famous emergency board meetings?"

Bob knew Halperin's game, but he was too smart to retaliate, and he needed Halperin immediately. "Rabbi, you'll be back in charge. Let's try to get along for the sake of the *shul*. I'll tell Serena to assure our members that Rabbi Stein's gonna be all right, and that you're gonna fill in until he comes back."

Just as Leora ended an unpleasant interchange with her mother, Halperin's phone rang. It was Bob's wife. Halperin handed him the phone he had brought with him after Shabbat.

"Sheila, baby, I can't talk now. I gotta finish a piece of business with Halperin. Stein's gonna be OK, but out of commission for a coupla weeks, and I'm taking care of it."

Sheila insisted, "Bob, hold on! This is important. After you left with the ambulance, I was coming into the foyer outside the social hall. I spotted that reporter who came to our house, the one looking for dirt about Rabbi Halperin's departure. He was hiding in a corner taking pictures with his cell phone, but when he saw me, he put it away. You better prepare yourself and everybody who needs to know that this story is big enough to get all over the place."

Bob scanned the hospital room, and assured himself that he alone heard his wife's report. He had to think about his next move, but he was so worn out that all he could say as he hung up was, "Shit!"

CHAPTER 49

When Josh opened his eyes Sunday morning, it took him a few seconds to adjust to the excruciating pain radiating up and down his arm. At that moment, a nurse came into his room to check his vital signs.

Taking note of the woman sitting by Josh's side, the nurse addressed Leora, "Your husband was lucky that the bullet didn't do more damage. He'll be out of here in a few days, and with rehab he should be fine."

At the words 'your husband', Josh and Leora looked at each other conspiratorially and neither corrected the nurse. When she left the room, Josh asked Leora, "Were you here all night?"

Leora answered, "You didn't think I'd leave you unattended, did you? My dad took me home last night. I showered, put my things together, warmed up some soup from Friday night dinner, and came back here to take advantage of this comfortable chair. As your devoted spouse, where else would I be? You wouldn't expect me to be at my parents' house with real food, in a real bed with a real sheet and pillow, would you?

Josh reached for Leora's hand. Even though he had been in and out of consciousness, he knew that Leora had been by his side, but what about Bob Small? Josh seemed to remember that both of them stayed with him after he was taken to the hospital, and he had a lot of questions.

"Leora, how did you get to the hospital yesterday? Did you come with Bob?"

"Bob was in the ambulance with you, and I was fortunate enough to have an energizing multi-mile walk."

Josh laughed, "You're lucky that I wasn't taken to Cook County! And I have another question. Does your mother know you're here?"

"Of course she does. You know how supportive she's been with my decision to move back here, right?" Leora joked.

Josh tried to sit up. "You definitely made the decision to move back?"

"Looks that way. First, I want to help finish packing my parents' things. After that, I have the Holocaust Memorial Garden to take care of. And now, with your unfortunate mishap, my dear Rabbi Stein, I suppose I'm going to have to attend to your needs, as well."

Josh tried to smile at her sarcasm, but winced instead. "I have more to say, but would you please call for pain meds and adjust my bed so I can sit up? I want to be able to look at you when I talk."

After Leora made him comfortable, she returned to her chair, and took Josh's hand again. "Speak to me," she urged.

"I couldn't ask for a more delightful attendant. I'm curious. Did anybody call my parents? Does Serena know? What happened to the guy who shot me? I hope you realize that I know him, and Bob and your father know him, too."

Leora wanted to quickly answer and then get him to sleep. "My father called your parents, and I'm sure we'll hear from them any minute. Bob contacted Serena after Shabbat and told her to inform the congregation about you. So rest assured that your friend, Rachel Berg, knows that you're currently incapacitated. And as for your last question, they immediately caught the man who shot you, and he's in jail."

Josh had one more thing to ask, "I wasn't out of it the whole time yesterday. I think I overheard a conversation between Bob and your father. Was I dreaming?"

Leora smiled, "You weren't out of it. Bob paced around all day yesterday, trying to figure out what to do next, now that his interim rabbi won't be able to work for a while. He told me about it. And then in walked my father! The answer to Bob's dilemma was standing in front of him. I'm aware that something serious had happened between the two of them, but Bob wouldn't elaborate. He needs my father, and to be perfectly honest with you, my father was flattered. I'm pretty sure that he'll accept. On the other hand, my mother will now have three people to resent--Bob, me, and my father."

Josh nodded. "I can't even imagine Bob admitting that he needs your father. You're right when you say that there's bad blood between them, but it's not what I want to talk about. So how did they leave the discussion?"

"Funny you should ask because they didn't have a chance to finish the discussion. My father's cell rang, and I'm pretty sure it was Sheila calling. Something else happened, and it sounded bad."

"So then what?"

"All I know is that Bob got red in the face and ran out of here yelling, 'Shit!'.

"Sounds routine for Bob," Josh noted, dryly.

Josh wanted to talk more but he was falling asleep. His last words before his eyes closed were, "I hope you'll be here when I wake up. Please don't leave."

Leora decided to get some coffee after Josh fell asleep. She liked the position she found herself in, and she knew that Josh did, too. Leora had a sudden desire to call Rachel Berg, just in case Rachel needed to be assured that Leora was now Josh's confidante. On further reflection, Leora realized that it would be childish and mean-spirited to talk about Josh with his former girlfriend. Leora wasn't that kind of person, but she had to admit that it was tempting.

CHAPTER 50

The congregation was abuzz with gossip about the shooting of Rabbi Stein. Even though at first everyone was afraid that it had been a terrorist incident, Serena's email to them confirmed and clarified what had really happened. Naturally, in the close-knit Lev Shalom community, members wanted to do something to help the young rabbi of whom they had become fond. Both Sheila and Serena found themselves inundated with calls from *shul* members offering assistance to Rabbi Stein.

It started early Sunday morning, when Serena's cell phone rang at seven-thirty am. It was the sisterhood president. "Serena, last night I set up a meal rotation for Rabbi Stein, starting with lunch today. Should people bring food to the hospital or do you plan on handling the deliveries?"

Serena firmly told her to put a hold on the meal rotation until the rabbi was home, then the phone rang again. It was Sheila Small. "The youth group is going to visit Rabbi Stein this afternoon. Honest to God, I tried to stop them, but apparently the *mitzvah* of visiting the sick has been drummed into their do-good heads, and they won't take no for an answer."

Serena tried to calm Sheila down. "One of us has to get to the hospital and sit outside Rabbi Stein's room to protect him from all the well-meaning congregants."

"Wait, Serena! I'm not finished. The men's club choir is planning to visit the Rabbi to serenade him with some peppy, upbeat songs. I don't know whether to laugh or scream. Hold on, Bunny Halperin's trying to get through. I'll call you right back."

A few minutes later, Sheila called Serena again. "I'll tell you what Bunny's upset about. Do you get a home delivery of the Sunday paper?"

"Yes, why?"

"Guess whose pictures are on the front page?"

Serena was afraid to guess, but she had a good idea.

Sheila confirmed Serena's thought. "That busy-body journalist saw the whole thing. I caught him taking pictures in the vestibule, and Bob called him last night demanding that he kill the story, but it was Traub's biggest scoop. Besides, he had already filed it. Then, Traub tried to get information from the hospital, but they wouldn't tell him anything or let him anywhere near Stein. Now Traub's all over Bob to reveal everything that happened after the shooting. And Bunny told me that he's also pumping her husband for information. I have no great love for Bunny Halperin, but she doesn't deserve this."

When the call ended, Serena ran to her front yard to get the paper. Sure enough, there was a full-color picture of Rabbi Stein lying in the Lev Shalom foyer with blood all over the place. *The Tribune* gave Traub's story a complete half page, which included an extremely unflattering photo of Bob Small screaming, and another equally embarrassing shot of Rabbi Ephraim Halperin looking confused. The banner headline spanned the entire page:

BLOODY SABBATH AT TROUBLED SYNAGOGUE!

Serena's phone kept ringing. "Herb, for God's sake, answer the phone. I'm reading something important in the paper."

Herb yelled back, "They all want to talk to you, and only you. This is no time to read the paper. What's so important?"

Serena brought the paper into the kitchen, moved her husband's cereal bowl to the side, and displayed the front page.

Herb jumped up in fury. "Why didn't anybody catch that guy taking pictures? How did a photographer get in on *Shabbos*? I'm telling you, Serena, that security guy is worthless. The *shul's* gotta come up with a better plan. Anybody can do anything there. Nobody's safe!"

Serena's patience was hanging by a thread. "Herbert Berg, all you ever think about is how the *shul* wastes money. Somebody shot our rabbi! Somebody else wrote about it, and now everybody in Chicago is talking about the poor security at Lev Shalom and the crazy people who get in. Do me a favor. Stay here and take phone messages. I'm going to the hospital."

"What good can you do there?" Herb called as Serena rushed out of the kitchen.

She changed her shoes and put on her jacket, shouting, "I'm going to help Rabbi Stein by standing outside his hospital room and fending off the youth group, men's club choir, sisterhood *yentas*, and anybody else who tries to visit. And I just dare Mr. James Traub to try to get past me!"

CHAPTER 51

Elijah Dalton threw down his Sunday paper and hurried into the kitchen where his wife and Kayla were debating her next move. Kayla hadn't slept more than a couple of hours, and she was overwrought with worry and fear. She couldn't shake the phone call with Daniel's brothers.

Dalton announced, "I just read the front page story in today's paper. Guess whose picture's there?"

Kayla was shaking. "Is it Daniel?"

"It's not Daniel! The story says that Rabbi Stein was taken to Evanston Hospital and the shooter's in custody. They identified him as Daniel Lewisohn. There's also a picture of Rabbi Halperin looking 'out of it'. I'm about to call him. Kayla, do you want to speak with him?"

Kayla didn't know what to do.

"I wouldn't know what to say to Rabbi Halperin. He was very cold to us, but now I realize that he knew Daniel was unstable and didn't want to deal with him. We thought it was because we're an interracial couple. I wanted both of us to join Lev Shalom, but even Rabbi Stein knew that Daniel was wrong for me. Now, look what happened? It's all my fault!"

Ruth stopped her, "Kayla, you and Daniel go way back, and you were probably the only good thing that ever happened to him. No matter what his brothers want from you, you now have a chance to start over. You're not responsible for anything! Daniel was never able to control his anger, and we all knew it."

"Yes! The two of you kicked him out of Bet Hillel," Kayla acknowledged, with an edge to her voice. "Don't you see why I feel responsible? I just moved Daniel's problems from one synagogue to another, and now Rabbi Stein's in the hospital."

Dalton cut Kayla off. "All this talking is a waste of time. Kayla, you stay here with Ruth. Under no circumstances should you contact Daniel's brothers until I find out exactly what happened. I'm assuming that Daniel will be unable to reach you, but if he tries, don't dare accept that call!"

Kayla suddenly realized how vulnerable and alone she really was. She found herself at her weakest moment, embraced by these two loving people. They knew what she needed. This was a place of safety and comfort. These were people who understood her in a way that Rabbi Stein never could. It was clear to Kayla that she belonged here with the Daltons. Kayla, who had always prided herself on being the strong, independent one, ironically was ready to surrender.

A few minutes later, Rabbi Dalton returned to the kitchen to issue a report.

"I had a short, productive conversation with Ephraim Halperin, and he's just as dismayed as I am. We both wanted you, Kayla, to separate from Daniel, but unfortunately that didn't happen."

"See, I told you it was my fault!"

"That's not where I'm going with this. I've already warned you to have nothing further to do with Daniel. Luckily, Rabbi Halperin told me that Rabbi Stein's condition is stable, but it's going to be a slow recovery. I'm leaving for the hospital now."

Kayla insisted, "I'm coming with you!"

"Absolutely not. There's nothing you can say or do. Stay here with Ruth."

"I'm not leaving Kayla's side until you get back from the hospital, Elijah."

As Ruth walked Elijah to the front door, he cautioned his wife, "Kayla doesn't understand the repercussions of staying involved with any of the Lewisohns. While I'm out, take advantage of your time together. She'll be much more comfortable talking openly with you than she would with me."

"I've been thinking about this, Elijah. Kayla should stay with us for a while and come back to our congregation, too."

"We'll talk about that later. As usual, you're probably right."

Kayla was waiting for Ruth to return to the kitchen. In spite of everything, for better or worse, she had decided to call Bobby and Will. Ruth couldn't stop her.

Kayla put her phone on speaker mode.

Bobby answered on the first ring. "Bobby, put Will on the phone."

Bobby, who was relieved of having to carry on a conversation with someone of superior intellect, handed the phone to his more capable brother.

"Kayla, I know you're as worried about Dan as we are," Will stated. "Here's what you gotta do. Get a hold of one of your rabbis and meet us at the jail. Since you're such good friends with these holy guys, they'll do it for you. Nobody lets us any place near Dan, but they'll hop to it when they see a *yarmulka* and a beard."

It was all Kayla could do to keep herself from laughing at the absurdity of Will's assumption.

"Not only am I not going to ask any rabbi to get involved with your brother, but I'm calling to clarify the situation, Daniel tried to kill somebody. That's why he's in jail, and he's not going to get out on bail, which you can't raise anyway."

Will wasn't going to give up. "This all happened because you drove Daniel crazy. That's why you can't abandon him now. You gotta get a rabbi to come help us."

Kayla was furious, "Yeah, Will, that's right. Daniel tried to kill a rabbi, in a synagogue, in front of hundreds of people, but I'm supposed to get other rabbis to help him. Are you serious?"

"Kayla, you always had a bitchy side, and now I see you're selfish, too."

"I'm glad you understand that because of my bitchy selfishness I'm finished with all of you."

She hung up and turned to Ruth whose hand was numb from Kayla's grip.

"Ruth, I don't know why I called them, but I just felt that I had to. I guess it's because it really is my fault, isn't it?"

Ruth answered gently, "You loved the guy and you were sure you could change him. Thank God he didn't kill anyone."

Kayla tried, but was incapable of containing her emotions. As she sobbed, she asked, "Daniel's brothers don't believe that I'm finished, do they?"

Ruth moved a box of tissues toward Kayla and answered. "No, they didn't believe you, but it doesn't matter. I want to believe you and you have to believe you."

The test came sooner than expected. Kayla recognized the caller ID and let it go to voicemail, but the women listened to the message. *Kayla, I guess I lost it a coupla minutes ago. What you gotta know is that me and Will have had enough with Daniel, too. We're his brothers, and all, but we can't help him. It's up to you.*

Kayla was angry. "Now that I called them, they have this number. What should I do now?"

Ruth insisted, "You have no obligation here, Kayla. No more of this!"

Kayla knew that Ruth was right. "I'm done. Is it OK with you if I go lie down for a while? I know you won't answer if they try again."

CHAPTER 52

The Steins got the news late Saturday night, and Susan Stein was on the plane to Chicago to take care of her son by Sunday afternoon. The fact that he had been a shooting victim, and was now in a hospital, terrified his family. While Josh's father, Dan, considered the family's next move, his mother, Susan, had no doubts. She immediately began to pack.

Early Sunday morning, Dan called Josh's cellphone to prepare his son for Susan's take-over. Josh didn't pick up the call, but Leora saw the caller ID and answered.

Hearing a woman's voice, Dan assumed that Rachel Berg was sitting by Josh's side. "Rachel, I'm glad you're there. Before you tell me how Josh is doing, I have to warn both of you that my wife is on her way to Chicago. She threw enough clothes into her suitcase to be able to stay a long time. I couldn't stop her. Now, Rachel, tell me all about my son."

Leora signaled for Josh's attention because she didn't want him to miss any of the conversation, which she was sure he would find enlightening. On speaker-phone, she began to clarify her identity.

"Mr. Stein, this is not Rachel Berg. You won't remember me, but we have met. I'm Leora Halperin."

"Are you the Rabbi's wife?"

"No, I'm Rabbi Halperin's daughter, just one of your son's many admirers. I've appointed myself his caretaker, but now I learn that I'll be turning that responsibility over to your wife."

Dan was confused. "Is Rachel there, too?"

"So far, there hasn't been any Rachel sighting, but I wouldn't be surprised if Rachel and her new boyfriend, Glen, come by in the next few days."

Josh was listening with great interest. He called out from his semi-reclining position, "Hi Dad! Meet my new best friend, Leora! I guess there's a lot going on here that I haven't had a chance to tell you and Mom."

"In all your emails and texts, you never told us that you and Rachel broke up. It would have been helpful for your mother to know all of this before she left."

"Dad, are you more concerned about Mom or about me?"

"Sorry Josh, but you know how your mother worries about you! Anyway, Rabbi Halperin called us last night and told us what happened. I know you'll be OK, but I'm not sure about your mother. What's the pain like? Did you lose a lot of blood? Is it hard for you to talk? Maybe you should let your friend do the talking."

"I'm right here, Mr. Stein," Leora assured him. "Josh lost some blood, and he's uncomfortable. His labs look much better today, and the pain management seems to be working. It's probably going to take more than a month until he's back at work, but he'll go home soon. I think I've told you everything. Is there anything else you want to ask me?"

"There is something that could be a problem. Are they going to hold Josh's position?"

"Funny you should ask. It looks like your son's job is safe, and my father may fill in for his former assistant. Crazy, right?"

Dan had to process everything Leora had just told him. "Weren't your parents about to move to Israel? Isn't that why my son got the interim job?"

"They're still planning to move, but my father's loyalty to Lev Shalom is paramount. To be perfectly honest with you, I think he was flattered that the *shul* president asked him to come back."

"I have just one more question because I'm confused, and I might be out of line asking you. I'm assuming that you don't know anything about my son and Rachel Berg."

"As it happens, Rachel and I are friends, so I'm aware that Rachel and Josh were close. And Josh does tell me personal anecdotes from time to time. Rachel's now dating a man who's perfect for her, and she's very happy. As for your son, well, in my opinion, he's happy, too."

Dan read between the lines and decided to offer some advice. "When my wife gets there, make sure that she understands the new situation, and if you think I have questions, get ready for an inquisition."

CHAPTER 53

Serena was the first of many visitors to appear on the scene. When she knocked on Josh's hospital door Sunday morning, she intended to monitor the groups of people who wanted to entertain or feed him.

Leora answered the door and greeted her, "Serena, what a surprise!"

"You're not the only one who's surprised. It's still early! What time did you get here?"

"Oh, I've been guarding the patient all night!" Leora explained.

Before Serena could figure out how to react, Josh gestured for her to come closer to him.

Serena was tempted to give Josh a hug, but decided it was unprofessional. However, her thoughts burst forth, "I've been so worried about you! Can I get you anything? I have a kosher kitchen, so just tell me what you can eat. You're probably full of pain-killers and just want to sleep. I'm only staying for one minute, and then I'm going to stand outside and guard this room."

"That may not be necessary, but it's great to see you, Serena. I guess by now everyone knows what happened yesterday. In fact, my mother's on her way to Chicago right now to nurse me back to health. Just knowing that you, Leora and my mother are ready to grant my every wish and be my devoted caregivers, makes me feel almost completely healed."

"Thank God, you still have your sense of humor!" Serena sighed. "Or, is it the drugs?"

Josh asked Leora to raise the bed so he could sit. Serena watched their casual interaction. She turned to Leora, "How long do you plan to stay in town? For some reason, I thought you were going back to New York after this weekend. Am I missing something?"

Leora had no reason to be secretive. "Last night, Bob Small asked my father to lead the *shul* until Josh recovers. I've been thinking seriously about selling my share of the business to my partner in New York, and I'm also interested in possibly managing the completion of the Holocaust Memorial Garden."

Serena grasped the new turn of events. To Leora, Rabbi Stein was 'Josh', and there was obvious intimacy between the two.

Serena mused, *Bunny Halperin must be beside herself. Now I understand Bunny's impatience with her daughter when they were packing Rabbi Halperin's office. Bunny kept trying to get the job done, while Leora and the Rabbi manufactured excuses to be together. Thank God my Rachel is moving on.*

Intent on fulfilling her mission, Serena was ready to personally control the flow of visitors, but Josh thanked her and told her that he welcomed company. He assured her that Leora and his mother would protect him.

Serena decided not to get her feelings hurt, and besides, she was now, de facto, in charge of the *shul* and of keeping the congregants apprised of the unfolding events that kept changing.

She didn't have long to wait. As she said her goodbyes, the man who would determine her assignments entered.

It was Bob Small, carrying a huge shopping bag. "How ya doin', Rabbi? You don't look as bad as you did yesterday. I know you probably can't eat these yet, but I got bagels for everybody else around here! Leora, go get the nurses. I have breakfast for the whole staff!"

Leora caught Serena's eye. "Mr. Small, the way it works is that we may offer food to the nurses, but they don't come to patients' rooms to eat."

Bob shrugged his shoulders, "Whatever."

Then, spotting the shul administrator, he gestured toward the food, "Oh, Serena, I didn't see you standing there. Stay and have a bagel and cream cheese. I got some whitefish salad here, too. And while we're eating, I can tell you what you're gonna do."

Even though she was used to Bob's rude behavior, Serena was still surprised at his insensitivity. Rabbi Stein was lying in a hospital bed, suffering from a gunshot wound that could have killed him. In addition, it was inconsiderate to talk about *shul* business, and probably Rabbi Halperin, in front of his daughter. Who was going to eat all those bagels? Clearly, Bob Small was hungry; therefore, he decided that everyone else was, too.

Bob was spreading white fish salad on his bagel when Rabbi Halperin came into Josh's room. The wisdom Halperin had acquired over his many years in the pulpit taught him to assess the situation before speaking or acting. Before him were his loyal administrative assistant, Serena, his nemesis, Bob Small, and his love-struck daughter, Leora. While Josh lay in his bed, possibly napping, the other three were having breakfast.

Bob greeted Halperin jovially, "Pull up a chair, Rabbi! Grab yourself a whitefish sandwich! I brought plenty for everybody!"

Now, Serena felt extraneous. "I'm just leaving, Rabbi, so take my chair. I came to make sure that Rabbi Stein won't be overwhelmed with visitors today, but Leora can do that. I sent an email to the congregation and I'm going back to the office to field calls."

Making a quick exit, Serena crossed paths at Josh's door with another visitor, Rabbi Elijah Dalton. Rabbi Halperin extended his hand to greet his colleague. Sensing unease in the room, Halperin took charge, as usual.

"Rabbi Dalton, let me introduce you to the president of Lev Shalom, Bob Small. Bob, this gentleman is Rabbi Elijah Dalton, the rabbi of Bet Hillel across town. Rabbi Dalton, this charming young woman is my daughter, Leora, who's visiting us from New York."

Bob winked. "Come on over, Rabbi Dalton, and have something to eat. If you knew me, you'd know that I'd have plenty for everybody."

Even though Bob was the only one still eating, the two rabbis joined him near the hospital tray where the food was displayed. Leora noticed that Josh was awake and alert enough to have a big smile on his face, yet he remained silent. He signaled to her not to give him away. He wanted to experience the triumvirate in action. He wasn't disappointed.

"So tell me, Rabbi Dalton," Bob began, "I guess Bet Hillel's all black by now, right? You know that my family started out on your side of town. I hear that it's a pretty rough area these days."

Josh caught the look of shock on Leora's face, but he was sure that her father could finesse the situation.

Before Dalton could answer, Halperin jumped in. "The old Jewish neighborhood is much improved since Rabbi Dalton took over that synagogue. In fact, Bob, that area is prime real estate for developers now."

Dalton also was a pro, "Mr. Small, I invite you to come visit us soon. I guarantee a personal escort and guard, just to make sure that you feel safe. We black Jews are a welcoming kind of people, and it's just possible that we know something about peoplehood that others haven't learned."

Bob realized that he had offended Dalton, and he tried to make amends. "But, you black Jews do eat bagels like we do, right? Come on, Rabbi, eat something!"

Bob had dug himself into such a deep hole that Halperin just shook his head and changed the subject.

"Rabbi Dalton, what's your connection with Rabbi Stein? He hasn't been here very long, but I assume you have extended yourself to him. Seeing you here reminds me of the joint mission to Israel that Federation asked us to lead. How's your family, by the way? I remember how helpful your wife was when my wife forgot her purse at the hotel."

Leora noticed Josh signaling to get her attention. She walked over to her father and pointed toward Josh. "I think Josh has had enough company. I'm sure he's grateful that you came to see him."

"Wait a minute, honey," Bob stopped her, "I haven't had a chance to brief Rabbi Stein about my plans. Rabbi Halperin, stick around and we'll get our act together." Leora saw Josh nod toward Rabbi Dalton, and she rose to offer him her chair. Instead, Bob took it and sat next to the patient.

Rabbi Halperin wanted to talk privately to Josh and had hoped that Bob and Rabbi Dalton would leave so that he could have some time alone with his former assistant. As for his daughter, Leora, who obviously wanted to stay with Josh, her attachment bothered him, and he didn't welcome the distraction she caused.

Rabbi Dalton was the only one ready to leave. "*Refuah shelemah*, Rabbi Stein! The next time I see you, you'll be so busy at Lev Shalom, this will just be an unpleasant memory of little consequence. I do have to tell you, though, that Kayla feels responsible for what happened. You know, don't you, that she had no control over anything Daniel did."

Josh finally got a chance to speak, "I'm glad Kayla was able to confide in you. Of course I know that she can't control Daniel. The next time you talk to her, please assure her that I don't blame her for anything."

"As a matter of fact," Dalton responded, "I'll be talking to Kayla within a half hour. She's staying with us until she's ready to get back to her own place. She wanted to come here today, but my wife and I convinced her to wait a while before she sees you."

"Who's Kayla?" Leora asked.

Rabbi Halperin didn't want to say too much and answered diplomatically, "Kayla is a teacher at Rabbi Dalton's school, and is a member of his synagogue, Bet Hillel. I met her some time ago, and I was impressed with her genuine love of Judaism."

Dalton turned to Bob and added, "Kayla Morales is the former fiance of the man who shot Rabbi Stein. She wanted to be a member of Lev Shalom and brought her fiance there to meet the rabbis."

"Yeah, I knew something was fishy about those two!" Bob exclaimed.

Halperin held his hand up to stop Bob. "Rabbi Stein and I discussed that relationship fully. Rabbi Dalton, I'm pleased to hear that Kayla is in a safe place. Enough said."

Leora walked Rabbi Dalton to the door, then tried to catch her father's eye. She was successful.

Halperin put his hand on Bob's shoulder. "Bob, Rabbi Stein is in no shape to discuss *shul* business. Let me put your mind at ease. I've decided to remain in Chicago until Rabbi Stein can resume his duties. I'm sure it won't take very long."

"And Mom agreed to that?" Leora challenged.

"Leora, everyone knows how devoted to our *shul* your mother is," Halperin lied. "She would never keep me from doing what only I can do."

Bob stood up to forcefully make his point to Josh. "Saved by the bell! It's a good thing that Rabbi Halperin isn't in a hurry to get outta Dodge!" Then he turned to Leora, with a wink, "And what about you, honey? You gonna stick around, too? It looks like you got something of your own going on, right?"

Ephraim Halperin had seldom found himself speechless, but there was no polite way to respond.

Leora, however, had no such problem. "Mr. Small, you seem to be a man who values straight talk, so here goes. You may want to do the right thing, but you're painfully insensitive. My father should be thanked for his sacrifice. Rabbi Stein needs kind words more than bagels and directives. And that woman Kayla, whoever she is, deserves a different description from 'fishy'. I've known you my whole life and I've always respected how much you and Mrs. Small do for the *shul*, but why insult both of these men and me, too?"

That stopped Bob. "Geez, you women get so emotional! What's the big deal? Sure, I'm happy your father agreed to stick around, and I brought breakfast for everybody so we could have a nice, easy conversation about the *shul,* didn't I?"

Once again, Fred Halperin eased the tension. "Rabbi Stein has had enough of us. Let's go, Bob. I'll walk out with you. Leora, are you coming with us?"

"I'll stay here until Rabbi Stein's mother arrives. I'm looking forward to meeting her."

Bob couldn't hold back, "That oughta be interesting!"

"Mr. Small, I guarantee that once Mrs. Stein meets me, we'll get along fine."

Unchastised, Bob rebounded, "Get well quick, Rabbi Stein. I'm gonna leave the rest of the food here. Now, I gotta get things straight with Rabbi Halperin."

Halperin wished Josh a *refuah shelemah* and, casting a knowing look in his daughter's direction, left with Bob. Leora turned to Josh, "Was that as much fun for you as it was for me?" She laughed.

"Thoroughly enjoyable, but not nearly as much fun as it will be when my mother comes!"

Josh fell asleep.

CHAPTER 54

After a long nap, it was late afternoon, and Josh was about to try the soup that Leora had brought. Just then, Susan Stein rushed breathlessly into the room, her arms full of shopping bags.

"Joshie, Joshie," Susan called out, dismissing the stranger sitting beside her son. "I got here as fast as I could. It's the first time I took an Uber, and I can tell you that I was plenty scared. You know what you hear about some of those drivers, but the man who came for me was a perfect gentleman. When I told him why I'm here, he already knew all about it. He heard it on the news, and he told me that they caught the guy who shot you. He should only rot in hell!"

Josh knew that his mother honestly meant her wish for his would-be assassin. When it came to her children, Susan Stein turned into a mother bear. "Mom! I knew you were coming, and you really made great time! I'm glad you're here, but I wish the reason were different."

"Rabbi Halperin called us late last night. He assured us that you'll recover. While your father kept asking questions, I started to pack.You know me, when my kids need me, I'm there!"

Susan stopped to catch her breath, giving Josh an opportunity to speak. She looked around the room and noticed Leora. *Who is that?* " she wondered.

"Mom, let me introduce you to Leora Halperin. You met her when you came to Chicago for the High Holidays."

Susan laid her packages down and neared the bed, the better to focus on the smiling young woman sitting beside her son. "Leora Halperin? Are you Rabbi Halperin's daughter? Don't you live in New York? Are you a nurse?"

Susan Stein wasn't the first overly inquisitive mother Leora had met. "Yes, I'm the Halperin daughter you met a couple of months ago, and yes, I do have a business in New York. No, I'm not a nurse. I'm just somebody who cares about your son."

It suddenly clicked in Susan Stein's mind. This woman was not a casual visitor to her son's hospital room. "So, did you make that soup for my Joshie?"

"I certainly did, and I'd be happy to give you some, too. I brought a lot, because right now, Josh can't have solid foods."

Susan was impressed. "I am a little hungry. I brought a lot of food with me from the freezer at home, but it's still mostly frozen. The soup looks good."

Leora pulled another chair up to the bed and poured from her thermos. Using the disposable bowls and spoons on Josh's tray, the three of them enjoyed the homemade vegetable broth. Susan noticed the tray of bagels and spreads.

She reached over and said to Leora, "We can't let this go to waste!"

Spreading cream cheese on her bagel, Susan relaxed. "Tell me what brings you back to Chicago. I mean, who's running your business?"

"I'm in the midst of selling my share to my partner. I think I'm moving back to Chicago, at least until I figure out if I have a good reason to stay."

Susan saw the look exchanged between Leora and her son. Josh hadn't told his family that he and Rachel were no longer a couple, so when did this other woman come into the picture?

I can see why Josh is attracted to her. She looks a little like his old fiancee, Debbie, but Debbie would never think of making soup for my Joshie. This one's probably the kind of person who makes her own soup all the time. Now, Rachel Berg, that's another story. Rachel would always be sure to do the right thing, but she'd buy the soup. And if she'd offer it to me, she'd make sure that I knew she was the one who brought it.

Josh closed his eyes again. All was well with the world. His mother was by his side, and he knew that wonderful food would soon be prepared for him at home. It looked like Leora's homemade soup had made it straight from his mother's stomach to her heart. Leora was his mom's kind of woman, and she didn't have to try very hard.

CHAPTER 55

It was Monday afternoon, and Kayla Morales was about to start teaching her sixth grade art class. The school secretary, Loretta, quietly came into the room to tell Kayla that two gentlemen were waiting for her in the office, claiming there was an emergency. Kayla immediately figured out who they were, and she asked Loretta to stay with her students while they worked on their collages.

Bobby and Will Lewisohn were sitting uncomfortably in the school's outer office. Kayla was relieved that neither of them smelled from beer and that they were dressed respectfully. They jumped up when they saw her.

"Kayla honey, now don't get all upset!" Bobby cautioned. 'We only came here to see if you found a rabbi to help Daniel."

"No, and I'm not going to try. Anything else you want to know?"

"You gotta do something. Are you gonna let him rot in jail?"

Kayla didn't know whether to laugh or scream. She decided to scream. "Your brother shot Rabbi Stein! Do the two of you shoot people when you get angry?"

Will brushed her off, "Now, don't get all snooty on us. Daniel probably didn't think the gun was loaded. It just went off by mistake."

Kayla turned to leave them. "I'm finished with Daniel, and I'm finished with you. The two of you don't want to mess with him, but you want me to do it. This conversation is over."

Rabbi Dalton, after hearing Kayla's raised voice outside his door, decided to come out of his office to find out what was going on.

"Gentlemen," Dalton said calmly, "Ms. Morales has to return to her students. May I ask if there's a problem that I can help you with? I'm Rabbi Elijah Dalton, and I'm the rabbi of the synagogue and head of the school here."

Will had nothing to lose. "I guess you heard the news about our brother, Daniel Lewisohn. He didn't mean to shoot anybody, but his gun went off by accident. We've been trying to find a rabbi to help another Jew who's in trouble. Daniel's always been a righteous Jew, so we figure that a good rabbi would be willing to stand up for him."

"It just so happens that I'm acquainted with your brother, and I have to suggest that he may not be the righteous man you're describing to me," Dalton informed them. " In fact, Ms. Morales brought Daniel to Shabbat services here a few times, but unfortunately, that didn't work out."

Even though he was surprised by Dalton's response, Will gave it one more try. "Daniel's always been under a lot of stress, with Kayla's Orthodox leanings and such. He just lost it. You know, that could happen to any of us."

Understanding the intellectual limitations and fantastical expectations of the two men standing before him, Dalton closed the conversation gently, but firmly.

"I regret that we have such different expectations for the outcome of your brother's unfortunate predicament. I'm confident that he'll receive adequate representation at his trial. I wish Daniel and the two of you well, but Ms. Morales and I must get back to work."

As Dalton returned to his office and closed the door behind him, Bobby whispered to Will, "That guy's not a real rabbi. Just because he wears that fancy suit and has his head covered, a big black dude doesn't turn into a rabbi."

Will nodded, "He's probably just a teacher, so he couldn't help us, anyway. We're outta luck."

Dalton watched as the brothers got into their truck and drove away. *At least they don't have Daniel's temper,* he thought. *The more I learn about the Lewisohns, the more I question Kayla's instincts. I know Ruth is concerned, too.*

That evening at dinner, Rabbi Dalton decided to bring up the subject of Kayla's future. The Daltons had talked about her situation at length, and they hoped that her desire for closure would work to their advantage.

"Now that Daniel's brothers know you're no longer involved with him," Dalton began, "we should probably discuss your next move."

Ruth was worried. "We want you to stay here with us until we're sure of the outcome of Daniel's trial, and after that, you can decide what's best for you."

Ruth looked at her husband and he nodded. She continued, "Kayla, I'm speaking for myself now, as if you were my own daughter."

Kayla laughed, "You're both beating around the bush. What are you trying to say?"

264 | Shapiro and Miller

"Kayla, you don't belong at Lev Shalom. You belong here. It's a good time to concentrate on your old friends whom you never see anymore, and to throw yourself into your artwork."

"And what do you think, Rabbi?" Kayla asked.

"I'm not as concerned about the synagogue you attend. I think Lev Shalom could be a fine *shul* for you. My concern is that ever since you tried to bring Daniel into your Jewish life, you have become more and more alienated from your old community."

Kayla couldn't let that go. "You mean that because I'm black, I have to stick with black friends?"

Dalton answered firmly, "That's not at all what I mean. When you moved to Chicago and came to our *shul*, you were open to both our white and black members. Our community is a working class group of people, and Lev Shalom is different from us. You're a teacher and you have aspirations to become a studio artist. I just want you to be honest with yourself."

Kayla didn't like the way the conversation was going. "With all due respect, Rabbi Dalton, Rabbi Stein was warm and welcoming to me. I can say the same for his administrator, Serena Berg. If it weren't for Daniel, I could have become happily active there. In fact, I was thinking of looking for a place to live near Lev Shalom, but I'm not even sure of that now. What I do know, is that after the school year is over, I'm going back to my family in New York for a while."

Then Kayla looked at Ruth. "You know that I respect your opinion. You want me to be happy, and you think that staying close to the two of you will resolve my problems and fix my confusion. What I really need from you is your support for whatever I decide."

The Daltons were surprised at Kayla's mention of going back to her family. "You moved here with Daniel. Don't you think you should give Chicago a chance without him? Don't run away from here only to find yourself in the place you were once eager to leave. I'm suggesting that you give yourself time to sort everything out. What I do believe is that running back home is a cop-out. You're not the same person you were when you left, and you don't want to be that same person again."

"I've been thinking about everything," Kayla sighed. "In spite of your joint advice and generosity, for now, until the school year ends, I'm going back to my own apartment. Daniel's in jail and we took care of his brothers. I just can't accept your assessment of Lev Shalom. I know you think I belong here, but I have to make that decision myself. I'm definitely going to my family in New York for winter vacation. I'll test the waters there, too."

Although Ruth had her doubts, Rabbi Dalton considered Kayla's determination. "I'm relieved that you're weighing your options and trying to get clarity about your life. Don't dismiss our ability to help you. It's important to listen to people who care about you, and we are those people."

All Kayla could answer was, "Thank you, both." Overcome with emotion, Kayla excused herself and went outside to take a walk. The Daltons looked at each other, sharing a single thought, *May God protect that headstrong girl.*

CHAPTER 56

Serena was caught by surprise and even a bit confused by the phone call she had just received from her daughter. Rachel announced that she was on her way and wanted to make sure her parents were home. Serena prayed that it wasn't bad news about Glen.

A few minutes after the call, Serena was loading the dishwasher and her husband, Herb, was watching the sports recap on TV, when they heard insistent knocking on the back door.

Rachel extended her left hand as she and Glen bounded in. "We're engaged!" the couple announced in unison.

Acutely aware of the faded warm-up suit she had on and the rubber gloves she was wearing, Serena simultaneously slammed the dishwasher door closed, whipped off her apron, ripped off her gloves, grabbed her daughter's hand and yelled, "Herb, get in here!"

Before her husband could reach the kitchen, Serena exclaimed, "I knew Glen was the one! A lawyer, just like you, Rachel! And such nice clothes, just like you, Rachel. And smart! And so handsome!"

"Mom, enough!"

Herb walked in, wearing his most comfortable sneakers, frayed sweatpants, and a snug 'Waukesha Wisconsin Berg Family Reunion' T-shirt.

Rachel was amused and took out her cell phone to capture her parents in their natural state of home fashion. "Mom, don't ever cross me because I now have proof that you don't re-apply your makeup when you're doing dishes. And, Daddy, even though I love that twenty-year-old tee, obviously it shrank at least two sizes in the dryer!"

"I think my future in-laws look perfect!" Glen laughed. "For the record, my parents still wear the sweatshirts we gave out at my Bar Mitzvah."

After extensive hugs and kisses, Serena couldn't wait to talk *tachlis* about wedding plans. Herb's contribution consisted of offering everyone a beer, but Serena pulled out a bottle of champagne she had been saving in secret, in high hopes that there would one day be the right reason to open it.

Rachel and Glen readily answered all their questions and, uncharacteristically, Rachel wanted to share all the details of Glen's proposal and their selection of the perfect engagement ring. Serena contentedly leaned back and let her daughter's happiness fill the room. Even Herb, who spent every evening glued to sports on TV, was drawn into his daughter's excitement.

Rachel did have one concern. "I want to make sure we're all on the same page. I grew up with Rabbi Halperin, and he must be the one to officiate, even if we have to bring him back from Israel. I'm sure that dear Rabbi Stein will be relieved when he learns that he's off the hook."

Serena added, "Rabbi Halperin may still be here, depending on the date you set. Bob told the board members that he'll be staying until Rabbi Stein recovers."

"I'm going to ask my family rabbi to co-officiate," Glen mentioned. "We haven't even told my parents yet."

Serena couldn't wait, "So, what date were you thinking about?"

"It depends on the honeymoon. I wanted to take Rachel to Hawaii, but that wasn't exotic enough for her," Glen laughed. "Then I said, 'How about Morocco'? But even that didn't suit your daughter. Fortunately, finances aren't a problem, so we settled on an island in the Bahamas, and it's so remote, I can't even remember its name."

"Glen, it's Erehwon Cay! We're renting a house for two weeks, and it comes with a personal chef. I already spoke to the owner with instructions to kosher the kitchen and grill."

Herb was a practical man. "I bet that costs extra, right? Does the place come with a boat? How far is it from the mainland, and what mainland are we talking about, anyway?"

Serena was practical, too. "Your decisions affect Daddy and me. Are you getting married at Lev Shalom? With Rabbi Halperin, I suppose you are, but where will the reception be?"

"As soon as my parents get the good news," Glen interjected, "my father will insist on having it at the club. Kosher catering is available, and there's valet parking. My mother will probably want to have it at a fancy hotel in the city. Honestly, I don't care. I just want to marry your daughter."

Even though Serena and Herb were secretly relieved to learn that Glen's parents, as well as Glen, seemed to be wealthy, Serena realized that they would have to coordinate plans with the Stemplers, including sharing wedding expenses. Glen's parents would probably want a lavish reception.

Herb shook Glen's hand and kissed his daughter. He excused himself and went back to the game on TV. Serena offered dessert, but Rachel and Glen were eager to give the good news to his parents. Rachel promised to call her brother from the car, assuming that he knew nothing about Glen.

As soon as they were out the door, Serena picked up the phone to call her sister and closest friends. She decided, *I'll call the Stemplers tomorrow morning and invite them over. I have a feeling that Glen's parents have a lot to learn about an Orthodox Jewish wedding. Now that Rabbi Halperin will be in Chicago for a while, it'll be easier to deal with Rabbi Stein. I wonder how Leora Halperin's going to react to the news. Isn't it ironic how things work out in the end? God must have had a hand in this!*

Rachel's call to her brother, Donnie, was short and sweet. Serena had told him all about Rabbi Stein, so he was surprised at Glen's sudden starring role in his sister's life. On speaker-phone in the car, Glen was able to introduce himself and be as likeable as possible. Donnie's wife was putting the kids to sleep, and Donnie promised that she would call Rachel during the week to get every last detail.

As predicted, the Stemplers had definite ideas about the wedding. Even though they had only met Rachel twice, they knew that she was right for their son. They were more than ready for Glen to settle down and start giving them Jewish grandchildren. The fact that their future daughter-in-law was stylish and successful was icing on the cake.

Glen's mother, Carol, was eager to meet the Bergs and decided to call them first thing in the morning. The fact that Serena and Herb would both be at work didn't occur to her. *I don't mind being late to my committee meeting at the Jewish Federation. I've waited a long time for this, and I'm going to enjoy it,* Carol thought.

Even though it was eleven o'clock at night by the time Rachel and Glen left his parents' house, Carol called her best friend, Margie, in whom she confided about her unmarried son on a regular basis. Margie had tried to set Glen up with many single women, but with no success. Finally, he had found the right one.

CHAPTER 57

Things were easier for Susan when Josh was finally home. She had just served her son a bowl of homemade chicken soup when the phone rang. "Keep eating, I'll get it!" Susan called out.

"How's the patient?" Leora asked.

Susan had not yet had a chance to fully question Josh about his relationship with Leora Halperin, but it was clear that something serious was going on between them. Susan hadn't been completely comfortable with Rachel Berg's assertive personality when they met in Chicago during the High Holidays, but at the same time, Susan wanted her son to find a strong wife.

Rachel's intentions had been more than obvious. When Josh left Boston, his goal was to learn if the rabbinate was right for him, not primarily to find a spouse. He had never been attracted to the polished, sophisticated type, and Susan had been surprised to see her son with Rachel. Leora, on the other hand, seemed a more natural match for her son.

"Leora, I'll bet you're on your way over here right now!" Susan laughed.

"I wish that were the case! Actually, I'm still in Chicago, on my way back to New York to tie things up with my business. Now that your son's in good hands I can concentrate on things there. I'll have to stay until everything's finished."

Susan took the phone into the other room in order to get information she wouldn't be able to get from her son.

"Leora, it's so nice of you to call to check up on Joshy. He's still on liquids. His appetite is back and he's eating the soup I made, so I have some time to talk. I really want to get to know you better, anyway, because it looks like you and Joshy are close. I hope you don't mind if I ask you just one or two little questions. You know how it is with boys; they're not as open with their mothers as daughters are. Or at least, that's what they tell me. I have three sons."

In comparison to Leora's own guarded mother, Susan was open and chatty. Leora wasn't the least bit offended by Susan's probing. "Ask me anything. It makes sense that we should get to know each other better. In fact, I'll probably have some questions for you, too," Leora said.

Susan was happy that Leora wanted a relationship with her. After briefing Leora about Josh's recovery and PT, she got right to the point. "So, do you think you'll be staying in New York for a long time? I mean, since your parents are still planning to move to Israel, you don't really have to rush back to Chicago, do you?"

Leora had to be diplomatic, "I want to finish up in New York as quickly as I can. I'm selling my half of the landscaping business to my former partner, who also happens to be my former fiance."

"May I ask if my son had anything to do with that decision?"

"Actually, Aaron and I broke the engagement before I came back to help my parents pack. We weren't a good romantic match, but we worked well together. The engagement kind of happened along with the business, and fortunately, we came to our senses in time. Now, I'm ready to move back home."

Susan wanted to dig deeper. "But why return to Chicago? I'm sure you have a lot of friends in New York, and just because the engagement's off, you wouldn't have to leave the business."

"That's true. If I hadn't met your son, I probably wouldn't consider moving back. I'm not at all sure this will be a permanent move, but I'm the kind of person who will chase a dream."

Susan was impressed. "I don't think I've ever had such an honest conversation with anyone I didn't really know. I'm happy that you're in my son's life."

"Well, I do have one other reason to move to Chicago. Remember, I design landscapes. The Holocaust Memorial Garden needs me, too!" Leora kidded.

Susan knew some of that story, but wasn't going to discuss any of Leora's father's involvement. She continued, "That seems to be a never-ending project. I bet your father and mother can't wait to move and leave all these unresolved matters behind."

"My mother is the one who can't wait to leave. My father has mixed feelings, and now that he has a chance to help your son, of course he's willing to do what he can. Their place in Israel is move-in ready, our house here is practically packed, and my father's home office is almost empty. If I didn't know better, I'd guess that my mother would leave for Israel while my father stays here to help the *shul*."

Susan was confused, "Are you and your father able to stay in your packed-up house if your mother leaves first?"

"Well, my mother and I haven't been getting along so well lately. She hasn't been confiding in me, but I'm sure she wouldn't go without my father. I'll bet that she's already unpacking some of their things for the duration."

"If I've learned anything in life," Susan affirmed, "it's that we never know what's going to happen next. Imagine my family's surprise when our biologist decided to become a rabbi. Believe me, I'm still adjusting! In fact, Solly, his brother, still expects him to come back to Boston to work with him. But, speaking for myself, if Joshy finds the right girl, wherever that is, I'll be the happiest person in the world."

The silence on Leora's end emboldened Susan. "I have a strong feeling that you just may be the right one."

"What makes you say that?"

"Mothers know these things. But wait, I think you called to talk to my son. Let's keep this little chat to ourselves, OK?"

Leora felt encouraged, but was careful not to push Susan further. "Mrs. Stein, I hope we'll have many more conversations about our favorite subject. Of course, I won't say anything about our private talk, but I want you to know that your honesty means a lot to me. Sometimes I have to remind myself that Josh and I have known each other a very short time and now that I'm not there, we'll both have a chance to think about things."

Susan had made up her mind. She had lived through Josh's serious girlfriends, and she was satisfied with Leora Halperin. She cautioned, "Don't think too hard, Leora! When good things happen, you have to grab them."

Leora was amused, "Mrs. Stein, that's how I got myself engaged to my business partner! I'm sure you can tell that I've set my sights on your son, but I don't really know what he's thinking."

Susan sighed, "I know my Joshy. I saw how attentive you were in the hospital, and you're sensible. My son needs somebody like you, and, besides, I saw the way he looks at you. That tells me everything. Finish what you have to do in New York and come back to Joshy as soon as you can."

Susan walked back to the bedroom and handed the phone to her son. "It's Leora. She called to check on you."

Even though Susan wanted to stick around and eavesdrop, she took the high road and carried Josh's empty soup bowl back to the kitchen.

Leora was heartened by the excitement in Josh's voice. "I feel like you've been gone a long time. I miss you. My mom's taking good care of me, but I wish you were here."

"I miss you, too, and I'm not even out of the airport! I'm glad I had a chance to talk with your mother, so I know you're in good hands."

"I heard the phone ring a while ago. So what were you talking to Mom about all that time?"

"I reassured her that once I come back to Chicago, I'm going to jump right into the Holocaust Memorial Garden project."

"Anything else?"

"The rest is classified information."

"And when you finish the Holocaust project, then what?"

"Well, I'm hoping you'll help me figure that out."

Did Josh want to go there? Yes, he did. "The most important thing for you to do when you get back is to spend time with me."

"My sentiments, exactly. Anything else on your mind?"

"I can't remember everything that happened in the hospital, but I know I haven't thanked you enough. I felt calm and safe when you were in the room."

Leora hoped it wasn't Josh's weakened condition that prompted him to display such unexpected affection, but she was willing to be optimistic.

After they hung up, Josh's mind drifted. *What is it about Leora? My mother and Serena expected me to be engaged to Rachel by now. How did I know that she was wrong for me? Rachel's smart, sexy, and religious, but she pushed me too hard, and I wasn't comfortable with her high-octane demeanor. Leora reminds me of Debbie back in Boston. If Debbie had wanted children we'd be married. So, here I am, confined to my apartment with nothing to do but daven, eat good food, stay hydrated, and endure physical therapy, while I fantasize about Leora Halperin.*

CHAPTER 58

At LaGuardia, Leora turned to grab her suitcase from the carousel and saw Aaron walking toward her. "Aaron, I didn't expect you to be here!"

"Nice to see you, too!" Aaron laughed. "When you texted me that you could get together tonight to talk about everything and start making plans about the business, I called your mother. Even though that woman never liked me, she let me know when you were landing. I figure that she was so happy that you broke up with me, she decided that it would be OK for me to pick you up."

Leora knew what her mother was doing. *Why did my mother tell Aaron anything? If she thinks that she can keep me away from Josh by getting Aaron back into my life, she's wrong. Just seeing him here makes me sure that there's no chance of that. Well, now that he's here, maybe we can meet someplace close to talk about the business, and I won't have to see him tomorrow.*

"Aaron, how about stopping for coffee now and straightening out the loose ends of dissolving the partnership?"

"I have a better idea," Aaron suggested, "I've been thinking about this, and I realize that taking over the business from you is going to be more complicated than we anticipated. I figured out a way for you to be in-volved, but not as a co-owner."

"That's not what I want, Aaron. I've decided to move back to Chicago as soon as I can. I already have somebody interested in my Manhattan apartment, and once that's finalized, I'll be ready to leave New York."

"Aren't your parents moving to Israel? Why in the world would you move back there? There's so much for you here."

"Like what? I'm tired of dealing with the business, and both of us know that our engagement was a mistake. We started out as friends, and I hope we can always stay that way."

Aaron had hoped to rekindle the relationship, but things were not going as he planned. "If you're as exhausted as I am," Aaron began, "we should continue this discussion tomorrow. Let me take you home, and I'll call you in the morning."

Instead of being relieved, Leora was disappointed. She didn't want to delay her return to Chicago any more than absolutely necessary. At the same time, there were things to sort out with Aaron, and it would be a bad idea to move too fast.

"Look, Aaron, we have to let our accountant look at everything carefully. When it gets to a lawyer, we can finalize the deal. I'm ready to do whatever makes it easiest for you to buy me out. Right now, I'll start packing everything I'll be taking to Chicago."

Driving to Leora's place, Aaron masked the silence by turning on the car radio. Both of them were saddened by the end of a romance, as well as the break-up of a flourishing business. Leora had not expected to feel that way, but sitting next to Aaron reminded her of old feelings. She didn't want to get back together with him, but her heart ached as she distanced herself from the man who had been her best friend.

Aaron had a hard time focusing as he drove. He had planned to win Leora back. Even though he had gone along with Leora's decision that the engagement was wrong for them, he was still in love with her.

As she got out of the car, Leora knew she had hurt Aaron deeply, but she was determined not to leave the relationship with any ambiguity. Tomorrow, when they would meet, it would be hard for both of them. Once they agreed on general business decisions, the lawyers could take over. Their personal separation would be much harder, and everything depended on her. A clean break was impossible, but an honest one was crucial.

While Leora was gathering her wits about her in New York, Josh back in Chicago was answering a call from his father in Boston.

"Josh, your brother, Solly, insisted that I give you a message."

"Hi, Dad, I'm doing much better now that Mom's nursing me back to health. Thanks for asking!"

"Sorry, Josh. Everybody here in Boston is worried, and Solly wants you to come home where you're safe from lunatic shooters and troublemaking congregants. For the record, I agree with him. You have a sweet set-up waiting for you right here in Solly's lab. If you don't want to work there, just come home and do the research you're meant to do. Mom called this morning and said that your job is up in the air, anyway. I know your mother, and as usual she's probably exaggerating, but really, do you even have a contract?"

"Hold it, Dad. I'm in no mood to have a debate about my future right now. I have a firm agreement with the *shul,* and I intend to honor it. If Solly wants to talk to me, he can call me himself. If you want to talk to Mom, she's in the other room and I'll call her. I'm too tired to continue this. I love you all, and I know you're worried about me, so let's talk more in a few days."

Dan wasn't finished with his son. "If you're staying in Chicago just because of the girl your mother told me about, that doesn't make sense to me."

"Mom told you about Leora Halperin?"

"Of course she did. Mom likes her and appreciates how much she helped you. I know she's in New York now, so once she closes her business, she can follow you anywhere. If the two of you are serious about each other, she'll move to Boston with you. Come home, Josh!"

Would the pushing from his family never stop? In order to control his temper, Josh called out to get his mother to talk to his father. What happened after that didn't concern him. Aggravated that even his taciturn father was on his case, Josh realized that his best option was a nap.

CHAPTER 59

After his favorite breakfast of a lox omelet with heavily-buttered rye toast, Bob Small patted his wife's rear end in gratitude and headed to Lev Shalom to strategize with Rabbi Halperin about the coming weeks while Josh was recuperating. Bob had promised Sheila he would remain controlled and focused and do everything he could to maintain peace.

When Bob came into the office, he found Serena trying to placate Bob's most unfavorite congregant, Cheryl Kleinmetz, whose daughter, Cicely, was about to celebrate her Bat Mitzvah.

Bob was a seasoned fixer, and he was proud of it. It was natural for him to take charge. *Thank God I walked in before Serena messed things up. This is what happens when there's nobody here with an ounce of common sense. Even Halperin could do a better job with this witch than Serena who gives in at the drop of a hat.*

"Serena, I'll handle this. What's the problem, Cheryl?"

Cheryl let loose, "Can't this *shul* do anything right? I have over two hundred people coming to the Shabbat service in three short weeks, and I expect at least four security guards to be on the premises. And, I'm not going to pay for it! It's not my fault that a deranged shooter broke in and practically killed Rabbi Stein. In fact, we probably need more than four. And another thing. We're paying for the *kiddush,* and we expect our family and friends to get more honors at the service than Serena told

284 | *Shapiro and Miller*

me we could have."

Bob forced a smile, "Cheryl, you know that rules are rules. Extra security is your decision, and therefore your responsibility. Rabbi Stein was only slightly wounded, and the perp's in jail. There's no danger at all. As for the honors, we have a set number that we give to all celebrants, and the other honors go to congregants who have *yahrzeits*. Got it?"

That's not what Cheryl Kleinmetz wanted to hear. "Bob, Serena and I were doing just fine before you walked in. I suggest you let us work this out."

Serena knew that Bob loved to be a hero. He was only too happy to step in. "Sorry, Cheryl, but that's not the way things work around here; not on my watch," Bob boasted.

Serena had something else to take care of. Rabbi Halperin needed to get back into his once comfortable office that had been totally packed by his wife and daughter. Instead of dealing with Cheryl Kleinmetz that morning, Serena had intended to spruce up the rabbi's office. She had to direct the maintenance staff to bring back chairs and a table that Bob and Rabbi Halperin would need that morning. Fortunately, Serena was able to leave Bob negotiating with the Bat Mitzvah girl's mother while Serena gathered some pens and pads of paper for the meeting.

Rabbi Halperin walked purposefully into the office after morning services, humming, as he used to do. Even though he dreaded seeing Mrs Kleinmetz just as much as Bob did, Halperin seized the moment to apply his rabbinic charm and, at the same time, make Bob look boorish.

"Mrs. Kleinmetz, delightful to see you! I understand that I'll have the pleasure of officiating at Cicely's Bat Mitzvah soon. I know that Cicely will deliver a splendid and meaningful *d'var Torah* after services."

Cheryl Kleinmetz turned away from Bob and focused her attention on the rabbi. "Thank God you walked in just now! Everybody's giving me such a hard time, but I know you'll understand."

"I wish I could stay to talk, Mrs. Kleinmetz, but Mr. Small and I have a very important meeting now. I'm sure you and Serena can work everything out. I'll check with her to make sure that your *simcha* goes perfectly."

Even though Halperin had trumped him, Bob was relieved that the pro took over. For his part, Halperin felt fortunate that Serena always had his back and would eventually manage the Kleinmetz case.

It was just like old times in the Halperin's office. He and Small sat facing each other, controlling their mutual animosity in order to keep things moving. Except for the two chairs and folding table Serena had set up, Halperin's office was bare. Everything of his had been packed to ship to Israel, and Bob had no desire to encourage redecorating the place until a new senior rabbi took over. Bob had made it clear that Rabbi Stein was to stay in his original office because he didn't want Stein to get any ideas.

Bob had one item on his agenda, and that was setting limits with Halperin. "The way I see it, Rabbi, is that Stein is gonna be out of commission for about a month, at most. So I figure that since you'll be taking his place, we'll just prorate his salary and pay you what he's getting."

Halperin couldn't believe what he had just heard. Ever the professional, he stood, thereby commanding the room. "Bob, I'm sure you haven't discussed this with the board. I suggest you go to them and explain that I expect my remuneration to be commensurate with my former salary. Until this matter is approved by the finance committee, I'm afraid that we can't come to any agreement. When do you think you can get back to me? Oh, let me add, I expect all my office furniture to be returned as soon as the carpet is cleaned."

Bob knew he was in a corner. "Rabbi, your furniture is in storage downstairs, and we've already hired painters to spruce up this place, not just the carpet. This unexpected emergency is hard on everybody. I'll see what I can do about the salary, and I'll postpone the painting. We'll bring your desk and chair back, but that's it. For the record, I'm going to have a hard time justifying a big salary."

"Bob, I've known you since you were a teenager, and nobody can match you for tenacity. Work out the salary issue, bring my desk back, and let me know when you're ready to talk again. Today is Monday, and Shabbat is five days away. As far as I know, there are at least two congregants in the hospital, and a *shiva* house that needs attention. Presently, Lev Shalom has no rabbi to take care of business. I'm going home now. We both know that time is of the essence."

As Halperin walked out of the office, Bob dialed the board treasurer. "Sam, I just worked out an arrangement with Rabbi Halperin. I got him to take over until Stein comes back, and he knows we're lucky he's still here. I don't like this but we're gonna have to give him his old salary while he's in charge. Can you work that out without getting the whole board involved?"

"Sorry, Bob, we'll have to call an emergency executive board meeting. Most of those guys love Halperin, so it shouldn't be a problem."

Bob got up and went to the already stressed administrator. "Serena, here's what you're gonna do, and it's gotta be done pronto. Call the executive board members and tell them we're having an emergency meeting at my house tonight at eight. Right after you do that, get Halperin's desk and chair back up here and tell the painters and rug guy they're on hold."

Serena sighed. "I'm still dealing with Mrs. Kleinmetz, who fortunately had to leave for a couple of hours. I'll do my best to contact the executive board, but the office furniture has to wait until this afternoon, and I won't leave until it's done."

Bob winked, "Serena, you're a doll!"

As he walked to his car, he dialed home. "Sheila, baby, the executive board's coming over tonight. See if you can get some snacks set up, and I'll pick up the drinks."

Always ready with homemade chocolate brownies in the freezer and blessed with a 'can-do' attitude, Sheila was up to the challenge. "Bob, it's OK to have a meeting here, but what are you up to now?"

"It's stuff with Halperin, as usual. While he's back in the saddle, he wants his old salary, and he's got me by the balls. I called Sam to see if we could finesse the money I need, but of course that man's afraid of his own shadow and won't do it the easy way. So now, I gotta do a song and dance for the executive board."

"It's not going to be a problem, Sweetie. Those guys love Halperin, and they're going to pay what he wants."

"That's what Sam said. They better come through or I'm up shit's creek."

"Bob, honey, do me a favor. When you get the pop at Mariano's, get some beer, too. If everybody's in a good mood, they'll do whatever you say."

"Beer? Are you kidding? We shouldn't even be having this meeting. By now everybody knows that I have a handle on *shul* business. I'm gonna tell 'em what we're gonna do, and they're gonna vote unanimously and go home. Period."

Sheila knew better than to try to convince Bob to make the meeting pleasant. When her husband was focused on something, it had to be done his way.

That evening, one hour after it started, the meeting adjourned. As expected, the entire group agreed to fulfill Halperin's salary demand. Naturally, Bob made it look like he was the one who wanted to be generous to Halperin, and it was easier than he thought it would be.

After everyone left and Sheila was clearing the table, Bob made the call. "OK, Rabbi," Bob stated, "Serena arranged your office furniture, and that was easy. I got you the money you wanted, and it was not easy. The first thing you gotta do is handle the Kleinmetz Bat Mitzvah, and I don't envy you. I'll swing by the office tomorrow morning to iron out details."

Halperin thought, *I bet Bob had no trouble at all meeting my old salary. He probably called the treasurer and Sam obeyed him. Bob just has to make himself the hero. As for Cheryl Kleinmetz, I've always had a wonderful relationship with that family, and Serena has probably done most of the work already.*

But, to Bob, Halperin replied, "I look forward to meeting you tomorrow morning. I'll be at services and then come to the office. It's a relief to know that Serena set up my office."

After the call, Bob was furious. He marched into the kitchen to find Sheila, "That bastard! I got him everything he wanted, and he didn't even thank me."

CHAPTER 60

It seemed as if Josh's phone had not stopped ringing from the time he had returned to his apartment from the hospital. Now, it was Rachel Berg. He was surprised to hear from her.

"Josh, I want you to know how concerned I've been about you. Remember, my fiance and I were talking to you just before you were hurt. I heard that your mother's in town to help you, so everybody is relieved that you're getting the best care possible."

"My mother has plenty of assistance. My refrigerator's full of meals and desserts from members of the *shul*. The sisterhood set up a rotation, and my mother's really impressed that so many people are helping us out."

"Well, they're not going to abandon their favorite rabbi! Even if the other women wouldn't have come through, my mother would've taken care of you. She certainly had high hopes that you'd be one of the family some day. My parents love Glen, but for some reason my mother had her eye on you from the start," Rachel admitted.

Josh laughed, "Your mother's not the only one with expectations. My mother also had hopes that I'd find a wife as soon as I came here, and she was convinced it was you."

"Well," Rachel noted, "there's a rumor going around that you now have a serious girlfriend, and things are moving pretty fast."

Josh decided to close that subject. "You know me better than that! I move slowly when it comes to romantic commitments."

"Fortunately, every man who's interested in me isn't like you. Glen can't wait to get married. As a matter of fact, I want to talk to you about that."

"Who knows when I'll be back in my office?" Josh replied. "I value our relationship, and I'll never forget how you helped me, and what you still mean to me. Now what's on your mind? I know you called about something important."

"Josh, Glen and I have discussed this with my parents, and because Rabbi Halperin, who has been my rabbi from birth, will still be in Chicago when we marry, we're asking him to officiate at the wedding. I hope you understand."

Josh wasn't surprised. "That makes perfect sense. You don't have to explain anything to me."

"Thank you," Rachel relaxed. "I have to admit that I was worried about hurting you."

"Rachel," Josh sighed, "I want you to be married to the right guy. I wasn't the right one, and now I'm glad you found him."

Rachel decided to make it perfectly clear, "Just so you know, Glen has been in love with me from the moment we met. If I hadn't wasted valuable time and emotion on someone else, we'd be married already!"

Josh smiled to himself. *Rachel hasn't gotten over the fact that I didn't adore her enough to rush to the* chupah *with her.*

"Rachel, thank you for calling," Josh yawned. "I wish I had more energy, but I've been sleeping a lot. I look forward to dancing at your wedding, and I think you know that I sincerely welcome Glen into the *shul*."

When Susan Stein came into the room with a cup of herbal tea and some crackers, she found her son sound asleep with the cellphone still in his hand.

CHAPTER 61

Elijah Dalton had been worried about Josh and decided it was time to visit him at home. He knew that if he told Kayla, she would insist on accompanying him, and that wasn't what he wanted.

Rabbi Dalton had taken a real liking to to the young rabbi and hoped that their collegial relationship would turn into friendship, unlike Rabbi Halperin's cool cordiality. Among other things, Dalton wanted to talk to Josh about Kayla's possible return to Bet Hillel for the time being and her eventual move home to New York, where her family still lived.

The visit was enjoyable for both rabbis. They shared pulpit anecdotes, and because Josh was having one of his better days, he was eager to prolong the visit. He quickly invited his mother to join the conversation, knowing that the experience would be unique for her. Susan found herself charmed by the warm and witty visitor. On his part, Dalton appreciated Susan's good-humored doting. It was clear that Josh was in good hands, and that Susan loved every minute of it.

While he was still on the north side of the city, Dalton decided to treat himself to dinner at Kalman's. True to form, Kalman welcomed him effusively, and led him to a center table, the better to display his exotic patron. Even though Dalton understood Kalman's intent, he cheerfully played along. Kalman pulled up a chair.

"Rabbi, what a pleasure to see you again. I bet I can guess what brings you to our neighborhood!"

"Obviously, I came for the food! Why else?"

"Since you put it that way, let me treat you to our featured appetizer, vegetarian spring rolls. It's a new item on our menu, and I want your opinion. But tell me, Rabbi, do you mean you came all the way here for dinner and didn't visit Rabbi Stein?"

Dalton nodded in feigned seriousness, "You're right. I definitely should have paid a visit to the recovering rabbi! What was I thinking?"

"You really didn't go see Rabbi Stein? Well, no matter. He's getting plenty of attention. I've already delivered three meals to his apartment from his admirers. That's in addition to the family-size lasagna I personally sent."

Dalton had come to the clearing-house of neighborhood gossip, and he did not want to be one of the subjects. He decided to get serious. "Kalman, of course I'm coming from Rabbi Stein's place. He was definitely well-fed and content. The combination of his mother's home cooking and your inestimable contributions seem to be doing the trick."

Kalman leaned conspiratorially forward, "Just between us, Rabbi, are you aware that Rachel Berg, who everybody thought would end up with Rabbi Stein, is out of the picture? I hear that Rabbi Halperin's daughter, Leora, took her place."

Dalton was uncomfortable and knew better than to get chummy with the restaurant owner. "I'm sorry if I gave the impression that I'm on intimate terms with Rabbi Stein. His love life is his own business, and that's the way it should be. Don't you agree?"

Kalman got the message and returned to work; he certainly wanted to appear professional in front of this distinguished man. "I'll be back with the spring rolls while you decide what to order. I bet we'll be seeing more of you now that you and Rabbi Stein are friends."

"You can count on it, Kalman. Next time, I'll bring Mrs. Dalton with me."

"When I have the pleasure of meeting your wife, dessert's on the house!"

CHAPTER 62

Leora, lying in bed completely exhausted at the end of the day in her New York apartment, thought about the past weeks. Dealing with the lawyers was nothing compared to handling her former fiance. Aaron tried to make himself indispensable by turning himself into her personal chauffeur, treating her to gourmet kosher meals and calling every morning to make plans for the day. Obviously, Aaron had put his personal and professional life on hold in order to be with her. He honestly believed that if he proved himself worthy, she'd change her mind about moving to Chicago.

When Leora and Aaron first met, it was a beautiful fall day at the Brooklyn Botanic Garden. They were wearing name tags to be identified as participants in a landscaping symposium. Aaron was sporting a brightly colored crocheted *kippah,* and at noon when it was time to break for lunch, the other participants went to the cafeteria. Leora and Aaron ended up walking together and discovered they were both scouting for something kosher to eat. They found a bench and got to know each other as they talked and snacked on chips.

The symposium lasted three days, during which time Leora and Aaron bonded. The fact that they were both religiously observant and shared a dream of working outdoors led them to believe that they belonged together. It took two years to establish and grow their business. Leora appreciated Aaron's devotion to her every need, and she admired his work ethic and big dreams. Aaron, on his part, was sure he had found his ideal mate in this creative and like-minded woman.

One day, they were strolling along the path where they had first met. Aaron romantically dropped to one knee and proposed. He plucked a vine and fashioned it into a ring. Leora was caught off-guard and was captivated by his passion. Aaron seemed to meet her criteria for a life partner. They got along in business, were physically compatible, and were in sync religiously.

Predictably, Bunny Halperin was less than thrilled with Leora's choice. Bunny felt that her daughter was 'settling' instead of choosing. Aaron didn't seem quite as intelligent or cultured as her daughter. Even though his family was well off and Orthodox, their lack of education and culture disappointed the Halperins. Was Bunny a snob, as Leora complained? Maybe so, but Bunny believed that her daughter would regret her future with Aaron and be bored by his family.

As Leora lay there, considering her present situation, she was over-whelmed with mixed emotions. In another week, the attorneys would be finished with her part of the business negotiations, and she could walk away with plenty of money. There were only a couple of months left on her lease, and she had a sublet in place. On the surface, she should have been relieved, and even overjoyed. Yet, she was breaking the heart of the man who loved her. But she knew she had to do it.

She didn't question whether Josh Stein was the right man for her. Everything about him pleased her. She knew the rabbinic life and she liked it. She and her brothers had grown up in a happy, fulfilled family. Leora respected the kind of life they lived and the kind of people they were. When she walked into Josh's office, she was warmed by the familiarity of it. Josh's manner was informal, but his suit and tie reflected the dignity of an Orthodox congregational rabbi, like her father.

Even more than that, she felt a powerful chemistry that she couldn't explain. She simply wanted to be with Josh. He was easy to talk to and unguarded with her, but not fawning like Aaron. Leora was happy that her 'credentials' as a rabbi's daughter negated the necessity of Josh having to explain how things work in his life as a rabbi.

Among other things, Leora was sure that she'd be able to successfully complete the Holocaust Memorial Garden to everyone's satisfaction. She looked forward to helping Josh handle people like Bob Small. The partnership she and Josh could have was different from the one with Aaron. That liaison started as a business and took an unfulfilling romantic turn. With Josh, it was just the opposite. Her physical and emotional attraction to him would enable her to build a more meaningful life.

Rather than becoming more drowsy, Leora felt energized. She got out of bed and went to the window. There were still a lot of people on the street. She put on sweats and sneakers, took the elevator down and started to walk. She was happy.

It was almost midnight by the time Leora returned to her apartment, too late to make any phone calls. In the morning she would call Aaron first, her parents second, and then Josh.

The phone calls went more smoothly than Leora had expected. When she told Aaron that the lawyers would handle the remaining details and she was leaving New York as soon as possible, Aaron begrudgingly accepted her decision; he didn't even suggest that they stay in touch. Leora wasn't worried about him and didn't feel guilty. It would only be a short time until a dozen wonderful women would pursue him.

When she called her parents in Chicago, Leora was prepared for an argument. Her father wasn't surprised. After seeing her interaction with Josh in the hospital and aware that she was eager to get involved in the Holocaust Memorial project, he had anticipated the news. Ephraim Halperin had always been proud of his daughter's independence and believed she had a sensible head on her shoulders. He knew that she was both sensitive and thick-skinned enough to be a congregational *rebbit-zin*.

Bunny, on the other hand, didn't approve, but she accepted the fact that Leora was determined to make changes in her life. Unlike other mothers, Bunny understood only too well the difficulties her daughter would encounter, if indeed she ended up with Josh. Leora had a habit of chasing her dreams, but not always fulfilling them. So, when she called to announce her plans of returning to Chicago for good, Bunny tried to concentrate on everything but that.

Josh was overjoyed and relieved to get Leora's phone call. He couldn't wait to see her again and hoped to be fully on his feet by the time she returned. Maybe he'd even meet her at the airport with a bouquet of roses. Josh wanted to surprise Leora with a romantic gesture. He wanted his future to be with her.

CHAPTER 63

Leora steadily closed the book on her life in New York. She found a reliable moving company, and spent hours on the computer looking for a place to live within walking distance of Lev Shalom. Even though her parents (who were sure that she would change her mind about Chicago after a few months) might have offered her their home temporarily, Leora wanted to find her own place.

After several false starts, Leora decided to enlist the help of Serena Berg, who knew everything about the neighborhood. Serena, who had always liked Leora and was thrilled that Rachel had found her *bashert,* was honored to be asked and trusted. Once Kalman became aware of Leora's search, he jumped at the opportunity to get involved, and he was successful. Before the week was out, Leora rented a two bedroom apartment close to Kalman's restaurant.

"Serena!" Kalman had announced, "I found the perfect place for Leora Halperin! It's so close to my restaurant, she can come here all the time!"

"Great, Kalman. Can I see it soon? In fact, I'll Skype Leora while I walk through it."

"I have to be there!" Kalman stated, self-importantly. "One of my customers is moving, and she's doing me a big favor by letting me show it to somebody before it goes public."

Serena did not relish the thought of going slowly through an apartment with Kalman offering his commentary along the way, while at the same time, Leora would have questions and comments of her own. But, in spite of her trepidation, it worked. Leora loved the place, and Kalman was proud to be the matchmaker. He was aware, too, that he had scored some extra points with the Lev Shalom administrator.

In passing, Serena mentioned that the future residence was close to Rabbi Stein's place. When Leora acknowledged that tidbit, Kalman was canny enough not to comment, but Serena saw him raise his eyebrows.

Leora threw herself into packing. It was stressful, hard to decide what to keep and what to discard, but exciting, too. She hadn't yet eaten, and she was exhausted. When her cellphone rang, her first impulse was to let it go, but she saw that Rachel Berg was calling.

"Rachel, what a surprise! I guess you know I'm in New York, not Chicago."

"That's why I'm calling. I haven't seen you since Josh was shot, and I really wanted to talk to you. You and I go way back, Leora, and my mother told me that you're moving here. I assume that Josh is the real reason, and I have to tell you that he's the kind of man who has a hard time making a commitment. When I think about it, you probably assume that you're the right kind of partner for him because you're the easy-going type. But be careful."

"Look, Rachel, you know what a realist I am. I've broken my engagement with my business partner, Aaron, and I'm leaving here for good. Aaron was ready to get married, but I accepted his proposal for the wrong reasons. You and I are about the same age, so you know that it's time for me to make some serious decisions about my life, and I guess that's what motivated me. I don't know what's going to happen between

Josh and me, but I'm determined to pursue it."

"Well, good luck with that! I have to admit that he's an exceptional man in many ways."

Leora took the opportunity to clarify her decision. "Rachel, I want you to know that I never would have considered getting close to Josh if you and he were serious. When my mother and I first went to pack my father's office, I was definitely attracted to Josh, but I was planning to go back to New York. There are many more eligible observant Jewish men to meet in the east."

"I know what you mean, Leora. Honestly, if I were in your place, I'd stay in New York instead of waiting in Chicago for Josh Stein. And, while we're on the subject, your father has agreed to officiate at my wedding. Once you get to know Glen, you'll love him. I hope you'll come to our wedding and that things work out for you, too."

CHAPTER 64

Bunny Halperin was in a dark mood. Now that her husband had agreed to stay at Lev Shalom as long as necessary, she was stuck. Not only that, but Leora was throwing her business away just to come back to Chicago to chase Josh Stein. Bunny hadn't approved of Leora's New York fiance, but this was even harder to understand. Leora would have to share Josh's responsibilities and stress if they got married. Although Bunny knew it was irrational, it surely felt as if God was testing her for some reason.

As Bunny was going through her jewelry, deciding what to unpack for the Chicago duration, her mind wandered back to the High Holiday diamond necklace fiasco. In her present state of mind, she began to obsess about it.

When Bunny diminished her husband's debt by selling her most valuable necklace to an upscale auction house in New York, in her wildest dreams she never thought she would see that necklace again. Unbelievably, flashy Sheila Small, who wouldn't know a Bulgari from a Swarovski, strutted down the *shul* aisle with that treasure displayed upon her ample chest.

Bunny finally figured out how the necklace ended up around Sheila's neck. Sheila's show-off husband, Bob, must have purchased it and convinced her to wear it at the very time the maximum number of people would notice it. Bunny never would have worn such an outstanding piece of jewelry to *shul*. That necklace was meant for grand events: weddings, museum openings, or celebratory dinners, and not a High Holiday service.

Bunny's obsessive thoughts continued. *I'm not going to let it go! I don't want my necklace back, but I'm going to make sure that Sheila, who didn't mean to hurt me, knows that, in fact, she did.*

Bunny had to talk to Sheila. She called to ask if they could meet to talk about something important. Sheila, assuming that Bunny wanted to improve the relationship between their husbands, readily agreed. Aware that the Halperin home was in disarray, she invited Bunny to her place.

That afternoon, over homemade apple cake and coffee, the two women started with small talk. After five minutes, Sheila asked, "So, Bunny, I have a feeling that you didn't just want to spend the afternoon eating cake with me. Am I right?"

"I do have something to tell you that will surprise you, and it has nothing to do with Lev Shalom. It's personal."

Sheila couldn't imagine Bunny sharing anything personal. It wasn't her style. "I'm all ears, and if I can do anything to help you, you know I will."

"You and I are very different," Bunny began, "so please try to understand me. It's about the necklace you wore on Rosh Hashanah."

"Do you think it made everybody jealous? I knew it would stand out and maybe other people would feel bad that they didn't have such nice jewelry, but Bob insisted. It was a special gift to me that he bought from some fancy auction house in New York. I don't even know how much he paid for it, but I bet it was too much!"

Bunny had no reason to be angry with Sheila, or even with Bob, but she impulsively continued. "That necklace once belonged to me. I, too, received it as a special gift. I sold it to help my husband repay the Holocaust money he borrowed. Can you imagine the emotions I experienced when I saw you parading down the aisle on Rosh Hashanah? It was all I could do to maintain my composure."

If Sheila had not noticed the tears in Bunny's eyes, she would have responded differently. Sheila was offended by Bunny's characterization of her as ostentatious, but she tried to respond with humor.

"I guess I couldn't help myself, Bunny. You know me, when I have something beautiful, I just want to share it!"

Bunny wasn't willing to accept an excuse, "That's what's wrong with you, Sheila. Rosh Hashanah, to you, is the same as opening day at a classic car show. And an irreplaceable necklace is the same to you as a common cubic zirconia bauble."

Now, Bunny was really crying, but she had gone too far. This was a cruel side of Bunny Halperin that Sheila had never experienced.

Sheila exploded, "What a mean, spiteful thing to say to me! For your information, I know only too well the difference between real and fake diamonds, and you're the only person I know who would be cruel enough to say what you just said to me! You know what, Bunny, you're a snob, and I'm not the only one who thinks so!"

"I didn't know this about you before," Bunny blubbered, "but you and your husband are two of a kind. You think that throwing your money around excuses your bad behavior and despicable manners. Well, it's not OK with me! You, Sheila Small, are a nouveau-riche wannabe!"

Sheila realized that Bunny was falling apart, and she was embarrassed for her. Instinctively, Sheila knew that she had to be kind.

"Bunny, you remember that Bob and I started out with nothing. We don't have the great educations and culture you and your husband have. We just do our best to help the *shul* and try to fix whatever we can. So, this is what I just decided. I'm giving your necklace back to you because you deserve it, and you know when to wear it better than I do. I'll figure out what to tell Bob."

Now it was Bunny who felt awful. She had lost her composure, and with it her self-respect, and she couldn't stop crying. What was happening to her? Her world was falling apart, and she was taking it out on poor Sheila Small. Who was the classier person now?

Neither woman knew what to say next. Sheila refilled the coffee cups, and both of them drank in awkward silence. Each was waiting for the other to clear the air.

Bunny had been in difficult circumstances before, but this confrontation was her own doing, and she knew she had to fix it.

"Sheila, I know you would never intentionally hurt me, and I shouldn't be taking my frustrations out on you. I'm not comfortable sharing personal problems, and I've trained myself over the years to behave rationally and not show emotion, no matter what. I've listened to people complaining about my husband's sermons. I've smiled when jealous congregants commented about our valuable manuscript collection. I've hosted sisterhood luncheons when I had a splitting headache. Our children have been criticized for everything from their clothing to their reluctance to volunteer when others got paid. Sheila, the life of a congregational *rebbetzin* is not easy, but I did it for almost fifty years. And now all I want to do is leave, but I can't."

309 | The Rabbi's in Trouble

Sheila was overcome with compassion. "You're a perfect *rebbitzin,* Bunny. When I was in the *shul* youth group, all of the girls wanted to be like you, and you were always nice to us. I remember when you taught us to bake *challah* and taught us songs at Sunday school. You were the best!"

Bunny couldn't respond. She took Sheila's hand in hers. "You're a good person, Sheila. I don't know why I said those things and took my problems out on you. The necklace looks great on you. Wear it in good health. Let's forget that this conversation took place, please."

"No, Bunny, I'm glad you came over. I won't forget the conversation, and I swear on a stack of bibles that I won't repeat it."

CHAPTER 65

After Susan Stein ended an impatient call from her husband back in Boston, she brought Josh's dinner to the table. She had been in Chicago until her son was able to move around more easily, and she was planning to return to her family in the next few days. She had hoped that Josh, after such a frightening experience, would come to his senses and agree to leave Lev Shalom.

"Solly is just waiting for the day when you come home and join him in the lab. It's crazy for you to stay here, and if it has anything to do with Leora Halperin, that's not a good enough reason. If the two of you are meant to be together, bring her to Boston. Joshy, you know as well as I do that you'll be safer in Solly's lab than on the *bimah,* where any crazy person can take a shot at you for no good reason."

Josh had heard this speech too many times. He was tired of stating his case, so he concentrated on his sandwich.

Susan was sure that something would happen to Josh again. She hated hearing reports of random acts of violence to innocent people. If Josh wouldn't come home, she'd have to check on him every single day, no matter what.

"Worrying about me won't keep me safe, Mom. I'm learning a lot here and I enjoy it. I have to live my own life. I couldn't have had a better, more loving caretaker than you, and now I'm better. It's time for you to go back to Dad and Ben, who need you more than I do."

Susan was torn, but she had prepared to leave. "There's plenty of food in your freezer, and I bought you some fresh fruit. Serena told me that meals will continue to come from the congregants for a while."

After a short pause, Susan added cautiously, "I guess when Leora Halperin moves back, she'll take over for me, right?"

Josh joked, "Let's call her and find out!"

"This is no time to make fun of me, Joshy. I'm serious. I refuse to leave unless I know that help is on the way. Daddy said we should hire somebody to come in to clean and make sure you keep doing your physical therapy."

Josh had had enough. "Mom, I can take care of myself now. I'll be back at work soon, and if Leora or anyone else wants to treat me like a king, as you do, I'll welcome the attention."

Susan took a minute to get a good look at her son. She saw a handsome, underweight, optimistic man, and she was proud of him. In her heart, she prayed that he'd be safe and secure. She did what always worked for her when she was stressed. It was time to start the soup.

CHAPTER 66

Josh had been looking forward to returning to the morning *minyan* at Lev Shalom, and the Monday after his mother left, he drove himself to *shul* where he reunited with his favorite congregants, the dwindling group of Holocaust survivors who were the core of the daily services. Rabbi Halperin, who had been attending every day, greeted him warmly, but hurried out of the room after *davening*, while Josh stayed to catch up on everything he had missed. He finally had the opportunity to thank them personally for their calls and donations, and he was intensely aware of the survivors' growing frailty. He treasured being with them.

Although Josh didn't yet have enough stamina to fully resume his rabbinical role, he couldn't resist stopping in the *shul* office before returning home. When Serena spotted him, she jumped up to welcome him.

"Rabbi Stein, I didn't think you'd be back so soon! Are you sure you're up to this?"

"I've missed being part of the morning *minyan,* and now that my mother has gone back to Boston, she can't keep me down."

"I'm a mother, too, don't forget! As happy as I am to see you, I advise you to head home! You know, of course, that Rabbi Halperin's staying until we're all sure that you're completely recovered."

Josh was about to defend his belief that he was fine, when Rabbi Halperin appeared at Serena's desk.

"Rabbi Stein," Halperin began, "I didn't expect to see you in the office, although it was encouraging to *daven* with you this morning at services. Now that you're here, come into my office for a few minutes and we can catch up."

Josh and Serena shared a quick smile and Josh turned to follow the rabbi.

"Make yourself comfortable, Rabbi Stein. I must say you're looking well, but I assume that you must be healing from more than the gunshot wound itself. Am I correct?"

Josh nodded. "I have to admit that I had a certain amount of anxiety when I came to Lev Shalom this morning. You know how we always advise congregants to work through their fears? Now that I'm on the other side, I'll be much more sympathetic to people who are frightened and anxious, because now I'm one of them."

"Believe it or not," Halperin offered, "Coming back under the present circumstances, and after clearing the air with a certain detractor, I've had my own moments of trepidation. But that's all behind us now. Rather than keeping you here too long, let me get right to the point."

Josh leaned forward, "Please do."

"As you know, the board has asked me to stay until they feel that you're ready to resume full interim responsibilities. In spite of my wife's hesitation, we'll be in Chicago as long as necessary. I understand that our daughter is moving back from New York, so that offers us an incentive to remain for a while. I'm willing to do this so that you can have a *refuah shelemah,* a complete recovery. That's why I allowed Bob Small to convince me to stay."

Josh wanted to respond to Halperin's veiled narcissism, but he answered without sarcasm. "Rabbi Halperin, I appreciate your sacrifice and I thank you!" Josh realized that what he actually owed Halperin was a greater form of gratitude. He had fathered the amazing Leora.

CHAPTER 67

By the time Leora returned to Chicago several weeks later, Josh was able to spend more time at Lev Shalom, slowly resuming his duties. He began hospital visits and leading services at *shiva* houses. During these weeks, there was one unfolding tragedy. Moish, who had cheerfully welcomed Josh on his first day at the Lev Shalom morning *minyan,* was hospitalized. Josh visited him every day, and when the end came, Josh led the *davening* at Moish's *shiva* every morning and evening. Moish's one wish had been to be present at the dedication of the Holocaust Memorial Garden, and the fact that he did not experience his dream, added to Josh's sense of loss and regret.

Rabbi Halperin wisely stepped aside to let Josh mourn with Moish's family. The few remaining survivors, with whom Rabbi Halperin had become more and more distant during the Holocaust Memorial debacle, bonded even more deeply with Josh. They knew that the young rabbi would do everything in his power to finish the project before it was too late for them.

Things between Leora and Josh were different now, and Leora couldn't wait to move into her own place. Each of them was aware of a tacit agreement that they were a couple, although it was not yet publicly expressed. Leora's parents had no choice but to accept the fact that Leora spent every day at Lev Shalom, working on the Holocaust Garden, sharing lunch with Josh (Bunny learned that her daughter prepared and packed a bag of sandwiches and fruit every morning), and frequently spending the evening with him. They often sat together. Josh studied, read history, and wrote sermons, while Leora read archaeology mysteries and studied gardening catalogues and landscape manuals.

Each of Leora's parents offered unsolicited comments about the relationship. Leora listened patiently, secure in her own decision.

Bunny never tired of trying, "Did you ever think why synagogues prefer not to hire unmarried rabbis? Synagogue boards know that women throw themselves at these men. Leora, are you that kind of woman? Do you really want everyone in the congregation to gossip about you? Beside all that, you aren't the circumspect type. What kind of *rebbitzin* would you be? Don't look at me that way; you know I'm right, and I say this because I love you and I don't want you to be hurt."

Ephraim Halperin took a different approach, "I see that you and Rabbi Stein have become close. He's a fine young man, but will he be a successful congregational rabbi on his own when I'm not here to guide him? I caution you to take your time to see how he weathers the storms that will definitely appear as soon as I leave."

Leora had the same response for both of them, "Even when you've had serious reservations, you've learned that I make my own choices. I'm not going to hurry into another relationship. That's why I sold my share of the business and broke my engagement to Aaron. I catch myself before I fall. That's what I've always done, and that's what I'll always do."

At last, the Holocaust Memorial Garden was ready to be dedicated. The significant donation from Bob and Sheila Small enabled Leora to complete the halted project that had been initiated by the late Nathan Wohl.

The dedication ceremony was more poignant than anyone had expected. James Traub, now a feature columnist at *The Chicago Journal,* wrote a lengthy description of the event in the Sunday edition. It was replete with wonderful color photographs of the survivors, the Smalls, the Halperins, and Rabbi Joshua Stein standing with Leora Halperin.

Among the candid photographs, there was one of Lev Shalom's administrator with her husband, daughter, and future son-in-law. Community rabbis were captured together in feigned amity, with Rabbi Elijah and Ruth Dalton front and center. Bob Small had instructed Serena to contact the Chicago media to make sure the event was covered. Traub appeared with Jenny, his photographer, which pleased Bob, who dismissed their previous unpleasant interaction. Bob knew the reporter would milk the event to the max, and that's what the *shul* president wanted.

Bob dedicated the Garden to the Lev Shalom survivors, and made special mention of his immigrant parents, the late Nathan Wohl, and the recently deceased Moish Graubart. Rabbi Halperin spoke briefly and recited selected psalms, declaring the Garden a holy spot, and likening it to other Jewish memorials. Josh had been invited to speak, but he declined. Leora, too, although she could have been the star, stayed out of the spotlight. It was Bob's show, and Bob deserved it.

Bunny was proud of her daughter's accomplishment. Leora had finished the project that her father had mishandled, and now Bunny prayed that his error could be put to rest. Leora had a healthy sense of right and wrong. She had no idea what her father had done. She hadn't taken on the Garden project to exculpate his wrongdoing, but rather in response to a need that she could uniquely fulfill.

Bunny looked at her daughter. Leora seemed so happy standing next to Josh. There was a comfort between them that kindred spirits share. Bunny, in her many years as a pulpit *rebbitzin* had rarely seen this closeness, but when she did feel it, she knew that the couple would be best friends, as well as lovers. There was no doubt that Leora and Josh had that bond.

James Traub had achieved his new position at the newspaper for a reason. He was first and foremost an aggressive reporter. Scanning the crowd, he noted the convenient proximity of all the players who had been present in his blockbuster expose of the Lev Shalom shooting. He lost no time in grabbing Josh's attention. Now, he was determined to dig deeper for a follow-up of the case.

Traub began, "I'm happy to see that you're up and about! Out of curiosity, when do you expect to be called to testify against the shooter?"

Josh wouldn't play into Traub's hands. "This isn't the time or place to discuss Mr. Lewisohn. I have a feeling that you know more about the case than I do, so I wonder what's behind your question."

Traub laughed, "Rabbi Stein, you could be an investigative reporter yourself. You're right. What I really want to know is if Daniel Lewisohn or his brothers have contacted you. I did some snooping about that family, and I wasn't surprised at anything I learned. In fact, I bet they had the nerve to ask you to request leniency."

"Do you really believe that they would try something like that when the shooting was witnessed by so many credible witnesses?"

"Of course I believe it. What I also found out is that Lewisohn has this amazing fiancee who's well connected with Rabbi Elijah Dalton, and I see him across the room. As you know, he's a big shot in Chicago, and maybe Lewisohn's girlfriend asked him to put in a good word for your shooter."

"Mr. Traub, put your fishing pole away. I'm not interested in pursuing this conversation."

Before Josh could extricate himself, Traub threw a curveball. "Maybe you can help me just a bit. It has come to my attention that Lewisohn's fiance also has some kind of a relationship with you and Lev Shalom. Word on the street is that she's the connection between the shooter and you."

Josh searched the area for Leora. "Someone important is waiting for me. Before I leave you, I'd like to make two suggestions. First, don't bother Rabbi Dalton, and second, don't get involved with the Lewisohn brothers."

As Josh walked away, Traub predictably headed directly toward Elijah Dalton, who was standing with his wife. They were chatting with a small group of Lev Shalom congregants, including Rachel Berg and her fiance, Glen Stempler.

Traub took the opportunity to eavesdrop, hoping to overhear information that he knew would not be forthcoming if he pushed too hard. He had interviewed Rabbi Dalton on several occasions in the past and knew him to be an insightful, articulate, and honest man, but not a gossip. Traub was rewarded when he heard Josh Stein's name mentioned by someone in the group.

The good-looking redhead, dressed in the latest fashion, was holding court. "Seems like Rabbi Stein has found his future *rebbitzin*! Don't look now but would you believe that they're actually holding hands in public!"

Rabbi Dalton stepped in, "I see all of your heads turning toward Rabbi Stein, so you will note that there is no hand-holding taking place. Of course," he laughed, "Rabbi Stein is standing quite close to that young lady, so I can see how Miss Berg could innocently misinterpret the situation."

"Let me step in here just to clarify the so-called misinterpretation," Glen interjected, attempting to maintain a straight face. "I am privileged to know Miss Berg intimately, and I have never witnessed this fine attorney misinterpreting anything. Therefore, I believe, that the Rabbi and Leora Halperin are indeed holding hands."

Once again, all eyes in the group turned toward Josh and Leora. Rabbi Dalton, although enjoying the light-hearted banter, knew better than to continue to be part of it.

"Please excuse Ruth and me, but I haven't had a chance to speak to Rabbi Stein for some time. I think you'll all agree that he looks well, considering the trauma he's been through. I've seen too much violence in my time, and some people don't heal as quickly. It helps that Rabbi Stein is young and brave. Besides, he's not the kind of man who will let an unhinged person stop him."

Traub grabbed his chance to join the group. "I was getting a drink, and as I passed by, I couldn't help hearing you mention the shooting. Can anyone tell me anything about that guy, Lewisohn, who shot Rabbi Stein?"

Before Dalton walked away, he decided to alert the group, "Let me introduce *The Journal's* star reporter, James Traub."

Turning to him, Dalton warned, "Mr. Traub, your reputation got a surprise boost when your coverage of the shooting made the Sunday front page, with pictures galore. Now I'm asking you not to sensationalize this festive event for another scoop."

"With all due respect, Rabbi, my job is precisely to maximize a scoop whenever I find one. It's interesting that you seem determined to keep me from asking questions. I know that you are in some way connected to Daniel Lewisohn."

Ruth Dalton wisely shielded her husband from talking about Kayla or their connection to Daniel. She took her husband's arm, and whispered, "Elijah, let's go speak to Rabbi Stein before we leave."

CHAPTER 68

James Traub watched the Daltons walk toward Josh who was deep in conversation with Sheila and Bob Small. A good-looking young woman wearing a black turtleneck sweater, long paisley skirt and high boots was standing with them. Her most outstanding feature, however, was her long curly chestnut hair. She wasn't a classic beauty by any means, but there was something alluring about her, and she was standing close to Stein--or was Stein standing close to her?

Traub had caught part of the conversation between the Daltons and Rachel Berg, and he identified Stein's companion. That sexy woman must be Rabbi Halperin's daughter, Leora! This might be another interesting Lev Shalom story. What Byzantine plot led Halperin's daughter to an attachment with her father's likely replacement? It had to be more than her landscaping expertise, and what did the Halperins think about this liaison? At the same time, Traub realized that it would be impossible to get anyone, except possibly Rachel Berg, to enlighten him. He headed back to her.

Traub used his most engaging smile and tone as he began. "Miss Berg, you're probably the only person both able and willing to answer my questions."

"Careful, honey!" Glen warned. "The guy's a reporter. You might end up on the front page of *The Chicago Journal*!"

Traub now had his entree. "And Miss Berg would look pretty good there! May I continue?"

Rachel turned toward Traub, welcoming his questions. "Glen, you know that I love challenges. OK, Mr. Traub, shoot!"

Glen laughed, "Rachel, honey, 'shoot' might not be the best word to use in the present context."

Rachel continued without hesitation, "Mr. Traub, feel free to ask me anything."

"What's with that bohemian-type woman standing with Rabbi Stein?" Traub asked.

"That's Rabbi Halperin's daughter, Leora. You're of at least average intelligence, so you do the math!"

Traub feigned surprise, "Rabbi Stein and Leora Halperin? Well, I can see how he could be attracted to her. She looks like she's pretty low-maintenance. You know, the landscaping, the earthy look, like that. Am I right?"

Rachel shot back, "Let me tell you something about Rabbi Stein. Forget low-maintenance; the only kind of woman who would put up with his lifestyle has to be zero maintenance!"

Glen put his arm around his fiancee. " Rachel, let's just say that Stein isn't as lucky as I am."

Traub wanted more of the story from Rachel. "Were you and Leora friends growing up?"

Against Glen's obvious wishes, Rachel answered, "As teenagers, we were in the same school and Jewish youth groups, but eventually I understood that our paths would separate. I mean, I'm a Chicago lawyer and Leora plants gardens."

Traub decided to challenge her. "If you're talking about the Lev Shalom Holocaust Memorial Garden, I'd have to say that she managed to complete a complicated project. It was on hold for a couple of years. And, I think that she had a fairly large business on the east coast."

Rachel smiled slyly, "Let me sum it up for you. I work with my head; Leora works with her hands."

Glen had to prevent Rachel from continuing. He looked at his Patek Phillippe. "We have to leave now, honey. I'm sure Mr. Traub has more important stories to chase. Let's go."

In spite of herself, Rachel allowed Glen to prevent her from revealing the antipathy she felt toward Leora and the disappointment she had experienced with Josh.

Rachel could have easily told more to Traub, but Glen was the obstacle, and the reporter wouldn't get anything else from this source. He would have to stretch and embellish the memorial dedication story without benefit of more behind-the-scenes dirt.

CHAPTER 69

After everyone had left the memorial ceremony, Josh asked Leora to come to his office. She saw that apparently the long afternoon had been too much for him, and she grabbed a couple of cups of punch and followed him. They sat quietly at the round table, slowly sipping their drinks in comfortable silence. Leora knew that Josh had a lot on his mind.

Finally, Josh began. "Leora, you're the only person I'm telling this to. I haven't even discussed it with my family. It's about my relationship with Lev Shalom."

"Go on."

"Bob Small made it clear from the outset that I'm not guaranteed the position of senior rabbi, and the truth is I don't know if I'm even ready for it. In the short time I've been here, I've worked as hard as I can to prove myself. Not only that, but I've inadvertently acquired an enormous amount of knowledge about the intricacies and politics of a big, prosperous *shul*. I dread countless weeks ahead being nice to visiting rabbis from all over, who will be vying for the senior position."

"Keep going."

"What you don't know is that I've been researching positions in smaller congregations -- places I can make a difference and continue to learn

330 | *Shapiro and Miller*

and grow."

Leora nodded, "I have a few questions, Josh."

"You wouldn't be Leora if you didn't!"

"If you could, would you stay at Lev Shalom? What if you're offered a permanent position here? Is it fear or is it ego that is making you look elsewhere?"

"I'm not sure. I didn't expect to get such a rapid education in the gritty parts of *shul* life. I truly believe that I'm ready to lead a congregation, but not this one."

Leora was clearly surprised at Josh's self-assessment. She smiled drily, "And now that I've moved back here, you're leaving?"

"Oh, I guess I'd better tell you the rest. I'm taking you with me wherever I go!"

"You're what?"

"Leora, I won't take you just anywhere. I've applied to a few small *shuls*, up and down the east coast, from Boston to Florida. We have to live in a city that has a Jewish school for our kids."

Josh let out a gigantic sigh, having presented Leora with his *fait accompli* plan, which he assumed would please her.

"Anything else you'd like to add?" she asked, matter-of-factly crossing her arms, leaning back in her chair, waiting for Josh to say the magic words.

"What else can I say?" he asked. Then he got it. He ceremoniously stood and faced Leora, "Please marry me, Leora. I love you."

Leora thought for a moment. "I probably fell in love with you that day I came to the *shul* office, but I was, and I still am determined not to make the same mistake I made with Aaron. You and I have to learn to work together. I'm disappointed, maybe even hurt, maybe even angry, that you've made important decisions about us without my input, even though you seem confident that I'll agree."

Josh sat down again, realizing that he had missed three or four steps in the relationship. He had to set things right.

"You've got to forgive me, Leora, I'm sorry. My imagination took over, especially during the weeks when I was recuperating and I had so much time to think. I can't imagine a future without you. If that means staying in Chicago because you want to be here, I'll find something to do. I'll look for a teaching job or another smaller congregation. Maybe I can open a branch of my brother's Boston lab. Whatever it takes."

Now, Leora stood. "No! That's not what I want!" Leora exclaimed. "I'm only in Chicago because you're here. Fortunately, the Holocaust Memorial gave me an excuse to come back. I'm convinced that you're meant to be a congregational rabbi, and I've learned in my own home how to be a rabbi's wife. I've given this as much thought as you have, probably more. I will always be with you. We're going to be a great team...as long as we live in a house with a big yard for my garden."

Josh wanted to talk about their home of the future. There would certainly be a big yard, and inside lots of bookcases, and probably a room with a microscope or two for the kids.

Suddenly, Serena walked into Josh's office, not expecting to see Leora there. Gathering her wits, she explained, "I heard voices in here and decided to check it out. I honestly thought that you had both left after the dedication. I'm so sorry that I interrupted you."

Serena was embarrassed, but as she backed out of the office door, Leora stopped her. "Serena, you're the first to know that Josh and I are getting married!"

EPILOGUE --
FIVE YEARS LATER

Serena Berg retired from Lev Shalom soon after the Halperins moved to Israel. She is an active volunteer at the Chicago Jewish Federation, and she travels frequently with her husband, Herb, visiting her children and grandchildren (see below). The Bergs, now in their seventies, are planning a cruise to the Baltic countries next year.

Kalman's Kosher Vegetarian Restaurant was the subject of a short documentary in the Chicago Jewish Film Festival three years ago. The scene in which Kalman demonstrates an innovative meatless wedding meal created so much buzz that his restaurant became a favorite of Jews and non-Jews alike. Yet, Kalman doesn't accept reservations, in order to ensure that he can seat customers strategically, at will.

Daniel Lewisohn, who shot Rabbi Joshua Stein at Congregation Lev Shalom, spent four years of his sentence in prison. Upon early release, he joined mandatory Alcoholics Anonymous and anger management groups. Multiple attempts to reunite with Kayla Morales failed. He is currently renting an apartment near his brothers and has started a small IT business.

Bobby and Will Lewisohn, Daniel's brothers, both moved to a trailer park near Pocahontas, Illinois. Will remarried, moved into his own mobile home and is the manager of the park. Bobby, who never remarried, works in the area as a handyman and is dating a local waitress named Charlene.

Kayla Morales moved back to New York and is teaching art at John Lewis Junior High School in the South Bronx. She is pursuing an MFA in Studio Art at the Pratt Institute. She recently married co-worker, science teacher Enoch Meir Schulman, and they reside in a co-op in Washington Heights in Manhattan. The couple enjoy returning to Chicago to visit the Daltons and attend services at Bet Hillel.

Rabbi Elijah Dalton, in addition to synagogue duties at Bet Hillel, teaches Old Testament Personalities at Morgan Interdenominational Theological Seminary in Evanston, Illinois. His book, *Shalom, Shalom: My Journey with the Chosen People,* is a best seller and has been translated into five languages.

Ruth Dalton, in addition to *rebbitzin* responsibilities, spends two afternoons a week as a social worker in a neighborhood youth center. She is a frequent guest who discusses difficult family dynamics on a popular morning Chicago radio show, *Been There Done That*.

Bob Small has set a record for years as president of Congregation Lev Shalom. After hiring Emanuel Reuben Dombick as senior rabbi, Bob continues to monitor him and currently supervises a multi-million dollar renovation of the main sanctuary and chapel.

Sheila Small started a kosher recipe swap website that went viral. Encouraged by her husband, Bob, she expanded her site, which is featured in *Home Kitchen Magazine Monthly*. Her goal is to use the profits from her site to purchase a Torah and new ark for Bob's synagogue renovation. Sheila remains her husband's power behind the throne.

Rachel Berg Stempler married Glen Stempler at Lev Shalom in the spring following their engagement. The reception at the Stemplers' country club was the most lavish kosher wedding ever held there. Rachel decreased her workload in order to focus on decorating a custom-built Highland Park home. Their red-headed baby boy was born on their first wedding anniversary. Rachel, now pregnant with their second child, works with select clients in her firm.

Glen Stempler continues to gain status with high profile cases in his law firm. Encouraged by his wife, he became active in their Orthodox synagogue in Highland Park, and is a member of the executive board. Glen's Jewish metamorphosis continues to puzzle his parents and delight the Bergs.

Bunny Halperin, from her large Jerusalem apartment, organizes groups of arts-minded people on excursions throughout Israel. She is an active participant in the Rechavia Walking Club and volunteers once a week at Yad LaKashish, a workshop for elder craftspeople. The Halperin children and grandchildren visit Jerusalem regularly, but Bunny returns to the States solely for family *simchas*.

Rabbi Ephraim Halperin enjoys every day in Israel, *davening* at various Jerusalem synagogues and studying classic Jewish texts with other learned retirees. Unaccompanied by Bunny, who vowed never to return to Lev Shalom, Ephraim Halperin lectures there annually at his endowed series. When together, Ephraim Halperin and Bob Small give each other a wide berth, and Halperin's heart has never been better.

Leora Halperin Stein is a busy *rebbitzin*. She surprised everyone by giving birth to their first child, a daughter, at home, and is presently pregnant with twins. Leora manages a community garden at their *shul*, while owning a small landscaping business near Boston. Susan Stein, Josh's mother, is Leora's business manager, and Josh's brother, Ben, installed and maintains sophisticated computer systems for both the *shul* and Leora's business.

Rabbi Joshua Stein, after making the decision with Leora to leave Chicago, went to Israel for six months, where they were married. Among family and friends joyfully attending the ceremony and *sheva brachot* were the extended Stein and Halperin families, Serena and Herb Berg, and Rabbi Elijah and Ruth Dalton. On their return, Josh and Leora accepted a position at a small Modern Orthodox synagogue in Natick, Massachusetts. In his spare time, Josh is working on his first novel, *I Married My Boss' Daughter.*

ABOUT THE AUTHORS

Meta Miller was a congregational *rebbitzin* for twelve years. She taught Judaic and General Studies in Chicago and Atlanta and served as Director of Early Childhood Education in an Atlanta Jewish Day School. She co-authored *Ha-Sefer Sheli*, used for Hebrew language enrichment. Meta is married to Dr. Paul Miller, a retired pharmacist.

Chana Shapiro has written and illustrated numerous articles in magazines and journals. She taught middle school English and Art in New York and Atlanta, was program director at the Atlanta Jewish Community Center, and supervised programming at an Atlanta Orthodox synagogue. She is a regular columnist for the Atlanta Jewish Times. Chana is married to Rabbi Zvi Shapiro, a retired university professor.

Chana and Meta have known each other for more than thirty years, sharing joys and surprises along the way. Clearly, it's not easy to collaborate when writing a novel (their second!), and they recommend it only for very close friends.

Made in the USA
Columbia, SC
04 May 2019